Obsidian Curse

Other Works by Barbra Annino

Opal Fire: Stacy Justice Book One
Bloodstone: Stacy Justice Book Two
Tiger's Eye: Stacy Justice Book Three
Emerald Isle: Stacy Justice Book Four

Sin City Goddess: Secret Goddess series Book One

BOOK FIVE OF THE STACY JUSTICE SERIES

Obsidian Curse

(IT IS HIGHLY RECOMMENDED THAT THIS SERIES BE READ IN ORDER.)

Barbra Annino

THOMAS & MERCER

This is a work of fiction. Names, characters, organizations, places, events, and incidents are either products of the author's imagination or are used fictitiously.

Published by Thomas & Mercer, Seattle

www.apub.com

ISBN-13: 9781477820124
ISBN-10: 1477820124

Cover design by Kerrie Robertson

Library of Congress Control Number: 2013920855

Printed in the United States of America

For the fans

And always, for George

Chapter I

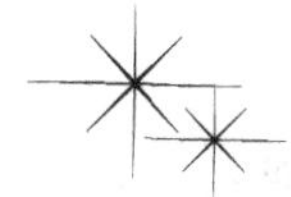

When I was a little girl, I used to love playing dress up. I would sneak into my mother's bedroom, slip into her black pointy heels with the shiny buckles, and explore her jewelry box, looking for colorful gemstones to accessorize the ensemble. I would sift through the clip-on jade earrings that matched her eyes, the obsidian necklace she wore every Samhain, the charm bracelet that my grandmother Birdie had given her one year for her birthday, and other baubles and shiny things.

After choosing the perfect glittery adornment, I would teeter off to her closet in search of a cape. Hers were more elaborate than my own, with intricate bric-a-brac and detailed embroidery accenting the sleeves or the hood. But what I really liked about them was how long they were. I felt like a queen, traipsing around our little house, a long train whooshing behind my every step. Then I would shuffle into the kitchen and dabble in spellcasting or potion making, relishing the charms I could come up with and the power I could wield with an herb or a gemstone.

You know, typical kid stuff.

One day, while I was balancing on a step stool near the sink, oleander leaf in one hand and dragon's blood root in the other, my father arrived home unexpectedly from work. My back was to him, but the lime and basil aftershave my mother crafted especially for his skin gave him away. He whisked me off the stool, twirling me in his arms, and I giggled. He kissed both of my cheeks and in a proper British accent said, "What regal beauty is this?"

I laughed. "It's me, Daddy. Stacy."

He feigned surprise. "Impossible. You are far too grown up to be my daughter."

"Nope. It's me. Honest."

"Why, I could have sworn you were a royal princess."

"I'm in disguise," I whispered, playing along.

He whispered back, "I see. Hiding from the queen?" He scanned the room, then shot a look over both shoulders as if an armed guard was about to leap from the pantry.

I giggled.

My father's eyes flicked behind me then, just over my head. He said, in a feigned worried tone, "Uh-oh. I'm afraid our cover has been breached, fair one."

He set me down gently on the step stool and we faced my mother. She was tapping her foot, her toned arms crossed over her chest. She shook her head first at my father, then at me in pointed disapproval. She aimed one long finger first at my right hand, then at my left, then straight at my nose. "Drop."

I let the oleander leaf and the dragon's blood root slip from my fingers at the same time. The leaf curled and swayed all the way to the floor and I could have sworn I saw a feather fall on top of it for the briefest moment.

My mother did not like me dabbling in magic without supervision. For someone so young, it was not only dangerous, it could be deadly. Even for someone like me, who had witchcraft coursing through her veins. That was a lesson I would eventually learn the hard way.

My mother cocked her head and raised one eyebrow at my father.

He performed a very graceful, sweeping bow. "Your majesty. A thousand pardons. Please do not punish the child for my misdeeds."

There was a sparkle in my mother's eye as she half smirked, half frowned at my father. Her hair was still damp from the shower she had taken and her feet were bare. "You may rise."

I stole a look at my dad, enjoying this little exchange between them.

He rose slowly, his gaze trailing the curve of my mother's figure, which was amplified by the spaghetti strap dress she was wearing.

"I am humbled, your grace." He stepped forward, kissed one of her wrists, then the other. Her face flushed slightly.

"As you should be. Oleander can stop a man's heart in minutes." She gave me another disappointed look. Her face was so expressive that I always knew what she was thinking—at least whenever she wanted me to know—even if she was clear across the room.

I shuffled my feet. "Sorry." It was a feeble apology, because I should have known better. Thankfully, while my mother could be strict, she wasn't one to hold a grudge.

My father stepped forward and extended his hand. "May I, princess?"

I placed my tiny hand in my father's large one and stepped off the stool, carefully tiptoeing around the plants I had discarded.

My mother looked at my father. "Honey, don't call her that."

He glanced up at her, weighing if she was serious or still playing make-believe. When he decided that she was all business, he said, "Why not? She looks just like a redheaded, green-eyed princess. Wouldn't you say?"

Mom crossed her arms and narrowed her eyes at me, drinking in my borrowed attire. She took a deep breath as if to smell my very essence. She paused for a while, then circled me like a shark.

I stood there in our cozy kitchen, the clock on the wall tick-tocking, the scent of my mother's vanilla-lavender body wash permeating the air, holding my breath in anxious anticipation.

Finally, she shook her head and a tiny line curved around her mouth. "Absolutely not. And do you know why?"

She turned her gaze to my father, who shrugged. "Do tell."

With the confidence of a woman who had no qualms about leaving the house without makeup, my mother said, "Because princesses can be rather stupid."

I gasped. *Was that true? Then why did everybody want to be one?* I thought about pigtailed, fresh-faced classmates who loved to wear tiaras, dress in pink and blue chiffon, and make up stories about fire-breathing dragons and knights in shining armor rescuing them. It made me wonder. *Do they know that their idols are dumb?* Because I would trade in all the sparkle and bling for some smarts.

Dad held his elbow and tapped his chin, considering this revelation.

I looked from him to my mother, hoping the game would continue a while longer. I couldn't wait for her explanation about why she felt this way and—more importantly—why Walt Disney wasn't privy to this information.

Dad said, "I see. Would you care to elaborate on that observation, my love?"

My mother began ticking off a list on her fingers. "Well, for one thing, they can't spot a disguise to save their lives. I mean, who mistakes a beautiful evil queen for an old decrepit hag?" She winked at me. "The eyes would give her away, would they not?"

She had a point. I nodded enthusiastically. My father gave me a high five.

Mom continued, "Plus, they are forever eating poisoned apples or some such nonsense. Everyone knows you don't eat anything given to you by a stranger." She grabbed some tea from the refrigerator and poured three glasses, handing one to my father first, then to me, emphasizing her meaning. "Not to mention, they tend to be rather careless, pricking their fingers, falling off mattresses, getting themselves cursed. And then there are the really daft ones who find themselves locked in a drafty castle for ages on end, all the while waiting for some Prince Charming to rescue them, when they should know how to save themselves."

She spun to face my father, parked a defiant hand on her hip.

There was a gleam in his eyes that I couldn't quite comprehend. "By stars, I do believe you're right, Sloane." He bent down, eyeing me. His breath smelled of oranges. "So what do you think our young Stacy Justice looks like? What sort of a nickname best suits her?"

My mother scooted up to his side. She thought for a moment.

I held my breath, waiting to hear the nickname she would bestow upon me. Movie star? Fairy queen? Batgirl?

"She looks like a truth seeker, if you ask me. A rebel spirit. All light, fairness, and fight. The kind of girl who doesn't burst into tears when life gets too tough. Who can defend herself with both her words and her strength." She narrowed her eyes at my father. "What do you think?"

"Hmm." He nodded. "So the word you're looking for is *warrior.*"

"I like the sound of that. Warrior."

She said that last bit with such strength and conviction that it has held me in good stead for many years. In fact, whenever I found myself in a tight spot and I began to lose confidence—like I was right now—I replayed her voice in my head.

Warrior.

I felt his breath first. Then his hands around my neck.

Chapter 2

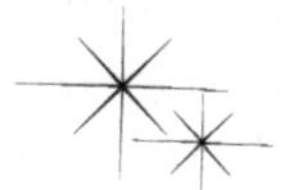

He was strong, to be sure. Tall, too, but that didn't matter. The strength and size of my attacker was not as important as intuition, sharp senses, and a quick mind. My training had taught me that. If he were standing in front of me, I would have head-butted him or kneed him in the groin. Instead, I stomped my heel into his left foot, jutted my right elbow into his ribs and, just as he doubled over, I grabbed both his arms and flipped him over my back. He bounced off the floor once before I pirouetted around and straddled him. The athame was tucked inside my boot and I whipped it out for good measure, placing one foot on his sternum.

He coughed twice.

"Um, Stace, honey, we need to get you a new sparring partner."

Chance looked a bit pale and a small, familiar panic gripped me. I could never hurt him, would never hurt him, but there was a part of me deep down terrified that I might one day. Not intentionally, but because of the secrets or circumstances that plagued my life and now, my role in this world.

There was a hint of mist in his blue eyes as if he had just stubbed his toe and was trying not to yell about it as I tucked the knife away. "I'm so sorry, Chance. You can't sneak up on me like that." I scanned his face, looking for signs of pain before I knelt down and kissed him. "Did I hurt you? Because you know I would sooner cut off my leg than hurt you."

"No, I'm okay." He grunted as he shifted beneath me. He gripped his hands on my hips and rolled me over onto the mat, hovering above me. His chest was bare with just a hint of hair trailing to his navel, his sandy locks damp near the temples where perspiration had broken out during our two-person fight club. "It's just that when you work construction like I do, you need all your parts in working order."

I grinned at him. "Right. We can't have you broken. I still need those shelves installed."

He blew a playful raspberry on my neck and I squealed.

"Is that all I'm good for? A handyman?" he asked.

I looked around at the addition he had built on to my little cottage. It was a good-size room that extended from the closet in my bedroom to a wide-open square space with a weight bench, boxing bag, and a treadmill. On the far wall were various martial arts accessories like Chako sticks and five-pointed stars, along with a few Taser guns and my newest find from the spy store—a tranquilizer gun. There was also a small room off to the right with a cedar door. Chance had surprised me with it last week, explaining he thought it would make a great post-workout sauna, but I had other plans for the space.

He assumed that this addition I had asked him to build, along with my relatively new obsession with self-defense, was all due to the fact that my job as a reporter, not to mention my wacky family, had often landed me in dangerous situations.

He didn't know the half of it.

Chance called the new area the Bat Cave. I called it the Seeker's Den. For that's who I was. The Seeker of Justice.

With a little bit of warrior whenever necessary.

I kept my voice low, seductive. "Oh, you're good for a lot more than that, you sexy beast."

He laughed, looked at me tenderly, longingly before he wove a web of kisses across my neck.

We made plans to see each other that night, before Chance ducked back into the cottage to take a shower. I hit the bag a few more times, did some flying roundhouse kicks and a quick set of sit-ups before I was all out of juice. I grabbed a water from the fridge and drank the whole thing in one shot.

There were three security cameras installed around the outer perimeter of the cottage. I'd had more than my share of intruders, so Chance was happy to help install this little peace of mind for me. One faced the space between the Geraghty Girls' House and the cottage, one was aimed at the back door and side yard, while the last one covered the walkway leading to my home as well as the front porch. I walked over to the laptop on the desk, hit a few keystrokes, and switched on the camera that faced the front of the cottage. It appeared that Chance had just opened the door to his truck. He tossed his overnight bag inside then hopped in after it, hair still damp, jean jacket unbuttoned. For some stupid reason, as if he could see me, I waved. As he drove off, the massive tires of his 4x4 crushing autumn leaves in their wake, I felt an overwhelming sense of remorse.

Guilt can be a crippling emotion. Even more so when the reason you're feeling guilty can't be washed away with an apology.

Because how do you apologize for a secret that must be contained?

I looked around at my new space that Chance had built in the weeks since I'd returned from Ireland. There were herbs drying on the peg rack behind the sleek metal desk; crystals of every shape and size packed into jars; knives, swords, and various other weapons covering most of the left wall; two laptops—one for home, one for work—a database system programmed with information that couldn't be found on the Internet (courtesy of the Council) that I was in the process of updating with pages from the Blessed Book; a large wireless monitor that talked to the database; and the cameras and a security panel on the door. This wasn't just a work space, or a workout space, it was a modestly armed, technologically fortified spy chamber.

I suppose that's what I was now. Sort of. A spy for witches.

My mind melted back to all that had transpired during my time in Ireland as I punched a code into the laptop and a tiny drawer slid open beneath the desk.

It had all been so extraordinary, even I had trouble believing everything that had happened.

Until I held the locket.

I extracted the tiny trinket from the drawer, careful not to open it, for that was where its heart beat, and held it in my palm. It was lightweight and caked with age, this gold piece of history. I dangled it from its long chain, allowing it to swirl and flutter in the air as I wondered how something so small, so delicate, could be the source of so much pain, agony, and betrayal.

Not to mention power. Oh, so much power.

And now, I was its keeper.

Or more accurately, its Seeker.

You see, Chance has known who I was ever since we were kids. At least as far as I knew who I was. I never shied away from telling my best friend all the stories my grandmother and mother had shared with me. Legends of myth, magic, and ancient treasures. Mystical tales of sorcery, healing, and spellcasting. Enchanting and frightening fables of fairies, gods, warriors, and wizards.

He would listen to me chatter away for hours on end, stretched out beneath the stars in his backyard, or on the floor of his little boy's room, surrounded by posters of race cars and monster trucks. As I waxed nostalgic about the long line of witches I hailed from, Chance would nod and occasionally ask a question that I was more than eager to answer.

What part of Ireland is your family from?

Kildare. It's the home of the great Goddess Brighid. That's who Birdie was named after. I'm going there someday.

Cool. And what did you say your ancestors were called?

Druids.

By the time we were in high school, Chance knew all about the Tuatha Dé Danann and the Goddess Danu. He knew about the battles fought and won on the Hill of Tara, where mortals and gods came together to protect the island, her gifts, and especially her secrets.

My secrets now.

Of course when my father died—when my prediction couldn't save his life—I left all of that behind. I refused my teachings, refused my training, refused my very heritage. But that had all changed now. It took fifteen years and some absurdly difficult lessons that I swore one day to write a book about, but I've come around to acceptance. Now, I could confidently call myself a witch. And a pretty good one too. In fact, the powers that be even gave me a promotion recently.

As the formally appointed Seeker of Justice, sworn to uphold sacred laws and protect ancient treasures at all costs, it was my duty, and truth be told, my honor, to abide by the Celtic order of a secret society known as the Council, of which my grandmother Birdie was now a cabinet member.

It took a long time for me to accept this position that I was born into—this calling, as my grandmother would say. A long time and a lot of blood, sweat, and tears. Literally.

But now that I had, I was lying to the only person I'd ever fully trusted. And even though I knew it was for his own safety, it was still a wretched feeling.

Secrets had ripped my family apart. I prayed they wouldn't do the same to my relationship with the love of my life.

I tucked the locket back into its safe spot and turned to head for a shower. I had to be at the newspaper office in forty-five minutes and I still hadn't fed Thor, my Great Dane familiar.

There was a soft glow emanating from the clear glass window on the "sauna" door when I looked up. The lightbulb had been engaged. I grabbed a towel off a nearby hook, punched in the security code for the small room, and slipped inside. The mirror on the wall was what controlled the signal to the light. I walked over to it, flipped it around, and faced the smooth black surface of the scrying mirror.

This was my connection to the Council. This was where I would be informed of any breach in security or urgent assignments. I checked it every morning, always hoping for good news.

My mother's freckled face appeared instantly. "Hello, sweetheart."

"Hi, Mom."

"I thought I'd try to reach you before you shuffled off to work."

My mother, who had been recently freed by the Council after spending fourteen years in exile for killing a man in my defense, would not stop calling me. She felt guilty, I thought, because she hadn't returned home with me to Amethyst, Illinois, the tiny tourist town where we were both raised. Yule was just two months away, however, and she was planning to come then, possibly even look for a house or move in with my grandmother and the aunts, but she had "a few things to take care of first." She said it with a flicker of unease too. At the time, I thought it was residual stress from everything she and I had been through, both of us nearly losing our lives, but it was there every time she spoke to me. When I pressed her on it the last time we chatted, she insisted it was "nothing to worry about."

Which, in my family, usually meant there was a whole lot to worry about, so I tucked it in the back of my mind, waiting for the right time—and if necessary, the right spell—to convince her to tell me what it was that had her on edge.

"Mom, you don't have to call me every five minutes. Honestly, I'm doing fine."

My last mission, which involved locating an ancient treasure, didn't exactly go as planned. I was hurt badly, but I recovered quickly.

"Are you sure? Because even though I don't receive the visions about you that I used to, I had the most powerful feeling that something wasn't right not minutes ago." She leaned in closer, her green eyes darkening as she examined my face.

I flitted my eyes away. "All good. Just preparing for Samhain."

Samhain was the pagan new year that some call All Hallows Eve.

"Oh really?" She crossed her arms, her brow furrowed. Her hair was floating just over her shoulders in a wavy, fresh style. She must have just had it done. "So how's that nice young man of yours?" she asked.

Dammit. She had the uncanny ability to extract my emotions like a surgeon taking out an appendix. My face contorted against my will.

"Aha!" She slapped her manicured hand on a table. "I knew it. What's the trouble?"

I chewed at a nail. "There's no trouble, Mom. It's just . . . you know."

Her face flashed with a hint of sadness, then resurrected itself into a stone statue. "You can't tell him, Stacy. We talked about this."

"He knows everything else, Mom, why can't I tell him this?"

She sighed, gave me a long, concerned look. "Look, sweetheart, I know it's difficult for you. I know you love him. But you know as well as I do that it's for his own good you keep this one thing from him. Do you think I told your father everything?"

I hadn't thought of that. Dad was always so easygoing, I just assumed he knew everything about her when I was little. Now, of course, those childhood illusions were shattered.

She went on. "There are people who would kill for the secrets we keep. And some, as you well know, will come looking for you to thwart any mission you're assigned. Do you really want them to come after Chance? Or his family?"

She was right. It was selfish to wish that everything could be like it had always been. To think that I would ever have a normal life with Chance, despite the fact that there was a huge part of me that wanted nothing more than that. But this was my life now. This was the path I had chosen.

"Sometimes we keep secrets from the ones we love to protect them," my mother said gently.

"Is that what you're doing?" I asked.

She stiffened. "I don't know what you're talking about."

I wiped my face with the towel and said, "I know something's been bothering you. I've known since we left Ireland. Don't think I won't find out, Mom."

"Don't you have enough on your plate without looking for trouble where there is none?" she snapped.

"Deny all you want, but if it's in the Blessed Book, you can be sure I'll find it."

The Blessed Book was a written history of our family's theology. It contained pages filled with the names of my ancestors and gods, lists of the ancient high kings, stories of legends, recipes, references, spells, charms, and even predictions for future generations. Some of it was hard to decipher without Birdie's help. After all, it was her mother, my great-grandmother, who compiled it. It belonged to me now.

"So how's your cousin Cinnamon?" my mother asked.

"Nice segue."

"I thought so."

She really wanted to keep this from me, whatever it was, and I didn't have time to argue about it. "Still pregnant and ornery as ever. We have a pool going to see how long and how many doctors she goes through in the delivery room before she completely snaps and takes matters into her own hands."

Mom grinned. "Put me down for twenty. I say four doctors in half an hour."

I heard Thor, my Great Dane familiar, bark. It was loud, penetrating as if he had trained his vocal cords to my thought waves.

Which, I decided, was exactly what he had done. I couldn't hear Thor, or anything for that matter, in this room. Chance had designed it to be virtually soundproof.

"Mom, I have to go. Gotta get ready for work."

"All right. I love you."

"Love you too."

I disconnected the call, stepped out of the room, and grabbed the tranquilizer gun. Thor barked once more. Urgently.

I was about to power down the laptop that still had the front security camera engaged when, on the monitor, I spotted a *Star Trek* baseball hat bobbing across the porch railing.

Chapter 3

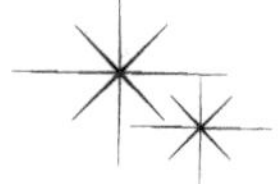

"It can't be," I whispered.

I ducked through the opening that led from the Seeker's Den to my bedroom and bolted out the front door, my tranquilizer gun tucked inside the back of my yoga pants.

Thor was right behind me, his muscular legs pumping fast, his massive black and tan head darting this way and that.

We covered the perimeter of the cottage, even checked in the bushes. We found no one.

But I knew that hat. And it didn't belong to a human.

"Pickle!" I hissed, careful to say his name just the one time. If I said it three times in a row it would surely summon him, although I didn't think my cottage was on a leyline, which is how he would travel here. The woods behind the Geraghty Girls' House—the bed-and-breakfast owned and operated by Birdie and her sisters—was most certainly linked to the realm of the Fae, however.

This, I learned all too well on my twenty-ninth birthday some weeks ago. That was the day I officially blossomed into a true Geraghty. A true witch.

I looked at Thor. He sat, ears perked and alert, one pointed forward, the other to the side listening for the slightest rustle.

"Anything?" I asked.

Thor harrumphed, frustrated that he didn't catch his target.

I crossed my arms, scanning the woods for signs of a fluorescent green light, a clear indicator that the fairies have come.

Again, nothing.

"Maybe we imagined it," I said to Thor. "It's getting close to Samhain. The veil between the worlds is thinning. Maybe it was just an energy surge. A crossed wire that picked up on their realm."

Thor cocked his head toward me.

"I know." I scratched behind his ear and looked back toward the woods once more. "Even as I said it, I didn't believe it."

But if it was Pickle I saw on the monitor, what was he doing here? What danger had he come to warn me about?

Because I had to say, I could have gone an entire lifetime without seeing Danu and the Morrigan again.

I showered and dressed in jeans, a purple sweater, and boots as quickly as possible, trying not to think of the Otherworld, or the Web of Wyrd, as I had since learned it was called, and prayed that I wouldn't wake up in a freaking birdcage tomorrow.

Yeah, those Celtic goddesses could be real whacknuts. They loved messing with humans. I wouldn't recommend mouthing off to one, as they desperately lack anything resembling a sense of humor. They're like the mean girls of the divine.

I tossed my work laptop into a bag along with a yogurt for me and some roast chicken and mashed potatoes for Thor, and we were on our way to the newspaper.

The office of the paper was only a few blocks away so we usually walked, but I was running late, so we drove through the fall morning sunshine down to Main Street.

There were a lot of cars parked along the street for a Monday morning, but fall was the busiest season for tourists. Many of the hotels, restaurants, inns, and bed-and-breakfasts were booked solid in October. In fact, though we were a town of just a few thousand, most years a million visitors passed through our neck of the woods. Amethyst, you see, was one of the gems of the Midwest. Perched on the corners of three states—Illinois, Iowa, and Wisconsin—it wasn't pancake-flat like so much of the heartland. Rather, it was hilly and lush, with gorgeous bluffs, the occasional waterfall, the mighty Mississippi, rolling green pastures, and a quaint Main Street filled with restored buildings that seemed to have sprung straight from a Dickens novel. It was an old steamboat and mining town, and it had seen its share of hardships as well as triumphs, including the nine Civil War generals and one president the locals were proud to claim as their own.

While business was excellent for the economy, it was hell on parking. The paper had a small parking lot, but overflow from the nearby lodging facilities often spilled into it. I finally squeezed my car into a spot after three loops around, and Thor and I headed inside.

Monday morning meetings were my partner Derek's idea. Personally, I hated meetings. I thought if you were adult enough to hold down a job then you were adult enough to work unsupervised. Besides, there were only five employees total, so anyone who needed to discuss an assignment could just walk across the hall, tap the person on the shoulder, and, well, discuss it. But Derek liked to think of himself as a young entrepreneur and he read in *Forbes* or somewhere that business meetings were a doorway to success.

Or maybe he saw that on a cat poster; I couldn't be sure.

Anyway, since I was responsible for getting him shot at once and I still felt bad about it, I didn't give him too much trouble when it came to business decisions, aside from the fact that I was the controlling partner of the *Amethyst Globe*.

The minute I walked into the conference room, I was smacked with an overwhelming perfume even a prostitute would find tacky.

"Well, it's about damn time you showed up," said a high-pitched, irritating voice.

So actually, there was one decision Derek made that I would never get used to, and there was a strong possibility it would be my only defense against a murder rap.

"Monique, lovely to see you as always. I guess this means there's a pole somewhere missing its stripper?" I unclipped Thor's leash and he sauntered down the hall to the water fountain and helped himself to a drink.

Derek licked his lips. "Um, ladies."

Monique snorted and winked one false blue eyelash at me. "Well, if I was a stripper, you could bet that I'd be on time."

"On time, on a lap, on your back," I said.

Iris, our gossip columnist, stifled a laugh.

Monique shot the grandmotherly woman a glare and Iris quickly pretended to read her notes.

"You know, I'm not sure, but I think that's sexual harassment." Monique stood and pointed a bright red talon at me. Her white blouse was unbuttoned so low, I was afraid one of her implants would jump out and dance across the table.

"Really? Because if anyone should know, it's you," I said.

Thor came back into the room, his huge jowls sopping wet, and shook his head, showering Monique with spittle.

"Ew!" She spun to face the dog, shaking her hands free of the slime. Her leather miniskirt didn't shift with her and we all saw more of Monique than anyone should before breakfast.

Thor sat, innocently blinking at her. I was so proud.

"And that damn dog! Why do you let him drink from the fountain? It's disgusting!" She ran her fingers through her hair.

"Well, to be fair, we let you drink from it."

Monique stepped forward aggressively as if she were about to strike.

I raised one hand. "You better think long and hard before you make your next move, Lolita."

Monique paused, shifted her eyes away.

Derek said, "Okay, that's enough."

I slammed my hand on the desk and both Gladys, the research assistant, and Iris jumped. "It is enough." I pointed at Monique. "I am your boss, so you better damn well treat me with respect if you want to keep your job. This arrangement was supposed to be temporary, if you recall."

Derek had hired Monique right before I left for Ireland and I warned both of them then that her sex column—don't even get me started on what a stupid idea that was for our conservative town—would be on a trial basis only.

Unfortunately, I didn't bank on our small hamlet being full of sex-starved geriatrics with adult toy collections and fetishes that would make Hugh Hefner blush. Needless to say, the column was gaining popularity.

Monique slithered over to Derek, wrapped a hand around his shoulder. "Oh, I hardly think that will be a problem."

I looked at her sternly as she smirked, her red lipstick thick as maraschino cherries. "What are you talking about?"

Monique feigned a "golly, gee, I don't know" look and sucked on one finger. I was about five seconds away from chopping it off at the knuckle.

I shot darts at Derek with my stare. "What is she talking about?"

Derek straightened his shirt, fiddled with his cuffs, but wouldn't look at me when he spoke. "I believe she means the new contract."

Stunned didn't even come close to what I was feeling at that moment. No, I think rage would better describe it.

"Office. Now." I said through gritted teeth.

Derek protested. "We're not done with the mee—"

I slid over the desk, grabbed my young partner by the ear, and dragged him through the door, down the hallway, and into the room with the title "Office of the Managing Editor" etched in the glass door.

"Ow, ow, ow, ow," he stammered.

I slammed the door shut behind him and whirled around.

Derek's chocolate-colored cheeks had a touch of red in them. "Damn, woman, how could you do that in front of the crew?" He rubbed his ear with his neatly manicured fingers. "That wasn't very professional."

"Are you kidding me right now?" I was flabbergasted. "I'm not being professional? You give that walking petri dish a contract without consulting me and I'm the one who's disrespecting you?"

"It was when you were away. I forgot to tell you." He kicked at a loose thread in the carpet.

"Are you sleeping with her?"

Derek looked up. "What? No."

I tossed my hands in the air. "Then why? Why in the name of all that is sanitary would you give the person I most loathe in the world a permanent position?"

Derek flung his arm in the air. "What is it about her that rubs you the wrong way?"

"You mean besides the fact that she acts like a stray cat in heat? Or that she's tried to steal every man both my cousin and

I ever had?" I pretended to think for a moment. "Well, let's see, perhaps it's because that woman has all the finesse and charm of a whoopee cushion."

Derek laughed. "I love those things."

Monday morning and already my patience was spent. "Show me the contract."

He reached into his desk just as Monique barged in on her platform thigh-high boots.

I gave her an exasperated look. "Monique, for Pete's sake, even a trained monkey knows when to knock."

She ignored me and said to Derek, "I'll be right back. I need to take care of that errand I told you about."

Derek lifted his head up, said okay, and went back to searching his files.

Monique stuck her tongue out at me and shut the door.

"Where's she going? What about the meeting?" I asked.

"You hate the meetings anyway." He shuffled through some paperwork, his smooth skin wrinkled in thought. "I thought it was in here," he mumbled.

"That's not the point. She gave me attitude for being late and now she's taking off."

Derek opened a file folder, shut it, and reached for another.

"Well, you should know where she's going. She'll be with your boyfriend."

I don't think I blinked for the next thirty seconds.

Derek stopped sifting through his files. "What, he didn't tell you?"

I shook my head.

No. No he didn't.

Chapter 4

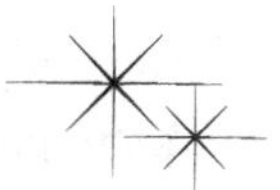

I had a hard time concentrating the rest of the morning. What was Chance doing meeting with Monique and, more importantly, why didn't he mention it to me? I suppose he could have been bidding on a job. Monique owned a nightclub called Down and Dirty, which was across the street from my cousin's bar, the Black Opal. Maybe she needed some work done. I guess I would find out that night from Chance because I had no intention of dealing with her anymore that day unless it involved a shovel and a bag of lime.

Thor was bellowing for food, so I loaded the chicken and potatoes into his bowl and fed him in my office. I was too pissed to eat myself, so I stuck the yogurt in my mini refrigerator and sat down to do some work.

It was going to be a busy news week. Busy for Amethyst, anyway. There was a town council meeting on Wednesday, a costumed parade on Friday—the day of Samhain—immediately followed by a multi-class reunion (costumes optional) that evening, and a Saturday morning farewell brunch for the classmates. At the park on Sunday, an Oktoberfest featuring the best homemade brats and beer contest was also on the agenda, but I'd be skipping that and spending time with my family.

A multi-class reunion may sound strange to some, but when you live in a town as small as Amethyst, the graduating class could be as little as thirty people, so the committees sometimes teamed up in an effort to cut costs, combining classes that spanned decades. This year's reunion covered the classes of 1930 through 2003. An interesting mix of folks to say the least.

Thor scratched at the door, so I let him out of my office to do his business and went to talk to Gladys.

Derek would be covering the parade and the Oktoberfest, since his specialty was photography and both events would certainly prompt some amazing photo ops. Iris would handle the meeting, because meetings were boring as hell and I fell asleep during the last one, while Gladys and I would take the reunion festivities.

The research room was in the basement, so I darted down there and found Gladys surfing the web for Samhain ritual garb. Gladys had a fascination with all things witchy. She'd been dying for an invitation to one of Birdie's Samhain festivals ever since I could remember, but Birdie's holiday guest list was restricted to a fairly tight-knit group. Mostly distant relatives, members of her original coven, her sisters, and myself. I don't even think Gramps was ever invited, which was just as well. Magic could be powerful on Samhain so the chances of my grandmother turning her ex-husband into a snail were pretty high.

"Hey, Gladys."

She turned around, a sheepish look on her face. "Oh, hello, Stacy," she said in her thick Polish accent.

I motioned toward the monitor. "Maybe this is the year."

Her face brightened. "Oh, yes, I hope so."

"Listen, Gladys, I was wondering if you could find me the names of any valedictorians from Amethyst High School for the years 1930 through 2003 and any updates on what they're doing now, special achievements, things like that."

She nodded. "I can do."

"Perfect."

My cell phone rang. It was Cinnamon. I thanked Gladys, asked her to call or e-mail me with an update at the end of the day, and stepped into the hallway to take the call.

"Hey, Cin."

"Stacy, come and get this damn dog before I string him up a flagpole."

"Thor? He's there?"

"Yes and he's driving me insane. He's following me all around the house. He wiped out a lamp with his tail, and he just ate three steaks I had defrosting on the counter."

"Three?"

"Yes, three. One for me, one for Tony, and one for the baby. You got a problem with that?"

Oy. Cinnamon's temper was volatile on a good day. Now that she was six months pregnant it was downright frightening. Like a cross between John McEnroe and Mike Tyson. On steroids.

"Be right there."

I popped my head into Derek's office to tell him I'd be back in a bit and headed for the car.

Thor was originally Cinnamon's dog. He showed up one day at the Black Opal a few years ago while I was living in Chicago. At the time, Cinnamon was separated from her husband, Tony, and she welcomed the companionship. It didn't hurt that the dog weighed in at 180 pounds, stood over four feet tall, and had a look about him that warned customers if they stepped out of line, they'd have a set of two-inch canines embedded in their backsides. Cinnamon had that look too, so I guess you could say Thor was the backup bouncer. When I came back to live in Amethyst, Thor quickly attached himself to me as if we had known each other in a past life. Since Cinnamon wasn't the type to get emotional over animals, she didn't mind sharing her dog until eventually he adopted me.

Fiona, my great-aunt whose gift was communicating with animals, once told me that Thor had been searching for me, biding his time with Cinnamon until I came home. After I had confided in her that I had indeed been having numerous dreams about a fawn-colored Great Dane while still living in the city, she confirmed that Thor was my familiar. He'd been with me ever since.

That is part of my gift. Dreams of premonition. The other part is something I don't think I'll ever get used to—communicating with the dead. At first, it wasn't so bad. They would come to me in a dream, via a spirit guide, or through the ethereal form at the most inopportune times. Like in the drive-through of a fast-food joint. Poof! I'd turn my head and a ghost would be sitting in the passenger seat coaxing me to order him a bacon double cheeseburger. And no, they can't eat, but those residual memories of life in corporeal form tended to linger. Or I'd be shopping for new boots and suddenly an old salesclerk would show up, insisting that brown was not my color. Luckily, no one has ever appeared in the shower, or I'd be sporting dreadlocks by now.

It wasn't until I began honing my particular skill set that they started touching me.

And boy did that freak me out.

So now, I can't walk past a cemetery without a ghost grabbing my arm and asking me to send a message. Usually it's something completely mundane like "Tell my granddaughter that my wedding silver was supposed to go to her except that sneaky cousin of mine made off with it." Things like that.

And if they can touch you, that means they can hurt you. A lesson I hold in the forefront of my mind at all times. This was why I took the car to Cinnamon's place. I had to loop around the long way to my cousin's house now, because the direct path would send me straight past one of the oldest cemeteries in the state. Those are the worst. Mostly, the ghosts there wanted to argue about politics, unsettled feuds, urban sprawl, and how screwed up today's young people were. You can only listen to so many "in my day" stories before your ears start to bleed.

I pulled up to Cinnamon's two-bedroom ranch over on Ruby Lane and parked the car in the driveway. There was a cement sidewalk that led to my cousin's door, and I followed that to three carved pumpkins sitting on the porch next to a plastic skeleton who leaned back in a wooden chair as if he'd just been reading the newspaper. Someone had propped up his hand and he was flipping me the bird. The pumpkins had to be Tony's doing, because Cin was not the type of woman to decorate, let alone acknowledge holidays.

I suspected that she was the one who arranged the finger.

I knocked once and heard my cousin yell, "It's open." That's the type of community we lived in. Everyone left their doors unlocked, the keys in the car, and the children unsupervised. That kind of thing made me uneasy because I'd written enough obituaries in Chicago to know that we were never that safe, no matter where we lived.

Predators roamed every town, in every form.

However, Cinnamon was heavily armed and could shoot a pen out of someone's hand from twenty yards away. Her father, my uncle Declan, was the chief of police in Amethyst for many years before he left this plane not so long ago. He was obsessed with making certain his little girl knew her way around a weapon and how to defend herself. I supposed my own mother, his sister, was the same way. Except the self-defense she had instilled in me was in the form of spellcasting, potion making, intuitive clarity, and inner strength.

The door creaked as I opened it and I was surprised at the sight before me.

Cinnamon was sitting on her blue couch looking like a bomb about to explode. Her dark hair was clipped high on her head in a mass of knotty waves. She had no makeup on and she was wearing one of Tony's Bears tee shirts, cut off at the sleeves, with a ketchup stain dribbled down the front. Thor was perched next to her, his rear on the sofa, paws on the ground, and his huge head in my cousin's lap.

They both looked uncomfortable. But here's the thing about Great Danes. When they don't want to move, it's nearly impossible to get them to do so, short of renting a forklift.

I bit my lip, knowing that if I laughed, which is what I really wanted to do, my cousin would disembowel me with a toothpick.

"Thor, buddy, are you bothering Auntie Cinnamon?"

Cin shot daggers at me with her eyes. "Do. Not. Call. Me. That."

"Oh, come on, it's kind of cute. He must be protecting you because he knows you're with child."

"With child? Do you want me to punch you in the throat?"

"Fine. Knocked up. Better?"

"Can you please just help me?"

I circled the coffee table and sat in a black leather chair across from them. "Thor, look at me."

He wouldn't take his eyes off of my cousin.

"Big Man, I promise that Cinnamon and the baby will be just fine without your protection."

The dog shot me a doubtful look. Like, *Oh please, I've had to bail you out of more crap than I leave in the yard.* Which was true, but still hurtful.

He turned his head and rolled on his back, eyes still on Cin.

I decided to try another approach. "Cinnamon has Tony to protect her, Thor."

At this, my cousin balked. I knew what she was thinking. *I can protect my own damn self.* I held up a hand warning her not to vocalize that thought.

I continued. "But who will protect me? I need you, buddy."

He swiveled his head my way and Cin shifted. He looked conflicted. The Great Dane stared at me, then Cinnamon. He decided I could take my chances and nuzzled closer to my cousin.

"You're not helping much," Cin grumbled.

I blew out a frustrated sigh. "Okay, Thor, you win. What do you say we come and check on Cinnamon and the baby once a week."

"What?" she flared.

Thor considered this. He lifted his head and righted himself. He looked straight at me and then flung his giant jaw on the back of the couch, pretending to watch the birds fluttering in the trees. He sighed as if the weight of the world lay solely on his broad shoulders.

I stood up. "Fine, twice a week."

"Stacy—" Cin growled.

I shushed her.

Thor turned his head and sat upright, scooting away from Cinnamon, but he didn't get off the sofa.

"Three times a week, Big Man, and that's my final offer." I parked a hand on my hip, letting him know I meant business.

Cinnamon said, "Are you nuts?"

I kept my eyes on the dog when I said, "I prefer the term *eccentric*."

Thor stood up on all fours, shot my cousin an *I'll be back* look, and sauntered over to the screen door. He smacked it open and walked out of the house like he was John Wayne looking for a man who had wronged his woman.

Cinnamon tried to extract herself from the sofa and failed. I didn't dare offer her a hand.

"Don't you dare offer me a hand, or I swear to God, I'll break your finger," she said.

Geez, we had two more months of this? Poor Tony.

After three attempts, she rallied and catapulted herself to a standing position. She blew a stray hair from her eye, adjusted her tee shirt, and glared at me.

"Why did you tell him that?" she snapped.

"What did you want me to do? Because I'll tell you right now, if Tony had seen that, he would have insisted something was wrong and you'd be spending the night in the emergency room with an armed guard blocking the door."

Cinnamon considered this. Her husband had become overly protective ever since she got pregnant and it was all she could do not to check herself into the Holiday Inn just to get some peace. While some women loved to be doted on, for a woman as independent as my cousin, it was I-want-to-pull-my-own-hair-out frustrating.

Finally, she acquiesced. "All right, but if he comes unsupervised again, I cannot be responsible for my actions."

"Understood."

We talked a little bit about the reunion to be held later that week. Cinnamon had won the bid to cater the party, but Tony insisted she turn it down.

"We're still going, just so I can watch Monique make an ass of herself and lose what little customers she has left," she said.

Monique had been the second choice, although her bar wasn't big enough to host the event, so the committees decided to rent out Grant Hall.

I walked toward the door as she added, "I'm just glad I don't have to work with her on the damn thing. Not like you." She nudged me.

I turned around. "I don't have to work with her on the reunion."

Cin frowned. "Oh, I thought you were on the class committee for your graduation year."

"No I wasn't."

She tapped her chin with her finger. "Well, someone I know was. Who was it?" She lifted her eyes to the ceiling just as I spotted Thor inspecting the detached garage. He was really taking this whole protecting-the-baby job seriously. I wouldn't be surprised if he called in a bomb-sniffing German shepherd as an extra precaution.

That's when Cinnamon's words finally registered. I wasn't on the class committee with Monique.

"It was Chance," I said.

Chapter 5

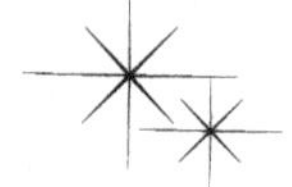

I decided to drop Thor off at the cottage and put him on lockdown until I could figure out what was going on with him. I would need to consult my great-aunt Fiona, whose prominent gifts were love spells and animal communication, and possibly the Blessed Book to decide if his sudden concern for Cinnamon was due to the pregnancy or something prophesied. As Cinnamon's connection to the Geraghty clan was threaded through her father, she wasn't gifted with the same abilities as the maternal line of our family. But perhaps we were all wrong about that. Maybe there was something magical within her. Literally. Maybe the baby was a girl and she held some sort of Geraghty gift that no one saw coming.

Or maybe the dog was just being overprotective of his first family. The first family I knew of anyway.

As I wove my car back through the streets of Amethyst and down toward my office, the sun was blazing and my mind was on Chance and the possibility that he'd be working with Monique on organizing the multi-class reunion. It must have just slipped his mind to tell me. Or perhaps mine. Maybe he had told me about this and I simply forgot. Either way, I didn't like it. While I trusted the man completely, I trusted Monique about as much as I trusted a pirate selling time-shares in Florida. And the way she smirked at me on her way to meet him intensified that slithery feeling I felt in her presence tenfold.

My mind was racing with horrible images of Chance clutched in Monique's arms as I sped down the street toward the newspaper.

Then I saw him.

That *Star Trek* hat was unmistakable. Pickle was flouncing in a garden of rust-colored mums, butterflies swirling around his head. He was holding a taffy apple in one hand and a giant, rainbow-colored lollipop in the other. The lollipop was stuck to his hair, but he didn't seem to mind.

I slammed on the brakes, threw the car into park right in the middle of the street, and jumped out of the vehicle. Didn't even bother to shut the door as I chased after Pickle.

I was ten steps away when a Cadillac Escalade plowed into my car.

At the excruciating sound of metal crushing against metal and glass glittering the pavement, I spun around, hands clutched to my head.

"Not my new car!"

I squeezed my eyes shut and smacked a palm to my head. *Stacy, you idiot!*

When I gathered up the courage to assess the damage, the Escalade seemed to be relatively intact and no one appeared to be injured, but my new Fiat looked like a crushed-up beer can. I had purchased it with the bonus money I received from the Council on completing my last mission. Special ordered to have the backseats removed so that Thor could ride comfortably.

At twenty-nine, it was the first new car I had ever owned. Now, it wouldn't even serve as a key chain. My stomach felt woozy and I swayed, biting back a tear.

A man who would have been a shoo-in for a *Vampire Diaries* casting call hopped out of the Cadillac. "Jesus, are you all right?" He looked at the Fiat—my first big purchase ever—and ran his fingers through his hair. "Are you hurt?"

"I'm fine, thanks. It was new," I said, my voice cracking, eyes on my tiny tin box.

The man looked at the crumpled car and scowled at me. "What the hell were you thinking? Stopping in the middle of the road like that? I could have hit you."

How to explain this? I saw a fairy traipsing through the garden across the street and since I had only ever seen him in a magical world that lies parallel to this one, I thought it best to investigate the situation immediately, lest there be some impending doom that would lead to total carnage of all life as we knew it.

That would have been the truth, of course, but I couldn't very well tell a perfect stranger that. "I thought I saw a bunny."

He looked at me as if he was certain there was a bottle of Prozac with my name on it and it was still full.

"A bunny?"

I shrugged. "I like bunnies. Didn't want to hit the little guy."

He crossed his arms, studied me a moment, and I shifted my stance. "But why would you get out of the car?"

Good question. I hadn't really thought through the whole bunny thing. Really wishing at that moment I had said "missing child" or something equally as urgent. *Good Goddess, Stacy, you have to start thinking on your feet.*

I glanced toward the mum garden. Pickle was gone. Naturally.

"I volunteer at a rabbit sanctuary. So, um, you see, a bunny can be very vulnerable at this time of year. Coyotes, you know. And, um . . ."

He waited as I searched for an explanation that would make some sort of rational sense.

"I didn't see the mother, so I figured it needed help. I was going to crate it and take it to the rescue. You know, to nurse it."

He cocked an eyebrow, clearly not buying a fricking word of the phantom bunny story.

"Nurse it?"

"Well, not personally." I flicked my eyes to his car. It looked like a brand-new model. It was practically painted with dollar signs.

"Right," he said in a deep tone.

I sighed. "Look, my cousin-in-law runs an auto body shop." I reached into the mangled monstrosity that was my car and grabbed my bag. "It was my fault for stopping in the middle of the road like that. I'll pay for the damages. I planned to take up cycling again anyway." I whipped out my wallet and pulled out Tony's card. My number was already printed on the back because, well, this was not the first wreck I'd had this year.

"My number's on the back."

"Of course it is."

I ignored that, flipped out my cell phone, called Tony, and told him I was sending him a customer and to get a tow truck over to Crescent Street.

The man's phone chimed then. He pulled it out, checked something, and said, "Look, I'm late for a meeting and there's not much damage to my car. You don't have to pay for anything. I should have been able to stop in time."

I breathed a sigh of relief. Biking on icy roads with monster hills was no fun. Plus, there wasn't a basket big enough to hold Thor.

He glanced over at my Fiat. Winced. "Thanks for this." He waved the card and headed for his vehicle.

"Wait, are you sure you don't want my insurance information or something?"

The man hopped inside his vehicle just as Leo, the chief of police of Amethyst, was motoring up the hill.

The man glanced back at the police cruiser. "No, it's fine. The damage is minor."

He fired up the engine as Leo rolled to a stop.

I called, "Well, don't you want my name?"

He stuck his handsome head out the window as he drove by. "I already know it, Stacy."

I stood there, mouth agape, as the SUV crested the hill.

Chapter 6

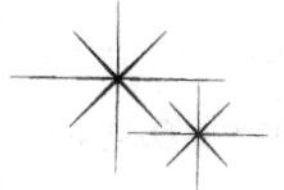

I remained in the street, wondering who on earth that man was and how he knew my name, as Leo hopped out of the cruiser. He took one look at the heap of red metal, another look at me, and said, "Do I want to know?"

"Probably not."

"You okay?"

His concern for me was still there in his hazel eyes, although we had been broken up for some months. When you're the Seeker of Justice working for a secret society of witches, dating a man with a badge can have serious drawbacks. They tend to get upset when you break the law, stumble upon various dead bodies, get yourself shot at, and talk to dead people. Leo was no exception. Our relationship didn't end badly, it just ended. It wasn't long after that when Chance and I rekindled the relationship we had begun all those years ago.

"Did you call Tony?"

"Yep."

Leo nodded, his strong jawline twitching as if he had something to say, but his lips couldn't quite form the words. His skin was perpetually tanned thanks to his Mediterranean parents, and he filled out a uniform better than Batman.

"Need a lift?"

I looked at what remained of the car, wondering how much I could get for the scrap metal, and kicking myself that I had been so incredibly careless. "Sure. Why not?"

Leo mentioned on the way back to the office that he would be attending the high school reunion.

"But you didn't graduate from our school."

He glanced at me, blew a thick, black lock of hair from his forehead. "I'll be there in an unofficial official capacity."

"What does that mean?"

"It means I'll be wearing my holster under my costume."

I rolled my eyes. "That seems unnecessary, don't you think? It's just a class reunion."

"One room filled with half the town and all your family. Sure. What could possibly go wrong?" he said sarcastically.

Leo was still getting used to our quirky town and its even quirkier residents. And, truth be told, Birdie and the aunts scared the bejeezus out of him.

"Good point."

I thanked him for the ride, sent out a silent wish that he'd find someone someday, and hopped out of the car. As he drove away, I couldn't help but notice the look of wistfulness on his face.

I settled back into my office, where I checked my e-mail and found a few notes Gladys had sent me on some of the valedictorians. I printed them out and scanned through the pages. There were doctors and lawyers, some homemakers, an archeologist, a fashion designer, a scientist, and one author. I jotted down notes and brainstormed some story angles before I shoved everything inside a manila folder.

I grabbed the yogurt I had tucked inside the fridge earlier and ate that as I contemplated the conversation I was going to have with Chance tonight. In my mind's eye, it went something like this:

Me: Why didn't you tell me you were meeting with Monique today?

Chance (looking completely baffled): I'm sorry, sweetie, I thought I did.

Me (relieved and totally calm): Oh. Well, maybe you did and it slipped my mind.

Chance (rubbing my shoulders): What do you say I cook us up a nice dinner, and afterwards we'll snuggle on the couch and watch *The Notebook* while I massage your feet?

Me (looking stunning in candlelight): That sounds wonderful.

The end.

My daydream was interrupted by a knock on the door. I tossed the empty yogurt carton in the trash can and went to answer it.

Derek was standing there holding a manila envelope. "Here's the contract."

I gave him a disappointed look and walked over to my desk. I tossed Monique's contract on top of the folder I had started for the reunion piece.

There was a second knock on my already-open door. I turned to see the man with the Escalade standing there.

"So, this is where the magic happens." He waltzed himself into my office and looked around the room. His sea-blue eyes were greedily drinking in every inch of my workspace. The walls, the computer, the photographs, everything. As if he was painting a mental picture.

I felt my heart skip a beat and my face grow pale. Who was this guy? Had he been sent by the Council? Was he a new member of the four corners? But why would he come here? Why wouldn't he have just told me that on the street?

The four corners consisted of myself, the Seeker; John, the Guardian; Ivy, the Warrior; and the Mage, who happened to be my grandmother, Birdie. Some quests, like the last one in Ireland, required all of our services.

"What are you talking about? There's no magic here," I said in a voice that sounded like a squeak toy.

Derek shot me a funny look. "Well, we haven't won a Pulitzer, but I think we put out a good little paper." He smiled, his white teeth contrasting beautifully with his dark skin.

The man walked over to the far wall and touched the new sword Birdie had given me to adorn my office. He shifted and I couldn't help but notice even his clothes reeked of wealth. His sports jacket was perfectly tailored, his shoes polished, his white shirt crisp, and his hair was definitely not courtesy of Cost Cutters.

"Interesting piece." He spoke clearly, enunciating each word as if he were savoring it like other people savored cake.

The man with the wavy chestnut hair plucked the shiny sword off the wall by the handle that featured the Morrigan, and a tiny yelp escaped my throat. I couldn't have strangers touching my magical tools. It left me exposed to attacks, both psychic and physical.

Plus it was rude. And rude people pissed me off.

I lunged forward to snatch the sword from his large hands, but Derek yanked me by the collar and I sprung back like a yo-yo. He hissed in my ear, "What's wrong with you, woman?"

Before I could answer, the man read the inscription aloud. "Between Destiny and Duty lies Faith. I'm so happy you found yours. Love, Birdie."

I swallowed hard. I couldn't exactly pinpoint why, but this guy made me incredibly uncomfortable, and the fact that he had his hands all over my sword tainted it. I would have to consecrate it again for it to be of any use to me magically. Although the tip was still pointy, and if he didn't stop manhandling my belongings, I might have to test its functionality on his perfectly pressed blue jeans.

"Who's Birdie?" he asked, cocking his head toward me as if he already knew the answer. As if he had a lot of answers wandering around that smug head of his.

I was beginning to feel vulnerable. And I had sworn I would never feel vulnerable again.

I ignored his question and found my voice. "I already told you I would pay for your damages. Now please take your hands off my office décor before I find a better place to stick it."

Derek pinched my arm.

"Ouch," I yelped.

"Stacy, I'd like to introduce you to Blade Knight." Derek's voice was layered with a twinge of annoyance.

Blade Knight extended his hand. I didn't take it at first, but Derek shoved me forward.

I shot a glare back at Derek, then faced Knight. "Forgive me for saying so, Mr. Knight, but that's the fakest sounding name I've heard outside of a Marvel Comics book."

"Stacy!" Derek said.

I braced myself before I shook the man's hand, anticipating an image, a message, or a feeling. It was warm and cold at the same time. Strong. Almost too strong. I held it until I got the message I was seeking and then I abruptly dropped it.

Blade Knight held his gaze on me. His eyes seemed to penetrate my very soul. One corner of his mouth curled up into a sly smile. “She’s right, actually. My editor thought I needed something a bit more . . .” He searched for the right word. “Dangerous.” His face told me he liked danger. Lived for it, in fact.

I lived to fight it.

“Your editor?” I didn’t like this. Not one bit.

Derek smiled wide. “Blade is a crime writer. He’s here to do some research on a story.”

“Research? What kind of research?”

Because I swear, if he’d said *witches*, I would have had to slip him some hemlock and put him on a cruise to Alaska.

Blade Knight looked at me and smiled as if he’d just been granted the key to the Emerald City. “Most of my novels are set in Chicago, but I wanted to set a story in a small town. This seemed like the perfect place.”

A tiny wave of relief flooded me. “So you write fiction? Thrillers? Murder mysteries? That sort of thing?”

“That’s right. I’ve been spending some time exploring and chatting with the locals.” He walked his eyes up and down my body and I suddenly felt the need for a turtleneck. “They have lots of interesting tales to tell.”

This guy was too put together, too classy, and too arrogant for Amethyst. My worry began to slip away, because the more he talked to the locals, the faster he would want to hightail it out of Dodge. “Well, don’t believe everything you hear. People tend to exaggerate in small towns when the biggest news of the week is who won the pie-eating contest at St. Mary’s and who got hammered at the Elks Club.” I motioned to escort him out of my office, far, far away from me, but he didn’t budge.

“Actually, Stacy, Blade was thinking of switching directions this time," Derek interjected, completely oblivious to my obvious unease.

Damn. I knew it couldn't be that easy. There was always a catch. See, the Universe and I have this little game we like to play. I preferred to get through the day without getting blown up, kidnapped, or set on fire, and *It* preferred that, at the very least, I spill hot coffee on my lap and crash my car just for giggles. I was like Mother Nature's personal jester.

"Oh?" I felt a tingle dance up and down my spine, confirming the message I had picked up earlier when I shook Blade's hand. I used to ignore signs like those, but now I searched for them. The more signals I received, both internal and external, the better prepared I was for anything. Or anyone.

Blade smiled wide. I was sure other women found that smile charming. To me, he looked like a tiger moving in for a kill. He paused before he pounced. "You know, I've learned so much since I've been here and I was so intrigued with the people I've spoken with that I decided to write a nonfiction book. True crime, if you will. With a touch of mysticism."

I flicked my eyes to Derek, who stood there grinning like an idiot.

I hurried to stop that thought train before it left the station. "I see. Well, I'm sure you might dig up a story or two in the archives of the library, but I doubt you could fill a whole book with them. Derek would be happy to escort you there." I couldn't have this man digging into my past, into my family, into all that I'd been sworn to protect. Not now, not when I'd come so far.

Derek said, "He's not here to talk to me, Stacy."

I suddenly wished I had insisted Chance install a trapdoor in my office while I was gone.

No one spoke, so I asked the question, despite knowing the answer. "So then, who are you here to see?"

"You, Stacy Justice."

Of course you are, I thought, just as a busy spider spun a web over the threshold to my office.

Which was the third confirmation of my suspicions.

There was an uninvited guest in our midst.

Chapter 7

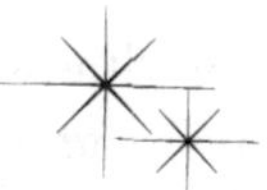

I walked over to the door, put my hand on the handle, and said, "Would you excuse us, please, Mr. Knight?"

I tried to smile politely but my mouth wasn't cooperating. I probably looked like I was constipated.

"Call me Blade, please."

Ugh. What a stupid name. "Would you excuse us, Blade?" I repeated when he didn't take a step toward me.

"Certainly." He flashed Derek the winning smile of an expert poker player holding a full house and sauntered out the door.

Derek smiled back. Until I shut the door. Then his face deflated like a punctured balloon.

"Derek, I don't like this man. I don't like what he's implying." I glanced back toward the spot that Blade Knight had just occupied. I could still see his dark blue jeans through the glass pane.

"What are you talking about? The man's a bestselling author. This book could ignite a ton of revenue for the town. Tourists eat that stuff up. It would be good for all of us." Derek crossed his arms. "What's really going on?" He eyed me suspiciously.

I licked my lips. Derek and I had a unique partnership in that he pretended I wasn't a maniac magnet with a smart-ass mouth and

I pretended he wasn't a cocky pinhead who consulted his crotch whenever he made a decision. It worked out well for both of us, although Derek was fully aware that there was more to me and my heritage than I had ever told him. Thankfully, his voodoo priestess aunt left him with a fear of anything supernatural so he didn't ask a lot of detailed questions and I certainly didn't offer any answers.

"Nothing. I just think he's here to make us look foolish. Small-town idiots and their small-town crimes. You know what I'm talking about." I spread my arms out like I was highlighting a headline. "Come to Hicksville, USA, see all the freaks."

"First of all, this place has had more murders than a prison riot. And second—"

I rushed to interrupt him. "I mean, what was that crack about mysticism?" What *was* that crack about? How much did Blade Knight know about our town? More importantly, what did he know about my family, and why did he want to interview me?

"Girl, please." Derek waved his hand away, dismissing my concerns. I hated it when people dismissed my concerns. Usually because it meant I was about to wind up in Crap Creek without a paddle. Or even a canoe.

Derek continued. "You know as well as I do that Amethyst is Kookytown on crack. The guy found an angle he liked and he wants to run with it." He shrugged. "He's a writer."

"Exactly. I don't trust them."

Derek made a noise that sounded like he was choking on a mosquito. "Do I have to remind you that you're a writer too?"

"I'm a reporter. There's a difference." I was grasping at straws, but I was desperate. Samhain was coming up, which meant a clothing-optional moon ritual; I was pretty sure Pickle was in town, accosting all the candy stores; and I had yet to figure out what was going on with my fidgety mother, my overprotective dog, and my insanely irritable cousin. So I wasn't exactly in a healthy position to be shadowed by a nosy author with a tape recorder and an interest in the occult.

Because, good Goddess, what if he exposed me? What if the world suddenly knew where I lived and every history zealot who believed in the ancient texts of the Druids came looking for me?

Or *hunted* me, as Birdie called it. The hunters came from all walks of life seeking to unlock the mysteries of the Universe. Looking for ancient texts hidden long ago, artifacts with power beyond human comprehension, treasures believed by most of the world to be only legends. These were just some of the secrets the Council kept, and I, as the Seeker, was sworn to protect them.

It was imperative for myself and everyone I loved that my role remain closely guarded.

Derek approached me and put a hand on my shoulder. "You need to get on board, because he's been pitching the idea all over town. Been talking to people and lining up interviews over the weekend, apparently. If you had gotten to the meeting on time this morning and hadn't had a cat fight with Monique, you would have known that."

That gave me the best idea I'd had in a while. I snapped my fingers. "That's it! Monique. Men love Monique. She can give him all the information he needs." And possibly a floor show.

He shook his head. "Nope. Gotta be you. He was pretty clear on that."

Damn. Who had this guy been talking to? He couldn't possibly believe I was a witch. I mean, people around town knew we were pagans, knew we cast spells here and there, but they didn't really *know*. Not the whole truth. Not that I was the Seeker of Justice, privy to information regarding very valuable, very ancient artifacts the world over. Not even Chance knew that.

Derek said in a serious tone, "If we don't cooperate with him, we could lose a lot of advertisers. I've been getting calls about this guy since you left. Personally, I had never heard of him." He leered at me in an attempt to look stealthy. "I prefer spy novels."

It didn't work. He looked more like a man being forced to eat a lemon against his will. "But I checked him out and he's pretty famous, especially with the folks around here. People are excited about this thing." He lowered his voice and gave me a stern look. "And I don't have to tell you that newspapers are dying all over the country. People want their news online these days. Lucky for us, this town is still stuck in the Stone Age, but that could all change tomorrow."

He was right, I knew, but that didn't set my mind at ease. If anything, it made me more jumpy.

When I didn't respond, Derek walked toward the door. He opened it, paused, and shifted to face me. I could see that the writer wasn't standing there anymore. "Oh, and one more thing. This guy?" He thumbed toward the hallway. "He's not looking to make us out to be small-town hicks. He's from Amethyst."

With that, Derek left me standing there in silent surprise.

Blade Knight was from Amethyst? He didn't look familiar, but that didn't mean anything. I had pegged him to be about ten years older than me.

So then, the question remained. Why was he so insistent that I help him with his research?

Before I went back to my work, I removed the sword from the wall. The vibration that had been attached to it from my consecration and the Morrigan's blessing was gone.

I placed it on my desk carefully. When I did, the folder I had tucked the reunion notes inside of earlier glowed.

Derek's words echoed in my head alongside Gladys's e-mail.

He's from Amethyst. A couple of doctors, lawyers, an archeologist, some homemakers, and an author.

Was Blade Knight the author Gladys had dug up?

The door to my office was ajar so I walked over to it, shut, and locked it. The light faded from the folder as I opened it to give the notes a more thorough examination.

"Let's see who you really are, Blade Knight."

The information on the author was buried five pages deep within the e-mail Gladys had sent me. But it glared at me all the same. As if a spotlight were shining on it.

When I read the name, I had to sit down from the shock of it.

Chapter 8

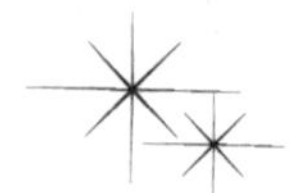

I stopped at the library on my way home from work to check out a Blade Knight book. The librarian informed me that none were available at the moment. She handed me a flyer and told me there was a signing scheduled for tomorrow evening at the bookstore on Main Street from six to eight. The front of the flyer featured the author's book covers. I counted thirteen titles in all. Five were part of a series featuring a female FBI agent named Tracey Stone. From the looks of the covers, Tracey was a badass who knew her way around a gun. I decided to just download the e-books. So I logged into the Amazon website via my smart phone and purchased all thirteen novels and sent them to my laptop and my Kindle. That way I could study Blade Knight where he lived. Find out what he was really up to.

The author's bio was on the back of the flyer. It read:

Blade Knight is the author of thirteen novels, numerous newspaper articles, and several short stories. He is originally from a small town in the Midwest, but now makes his home in Chicago.

No mention of his given name. No mention of what had happened to him when he was a child.

Interesting.

I tucked the flyer into my bag and circled around and out the back door of the library, down the steps, and across the alley. It was getting late. The sun had slashed the October sky with streaks of crimson, magenta, and violet before I had entered the stone building. Now the colors were darkening, making room for the night sky and the moon that would plump to fullness later in the week—the Blood Moon. Someone was burning leaves a few doors down as I made my way across the alley and up the street toward the cottage.

I was thinking about Chance and Monique when I heard a crunching sound behind me. Like a foot stepping on a brittle maple leaf.

There was a knife slipped inside the heel of my boot and a stun gun in my bag. I didn't slow my pace down, but I set my senses to full alert. It was better to be cautiously aware of the surroundings than to appear paranoid. That way, a would-be attacker who thought he had the upper hand would get the shock of his life when the tables were turned on him.

Another crunch. Closer this time.

I sniffed the air, tuned my ears to the vibration that was fluttering behind me. The soft music of a jazz pianist drifted over from my left. From my right, I smelled catnip that had recently been cut or rolled in by a happy feline.

Crunch, crunch, crunch. Louder. Closer.

Too close for my liking.

I whipped the knife out from my boot heel and, in one swift motion, whirled around and aimed it at the man who was following me.

Except it wasn't a man. It was Pickle.

At first, I wasn't sure who was more shocked, the fairy or myself. The poor thing was a wisp of a boy who looked to be no older than the age required to secure a driver's license. His skin, which was already pale under normal conditions, grew fright-white as he stared at me, wide sky-blue eyes filling up with water.

He was eating a peanut Munch bar.

I quickly plastered a broad smile onto my face, held my hands up slowly, and said, "Easy there, buddy. It's okay. I'm going to put this away, all right?" I slid the blade into my back pocket.

My Fae guide still hadn't made a sound, but his eyes started bubbling over like a burst pipe.

"No, no, don't cry, Pickle. Please don't cry."

Why in Goddess's name was this race so freaking sensitive? Sugar overload?

Pickle jutted out his lower lip, wadded up something in his hand, shrieked, and launched it at me. Then he ran straight into an oak tree and disappeared.

"Perfect. That's all I need is a pissed-off fairy." I removed my jacket and tried to extract whatever the hell it was he had thrown at me that was now imbedded in my hair. I managed to free a piece of it. It was a tan, sticky substance. I took a whiff of it. Mashed-up Bit-O-Honey.

"Son of a pusbucket. I'll never get this out," I grumbled.

I spun around to rush home.

That's when I saw the author.

He was standing next to his car looking as if he'd just seen a ghost.

I dashed through a row of houses and ran all the way home. I flung the door open to my cottage, thrust myself inside, and bolted the door shut, trying to catch my breath. How much of that had the writer seen? Could he see Pickle? Was that even possible? Or was it only me who could see my Fae guide?

I leaned up against the door, closed my eyes, and blew out a sigh.

A loud whinny drifted over to me from the general direction of the living room.

Thor was lying on the couch, his paw tapping the cushion as if he were a parent waiting up for a child who had missed curfew. I opened one eye as the dog jumped down, lumbered over to me, and sniffed the wad of candy in my hair.

He sat down in front of me and glared.

"Don't give me that look." I walked into the galley kitchen of my small cottage and filtered through the cupboards, searching for peanut butter. I heard it worked to remove gum from hair. Maybe it would work on Bit-O-Honey. "If you hadn't invaded Cinnamon's home, I wouldn't have had to lock you in here."

Thor harrumphed and stood by the back door. I let him out just as the front bell rang.

I grumbled, knowing very well it was Blade Knight. I was really growing tired of this man following me all over town. Didn't he ever hear of appointments? Cell phones? Geez, I felt like I was living in a fishbowl, just swimming around, waiting for him to pluck me out and flush me down the toilet.

There was no peanut butter, so I stuck a Cubs hat on my head and went to answer the door. I flung it open.

"Look, I've had a long day—"

Chance stood there, a bouquet of daisies in his strong arms, looking sexy and confused at the same time.

"You want to tell me about it?" he said.

I moved aside and let him pass through the threshold, shutting the door behind me.

"Not now." I followed him to the kitchen, where I watched as he put the flowers in water. I snaked my arms around his waist, laid my cheek on his back, and said, "Maybe we could talk about it over dinner. How does salmon sound?"

Chance lifted my arms and turned to face me. He pulled me close, secured my arms back around his waist, and kissed me. It was a deep kiss. The kind you can feel all the way down to your toes and back.

He sighed. "I can't, baby. I completely forgot I agreed to help with this reunion thing. Rain check?"

My body stiffened, despite my brain warning it to relax. *Be cool.* I turned to wash the dog dish left in the sink from last night. "Sure. Why not?"

My foot was shaking as tension in my body rose to the surface. I could feel the unreasonable bitch that lay within me fighting to make her way out. *Down, girl, down.*

Chance took a step to the side. He leaned in to get a look at my face. "Hey, what's wrong? Is something bothering you?"

The only other thing in the sink was a glass and I scrubbed the hell out of that thing with a Brillo pad. Had I scrubbed any harder, I could have molded it into a candy dish.

"Nope. All good."

I could feel myself losing it. I mean, really losing it. There was heat rising up from my belly. I bit my lip to keep my mouth from turning against me.

Chance put a gentle hand on my shoulder. "Hey, Stacy, what is it?"

Could he honestly not know? I mean, really? Were men that clueless? I turned to face him, trying very hard to soften my voice and calm that little vein in my throat that throbbed whenever I was upset.

"You're cancelling our date so you can hang out with Monique and now you're standing there asking me what's wrong?"

He moved back as if I had slapped him.

Chance put a hand out in a calming gesture. Oh, I just hated it when they did that! His voice was so irritatingly steady when he spoke that I wanted to pinch him, just to hear a different octave.

"Okay, first of all, I'm not cancelling to hang out with Monique. And secondly, I completely forgot about this thing or I would have told you sooner."

"You know what? It's fine." I tossed the glass back in the sink and it rattled around the drain for a while. "Hey, at least you brought flowers."

I turned to walk out of the kitchen and Chance grabbed my shoulders. He tried to look in my eyes. "Stacy, come on."

I flicked my eyes away. It wasn't just that he was cancelling a date. It wasn't just that he might be working with Monique. It was me. My own guilt for not telling him everything about what I had gone through lately. For not being able to share with my partner all the things I so desperately needed to talk about.

Guilt is a nasty bitch. And she makes you do really stupid things.

When I wouldn't look at him, Chance dropped his arms and backed up. "You don't trust me? Is that it? After everything we've been through?"

Everything we've been through. Everything I've been through. Now, so many secrets.

"Of course I trust you. But I don't trust Monique."

Chance's eyes darkened as he stared at me. "No. That's not it. It's something else. It's that thing that's always come between us. It's your fear."

My head shot up. "What? What are you talking about?"

He backed up, slowly nodded as if he had just come to some sort of epiphany. "That's it, isn't it? You don't trust yourself to open up to me completely, so you're terrified that someone else might."

"That's not fair!"

He rapped his knuckles on the counter, looked at me with a doubt I had never seen before. Never wanted to see again. "You're right. It's not fair. For either of us." He turned to walk out of the cottage.

I didn't bother to call him back. The way he carried himself as he walked out the door told me everything.

There was a crack in our foundation. And I was the only one who could fix it.

Except I couldn't. Not without risking his life.

And that was a chance I wasn't willing to take.

Chapter 9

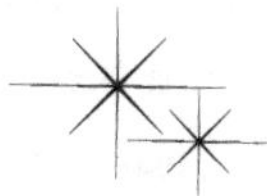

I sat there on the front porch of my cottage, sobbing, a wad of Bit-O-Honey stuck in my hair, my hat glued to that, and an empty carton of Ben & Jerry's Cherry Garcia tucked between my legs. Salty tears marched down my cheeks as Thor settled in next to me and passed gas.

It was not my finest hour.

I was just about to hunt down a bottle of tequila and order a meat lover's pizza when a familiar voice that I thought I'd never hear again pierced my ears.

"Stacy Justice, pull yourself together!" Danu barked.

I looked up. A large orb floated in front of me with the Goddess Danu's image imbedded in it. Her fiery red hair engulfed most of the frame and her emerald eyes were blazing at me.

I was so not in the mood for a lecture.

"What are you doing here, Danu?"

I glanced around but I didn't see Pickle.

Badb, the Morrigan, poked her head inside the orb. "Good Goddess. She's a mess." She shot Danu a look. "Honestly, this is the Seeker?"

I considered poking the orb with my fingernail just to watch it pop, or telling Badb to take a long walk down a short pier, but I had neither the energy nor the cojones to do so. Instead I said, "I'm not in the mood. Leave me alone. Both of you."

Danu ignored my request. "Did you make Pickle cry?"

I threw up my hands. "That's why you're here? To lecture me about some overly sensitive fairy who's hopped up on so much sugar even Willy Wonka would be disgusted."

"Who's Willy Wonka?" Badb asked.

I stood up. "I said go away."

The screen door slapped behind me as I made my way into the house in search of booze.

The goddesses floated behind me.

"Stacy Justice, you're beginning to anger me," Danu said. "Don't think I won't yank you back through the portal."

"Yeah, well, I have news for you, Danu. I had a door installed where your painting used to be." That was how I got myself sucked into the Otherworld in the first place. A portrait of Danu once hung in my grandmother's house and served as a doorway that led to the Geraghty Girls' Chamber of Magic. I asked Chance to put a door there so that would never happen again.

A sob choked in my throat at the thought of Chance. I needed wine. Something, anything to make this nightmare of a day a little more bearable. Where the hell was it? I was sure there was a bottle of Pinot Grigio somewhere. I slapped the cabinet door closed when I couldn't find any.

Danu scoffed. "Do you honestly think a door would stop me?"

Slowly, I turned around. "Don't do it, Danu. I can't take any more surprises today."

Badb said, "Then show some respect. And for Goddess's sake, wash your face and stop blubbering."

I rolled my eyes, wiped my nose with my sleeve. "Fine."

Before I headed into the bathroom, I checked one more cupboard for the emergency Kahlúa I always kept on hand when Lolly visited me. My great-aunt was the oldest Geraghty Girl and the one whose train didn't quite pull all the way into the station. Liquor sharpened her senses so we usually kept a steady supply on hand to spike her coffee when the need arose.

"Yes!" It was there, behind the chicory coffee can. I knocked back a shot, then poured another into a tumbler and mixed it with cream. The daisies Chance had brought were sitting on the counter and I burst into tears all over again.

Badb sighed. "This is pathetic."

Danu was a little more understanding. "Perhaps we should slap her?"

Badb and Danu discussed the best methods to penetrate the worlds so they could properly torture me, while I tried to gain my composure.

I stuck my head under the kitchen faucet and washed my face with Dawn dishwashing liquid because I didn't want to turn my back on these two sadistic banshees.

I took a deep breath and faced them. "Okay. I'm better." I sipped my cocktail. "What did you want to discuss with me?"

The orb bobbed up and down. "Tell the Mage that the Leanan Sidhe has escaped. You must find and bind her. Pickle is there to escort her back to the Otherworld."

"That's it?"

Danu smiled. "That's it."

I downed the rest of my drink, rinsed the glass out, and put it in the sink. "Sounds simple enough."

Danu and Badb exchanged a look that sent a chill through the room.

I narrowed my eyes. "Wait a minute. Who is the Leanan Sidhe?"

Danu said, "The Mage will fill you in. That's all for now."

"No, Danu, wait."

The bubble popped and they were gone.

I grabbed the Blessed Book and a sweatshirt and slipped outside to head to the Geraghty Girls' House, wondering who the Leanan Sidhe was and how I was supposed to find and bind her.

I didn't get very far because Blade Knight was standing on my porch holding a pizza. I checked his other hand for a tequila bottle, wondering if he had read my mind, but saw nothing.

The sweatshirt was covering the book, thankfully. I clutched it to my chest.

"Mr. Knight, what are you doing on my porch?" This guy was starting to creep me out. If we didn't have something incredibly painful in common, I would have stabbed him in the shoulder already.

"I brought you a peace offering." He held up the pizza box. "I'm afraid we didn't get off on the right foot and since we'll be working together, I wanted to make it up to you."

How did he know I hadn't eaten? "First of all, we"—I motioned from myself to him—"are not working together. Second"—I crossed my arms—"how did you know I wanted a pizza? What if I'd had a dinner date?"

The author glanced behind him. "Well, I imagine you did, but the man who came in with the daisies and left in the truck didn't stay long enough to eat. Didn't look too happy either."

"Are you stalking me?"

He looked confused at that, hurt even. "What? No. I just wanted to talk with you."

I glared at him. "How did you know where I live?"

"Well, I—"

"Who sent you?" Had he seen Pickle disappear into the tree? Or had he assumed I was talking to myself? Neither option appealed to me.

"No one—"

"What's your game?" I stepped forward.

"I don't have—"

I poked him. "And don't lie to me!"

"I'm not lying. If you'd just let me explain."

"I really don't think I want to listen to anything you have to say."

Thor came around the corner then, eyeing Blade Knight first and then the pizza box.

The man shot a glance at Thor and swung back to me. When he spoke, the words tumbled out. "Look, I was here earlier. I stopped by to talk to you. I saw the man leave, figured he was your date and you got into a fight, maybe you skipped dinner." His brow furrowed as he glanced at my head. Probably the Bit-O-Honey wad was making an escape. "So I thought I'd be chivalrous. Bring you hot food and maybe you'd be more open to my proposal."

"Why?"

He shrugged. "That's how I would write it. A mysterious stranger swoops in to save the day." He raised one eyebrow like he was Clark Kent.

I rolled my eyes. This guy had me very confused. At first he seemed threatening, then he seemed threatened by me, now he was being sweet and arrogant at the same time. Which irritated the hell out of me. I say pick a personality and stick with it.

Thor inched over to our visitor, still eyeing the pizza box. A long trail of drool clung to his muzzle. He licked his lips. He didn't seem too concerned about Knight, but I suspected maybe the aroma of fresh mozzarella and oregano was impeding his instincts.

"What kind of pizza?"

"The works. Extra pepperoni."

My stomach rumbled at the sound of that. Thor looked at me hopefully. Like, *Can he stay? Please, can he?*

"Before I even entertain the idea of sharing a pizza with you, I want to know how you found out my address."

He nodded toward the Geraghty Girls' House. "I didn't. I'm staying next door and I saw you come up the driveway through the window."

Damn. Now I'd never be able to shake him.

I sighed. "Okay, but before I invite you in, I want you to know you're not that mysterious."

He smiled. "I'm not?"

I shook my head and turned to open the door. "I'm afraid not. I know exactly who you are, Joseph Conrad."

The author's Adam's apple bobbed up and down as he swallowed hard. He wasn't smiling as I held the door open for him.

Chapter 10

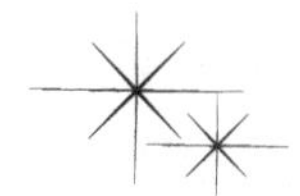

My cottage was too small for a dining table, so Blade Knight set the pizza box on the counter and stood in front of the breakfast bar. Thor sat near him, smacking his lips and looking at the man with hope and hunger in his eyes.

I didn't say anything more for a few minutes. I just let him stew on the revelation that I knew his real name, what happened to him all those years ago, and that I could also shake up a person's nerves if I had to.

There were paper plates in the drawer next to the refrigerator. I grabbed those along with some napkins and two waters.

When I turned around, the author was staring at me with a look I couldn't quite make out. Apprehension? Curiosity? Anger? He shook his head as if trying to erase a thought and the confident demeanor returned.

"I was going to tell you who I am. I just didn't want to mention it in front of the editor," he said.

"Why not?" I handed him a plate and a napkin, set the water in front of him, and opened mine.

Blade Knight took a long pull from the bottle. "I was afraid he'd want to do a story on me, and that's not why I came back here."

I pulled some crushed red pepper from the spice rack near the stove and set it on the counter between us. Blade opened the pizza box and the tangy aroma of pepperoni and tomato sauce made my stomach rumble. I grabbed a slice and slid it onto my plate, sprinkling it with the red pepper flakes.

Then I focused my gaze on Blade. "Why *did* you come back here?"

He met my eyes, steadied himself and said, "To find the son of a bitch who killed my parents."

Joseph Conrad had been nine years old when his parents were bludgeoned to death in their own home. I was just a baby myself, but when you grow up in a close-knit community, stories tend to travel through time. The police had determined it was a robbery gone wrong, except the only items the thief or thieves actually made off with were a few books, some artwork, and a computer. The boy was an only child, his parents had no close relatives that anyone could find, and so he entered the foster care system and became a ward of the state.

When the man standing in my kitchen became Blade Knight, I didn't know.

He reached for two slices of pizza. He put one on the paper plate and flipped the other one to Thor, who caught it midair and swallowed it whole. The dog sat down patiently waiting for a second serving.

I gauged the man's body language, the easy way he seemed comfortable in this situation. Most people find Thor threatening, but Blade didn't seem to have any qualms about my 180-pound Great Dane.

But if he was in Amethyst to find out who murdered his parents, what did he want with me?

I grabbed another slice of pizza, dabbing the grease with a napkin, and contemplated my next question.

"Why now? Why after all this time?"

He thought for a time before he spoke, measuring his words carefully. "A lot of reasons. First, because I'm older, wiser, and I have the money to track this thing wherever it leads. Second, I'm tired of finding justice only through my work. I can put a hundred killers away between the pages of my books, but all the while, a real killer—or killers—is still out there roaming free. My parents deserve better than that."

I was surprised to hear his voice crack. Surprised too at the wave of empathy that washed over me.

We had a lot in common, Blade and I.

His leg twitched suddenly. It wasn't obvious if you weren't looking for it, but I was. It was an unconscious movement, his body betraying him. He was holding something back. Either that or he was lying to me.

"What's the real reason? The smoking gun?" I asked, an edge to my voice.

Blade reached for two more slices of pizza and tossed one to Thor. He didn't meet my eyes for a moment. He drank more water and I did the same.

Finally he said, "Before I tell you that, you have to agree to help me."

I wasn't fond of ultimatums. "And why would I do that?" I asked, eyes narrowed.

He reached his hand into the inner pocket of his jacket and I whipped the athame out of mine and put it to his throat.

"Whoa! Easy, Miss Justice. It's just some newspaper articles."

I kept the knife to him, told him not to move, and reached inside his coat pocket. I pulled out a stack of newspaper clippings.

"Sorry," I mumbled. "I'm . . . cautious. Single woman living alone and all."

The author glanced at Thor, whose head was cocked. The dog was looking at me as if I'd just shot the man who invented Milk-Bones. The dog snorted off to the couch.

"Yes, I can see why you'd be jumpy. I mean, when your only safeguard is an animal the size of Chewbacca," Blade said. He rolled his eyes.

Get a grip, Stacy.

I put the knife on the counter and sifted through the articles. Most of them were written by or about me. The first was the story regarding my father's murder. Then there was the cold case about the dead girl bricked up inside the wall of Cinnamon's bar, along with a few other crimes I had helped put to bed. There were articles about my family, the town, historical pieces regarding Amethyst. Murders that had taken place here, missing persons reports, unusual unexplained sightings, and more.

"Okay, now I'm convinced you're stalking me, Mr. Knight." I slapped the papers to his chest.

What was he doing with all of these articles? Did he actually think I knew something about his parents' murder?

"Call me Blade, please." He shoved the news pieces back inside his coat.

"Do I have to?"

He ignored that and said, "It wasn't about you. It was about Amethyst. I've always felt that the key to my parents' murder—the reason they were killed—had something to do with this place. I've been a longtime subscriber of the *Amethyst Globe*. By the way, I like the new sex column."

I moaned. Of course he did.

He continued. "Come on, Stacy. May I call you Stacy?"

"I'll think about it."

"You have to admit there's something strange about this town." He glanced out the window in the direction of the Geraghty House. I could see that the lights were still on in the kitchen. "I suspect, too, that you know a lot more about it than I ever could."

Oh boy. How deep was he going to dig? It was my turn to twitch. "I still don't see why you think I could help you with this. I was barely crawling when the murders happened."

Spellcasting, yes. Crawling was new.

He tapped his jacket where he had tucked away the articles. "I don't just think you can help, I know you will."

"Are all bestselling authors as cocky as you?"

"Only Patterson."

"And what has you so convinced that I'll agree to this?"

Blade Knight shifted so that we were toe to toe. He was several inches taller than my five-foot-six frame. He lowered his head to stare right at me, right through me, to the hidden parts very few had ever reached. I sucked in a breath.

His voice lowered to practically a whisper and my heart thumped. "Because there's a hunger inside of you that lives to see the bad guys get theirs. It's a need you have that refuses to fade away no matter how many killers you put behind bars. You're driven to see things through to the end of the story wherever it leads, and what's more, you're good at it. Maybe the beast is fueled by your father's death. Maybe it grew from your mother's abandonment. Or maybe it's an insufferable fear that you can only keep buried when the world is balanced. When right wins over wrong. Whatever it is, Stacy Justice, I know you can't turn away from it or it'll consume you from the inside out."

His words tore through me and for a moment, I was stunned. Everything he said was so personal, so intimate. It was like he had his finger on the pulse of my subconscious. As if he could read the map of my soul with the touch of a button. I stared at him in bewilderment for several heartbeats.

When I regained my composure I said, "Are you always this dramatic?"

"Yes. It's my one flaw."

"Besides your name."

He smiled. "Besides my name."

I turned away from Blade to wash the pizza grease from my hands and to think.

He was right about one thing. I knew what it was like to feel forgotten. To feel as if there was no hope, no justice in the world when it came to the people we loved the most.

Except I had found justice for my parents. And didn't Blade—irritating as he may be—deserve the same for his?

I took my hat off and ran my fingers through my hair, forgetting I still had a wad of Bit-O-Honey stuck in it. Then I plopped the hat back on my head.

Blade gave me a curious look as if he had completely forgotten to ask me about something, and since I still didn't know how much he had seen on the street with Pickle—or if he could see Pickle—I stopped him as soon as he opened his mouth.

I held up a finger. "Rule number one. No questions."

He grinned. "Is that a yes?"

I nodded. "I'll help you. On my time. On my terms."

He smacked his hands together and said, "Yes!" Then he picked me up and swung me around.

"Okay, rule number two. No touching, no picking up, no swinging of any kind."

He set me back down. "Sorry."

"Now tell me about the smoking gun."

Chapter 11

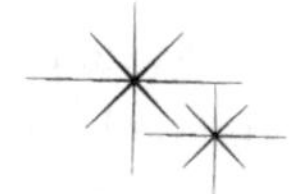

I looked at Thor, whose eyes were growing heavy as he snuggled deeper into the sofa. "What do you think, buddy? Did I just make a huge mistake?"

He pawed at the air, grunted, and flipped onto his back to settle in for a nap, unconcerned about anything but his full belly and his sleepy head.

While I was waiting for Blade Knight to retrieve something from his car, my phone made a typing sound, indicating I just received a text.

It was from Chance. I hate fighting with you.

I texted back. Me too.

Chance: You know you have nothing to be jealous about.

Me: And you have nothing to be nervous about. I'm not afraid. Not of you. Not of us. It's complicated right now, but there are things I need to tell you. I will as soon as I can.

Chance: I know you will. TTYL. xoxo.

Me: XOXOXO

I slipped the phone into the back pocket of my jeans as Blade Knight walked through the door carrying a beat-up-looking camel-colored satchel. He carefully closed the door behind him.

He set the bag on the counter. I pulled a stool up to where he stood and hopped onto it.

Blade launched right into the story. "I moved into my first foster home with only one box of belongings. That was the rule. Take only the essentials, leave the rest. Over the course of the years of being shuffled around from one dysfunctional household to another, I had forgotten all about the box."

He looked at me, eyes dark, defiant. Sincere. I felt for him in that moment. For the frightened little boy he must have been.

Blade ran a hand over his face. "When a person is under that much stress, with no room to breathe in between blows, the only way to survive is to bury it. All of it. Lock away every bit of garbage, every shred of fear, so no one can find your vulnerabilities."

"Because vulnerabilities can get you killed," I said softly.

He was taken aback by that remark and gave me a curious stare.

"I wrote a story on repressed memories," I said, which was complete baloney. I knew all about the dangers of exposing your weak spots strictly from experience.

Blade nodded, satisfied with that answer. "I repressed so many memories, my therapist had to use a shovel to dig them out. All but one. That one, I still kept in here." He pointed to his heart. "Until recently."

"Your parents' murder?"

Blade snapped his fingers as if to say, *bingo*. "It wasn't until I received a call two weeks ago from a social worker that I opened up that floodgate." He glanced at the satchel. "After losing my parents, and then the experience of the first few foster homes, I decided to cut all ties to anything painful. I brought only a book with me from house to house until eventually, I forgot all about the box. But it was labeled with my name and the contact information for the social services office. My last foster home was here in Amethyst. The man who owned it died recently and someone found the box in his attic and contacted the agency." He tapped the bag, right where it was buckled. "As soon as I opened it, the memory of that sticky summer day came flooding back."

"So what about the memory of that day makes you think it wasn't a robbery gone wrong?"

Blade looked at me, deadpan. "Because, Stacy, my parents knew someone was coming for them."

His words sent a shudder through me that chilled me to the bone. My mother knew someone was coming for me too. And her split-second decision that day sent a ripple effect through our entire family that would last a lifetime.

"Then why didn't they take you and leave?" I asked.

Blade sighed and started pacing the room. "I've been asking myself that question ever since I opened the box two weeks ago." His gaze met mine. "All I can figure is that they didn't think whoever it was was there to kill them. They must have only thought that the intruder wanted something from them." He slid his eyes over to me. "That was obvious, judging from the state of our house after the murders. The place had been thoroughly tossed."

"Then why didn't they just give it up? Whatever it was."

Blade turned to me, leaning on the other stool. His voice was rising, excited and frustrated at the same time. "I've been thinking about that too. What if they didn't actually have it, but the killer was certain they did? What if they never had it? What if it was hidden? Or it belonged to someone else?"

We stared at each other for a moment trying to piece the puzzle together. Blade broke his gaze after a while. He looked off toward the window and into the night sky, toward a past he had fought to forget.

But the past can only be buried so long. Eventually, it catches up with all of us. It's how we face it again that's important. Do you run away from the horror? Or do you challenge it head-on and give it the fight of your life? I suspected Blade had struggled with that decision. He had a lot to lose, after all. A solid career, money in the bank, a job he loved.

But looking at him now, it was obvious that he was tired of running.

"So what happened, Blade?" I prodded gently.

He snapped back from the fog and his voice rose an octave. "There was a hidden room inside our house. One of those Cold War bunkers that led underground. My mother stashed me in there that afternoon as soon as I got home from school. She told me to lock the door from the inside and not to come out until she came to get me. The walls were relatively soundproof, but I could hear footsteps on the ceiling and furniture crashing to the floor as if a fight had broken out."

"Or as if someone was ransacking the place."

"Exactly."

"So you never saw anyone. Do you know how many people came to the house?"

"No. I couldn't even tell you if it was a man or a woman, although if it were a woman, she would have had to be pretty strong to overcome my father, unless he was caught off guard." He paused, thinking. "And considering the way he was killed, he could have been."

"What was the murder weapon?"

"A hammer. The police believed my father was struck first, then my mother. All they took was some artwork, a clunky computer, and a few books."

"First-edition books?"

Blade shrugged, shook his head. "No. Just commercial fiction."

"And the artwork. Was it valuable?"

Another shrug. "Not that I know of. Purchased at garage sales and flea markets. My mother was an artist. She appreciated and supported modern painters."

I leaned against the counter, struggling to find a clue, anything that would make this story fall into a rhythm.

"There's more," Blade said. "When I finally emerged from the bunker there was something in our house that wasn't there before. Something I was certain the killer brought with him and left behind. A sculpture lying right there on the floor next to our shattered coffee table."

This piqued my interest. "And the police couldn't trace it to anyone?"

Blade shook his head. "They dismissed me as an imaginative child." His eyes shined a bit brighter for a moment. "I've been writing since I could hold a pen," he explained. "Blade Knight isn't my only pseudonym, it's just the one that pays the bills."

I nodded. "So they dismissed your claim."

"They couldn't fathom why anyone would bring a piece of art to a crime scene and leave it there. In fact, I remember the exact words of one of the officers." He scrunched up his face and in a gruff voice said, "*Usually works the other way around, son.*"

I suddenly had a horrible feeling in my gut. "Who was the officer? Do you recall?"

He looked at me, getting my meaning. "It was the chief at the time, not your uncle, if that's what you're getting at. Actually"—he scratched his chin—"now that you mention it, Officer Geraghty was the only one who believed me. He tried to bag the sculpture, but the chief ordered him not to."

It made me feel proud that my uncle wasn't as narrow-minded as his fellow lawmen.

"So this is the smoking gun? The thing that was left behind?"

Blade nodded.

I pointed to the bag. "May I see it now?"

Blade gave me a small smile. He twisted his body around and reached his arms into the satchel. "It's been packed away all this time."

When he turned back to face me, he was holding a small black skull. He placed it on the counter between us and sat down on the second stool.

I studied the piece for a moment. It seemed to be manufactured from some sort of gemstone. Obsidian? I trained my concentration to the energy of the skull, cupped my hands around it, and closed my eyes, centering myself with white light. I waited for a signal, a message.

Nothing came.

I leaned closer toward the skull, touched it, allowing my hands to linger near the eye sockets, but didn't get a vibration from it.

I sat back and scratched my head.

That's when a bullet shot through the window, exploding the skull into a million little pieces.

Chapter 12

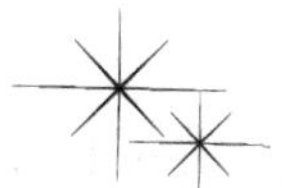

I launched myself at Blade Knight, toppling the author and sending both bar stools crashing to the tile. I clapped my hands to kill the lights and shouted for Thor to get to the Seeker's Den.

The dog whooshed past my right arm just as another bullet whizzed over my head, plunging into the door frame near my bedroom. Splintered wood crackled to the ground.

"Stay down!" I told Blade. Crawling around him, I stuck my hand in the back pocket of my jeans and extracted my iPhone. I tapped the app and punched in the code to unlock the den.

Thor and I had practiced this drill dozens of times so I knew exactly how many steps, dives, tail lengths, and arm reaches it took to reach my bedroom from anywhere in the cottage. I had to get to the closet—to the passageway and my lair. Thor was most likely waiting for the door to the Seeker's Den to open by the time I had punched in the code. I quickly slipped the phone back in my pocket and the cottage was inky black again. Not even the microwave clock cast a glow.

That was another trick I had picked up in training. It was amazing how a household staple as simple as a digital timer could get you killed.

Blade's heart beat loud through his shirt and I thought I heard a wheeze escape his throat.

"It's going to be okay," I assured him. "Grab my foot." I hustled in front of the author, dusting shattered glass from our pathway with the brim of my hat, except for one shard I held on to, and kicked my heel back so he could better find it in the dark.

"Ouch!" he said.

"Sorry."

I felt Blade's hand wrap around my ankle and we both belly-crawled as fast as we could through the bedroom, the closet, and finally the open doorway of the den.

Still lying on my stomach, I whipped out the phone and initiated the lockdown code for the first time. The door slammed shut and the digital keypad lit up in the pattern of the Celtic symbol triquetra. After a few seconds, a soft computer voice said, "Den secure" and the lights activated.

I jumped up from the floor and rushed to turn on the laptop that hosted the security cameras, setting the shard of black glass on the desk. I opened the application and punched in some codes and three windows popped up on the screen. The camera guarding the back door was the one I checked first because that was the side of the house the shots had come from. Nothing. Next, I turned my attention to the video coverage of the space between the Geraghty Girls' House and mine. The light was now off in their kitchen and I saw no one outside in the yard. I checked the time. Eight-thirty. They would be done cleaning up the dishes from dinner already. Fiona might be reading or crocheting. Birdie would likely be making a grocery list for the Samhain party. And Lolly would either be strutting around in a tangerine ball gown, a tiara pinned to her head, or she'd be on her third tumbler of Jameson and fashioning a special cape for the Samhain festival.

I didn't worry too much about the Geraghty Girls. They could take care of themselves pretty well and, aside from continuously casting protection spells along the property, the house itself had its own security measures in place thanks to the ingenious design of my great-grandmother and the carpentry talent of my great-grandfather. The Geraghtys called their safe room the Magic Chamber and it was nestled in the upper far left corner of the inn with a direct connection to the Seeker's Den via the scrying mirror. If any of them had heard the shots, they would have contacted me there, but the signal was silent.

I did a mental inventory of the perimeter of the cottage. The windows had all been locked, except now there was a hole in the one that was shot out, but it wasn't a large window. At least not large enough for a person to climb through. The back door was locked, but I wasn't certain about the front door since Blade had been the last one to use it.

I looked up to ask him if he had bolted the front door behind him, but stopped short when I saw how wide his eyes were. The writer had a sheen of perspiration lining his forehead and he looked less collected than I had ever seen him. Granted, I hadn't known the man that long, but I got the distinct impression that he was one Joe Cool.

He gaped at me. Slowly his eyes drank in the weapons lining the walls, the crystals, herbs, the dog, laptops—all of it. Then he asked the question I suspect he'd been wondering since we first met.

"Who *are* you?"

I held up my index finger. "Rule number one, Blade. Rule number one."

I circled around to the wall, liberated a five-point Chinese star from the peg rack and slipped it inside the pocket of the belt Aunt Lolly had made for me, then grabbed a tranquilizer gun and tucked that in the back waistband of my jeans. Next, I reached for a Taser made to look like a smart phone and tossed it to Blade. He caught it effortlessly.

There were only two shots fired. One aimed perfectly, the other way out of range. I didn't think the perpetrator was loitering around the area or that we were in any real danger, but better safe than snuffed.

"The question you should be asking is who was *that*?" I thumbed toward the door.

Blade stared at the Taser in his hand. "I have no idea."

I plucked a fresh knife from the wall and slid it in the hollow heel of my right boot. "Well, either it was an art activist on a mission to rid the world of its ugliest sculptures or someone doesn't want you poking around your parents' murder."

He was still staring at the Taser. He flipped it over and read the back. "iStun?"

"Clever, isn't it? It's pretty much foolproof." I walked over to him "See these two small points here?" I pointed to the top of the device.

Blade nodded.

"The current fires from there. And here"—I pointed to a small button on the side of the stun gun—"is the trigger. Press the pulse points to an assailant's neck and he drops like a sack of wet flour."

Blade nodded, still in a state of shock.

I touched his elbow. "If it makes you feel any better, the shooter wasn't aiming for either of us. Whoever it was just wanted to destroy that skull."

"Then why were there two shots fired?"

I shrugged. "To scare us. The fact that both shots missed us, even in the dark, means that it was the skull the shooter really wanted to kill." I tapped the stun gun in Blade's hand. "But just in case, carry this at all times."

Blade nodded. He shifted to face me. "So now what?"

"Now, I escort you back to the inn and figure out what to do next."

I whistled for Thor. The Great Dane trotted over to my side. I turned on the tiny camera imbedded in his collar and opened up the tiger's eye locket that hung from his neck. I slipped the wireless recording chip inside and clicked it shut. My expectations of picking up video of a sniper crouched in the azalea bushes, confessing to blowing up the World's Ugliest Piece of Crap, were pretty low, but I thought it couldn't hurt.

"Shouldn't we call the police?" asked Blade.

I had considered it, but I put the thought immediately out of my mind. If Leo knew what had happened here tonight he'd launch into overprotective mode and probably camp out on my doorstep 24/7, which, aside from putting a damper on my love life, would also set me up for Life's Most Awkward Conversation when Pickle decided to pay another visit. That was an introduction I hoped to avoid at all costs.

"I don't think that's a good idea right now." I faced him. "But that's my choice, Blade. You need to make your own choices. If you're scared, or you want to back out—"

"No." His voice was sharp, his eyes stern.

"Okay then."

I shuffled back over to the laptop and picked up the shard I had salvaged. I flicked on the desk lamp and held the black piece beneath the bulb, frowning. I switched the light to a brighter setting and gave the piece from the skull a closer study. Deeper frown.

"What is it?" Blade asked.

"I don't think the skull was very valuable. I thought it might have been made from the gemstone obsidian, but it's just glass."

Obsidian comes in many different colors, with specific magical properties attached to each shade. Black obsidian is the most powerful of all. It can open a gate to the Otherworld, ground a spiritual energy to the physical plane, and has the power to tap into one's subconscious mind. Or even, it's been rumored, the human soul. It's also believed to banish demons and can provide protection from impish spirits. Its most important function, however, is to remind us that birth and death are always present, one clasping hands with the other. For this reason, it's associated with spirit guides and is known as the "stone of truth," reflecting back the holder's true self when gazed upon.

"Are you sure? You can tell just from holding it up to that light? Is it an infrared bulb or something?"

"No." I held up the glass. "It says *Made in China*."

"Oh."

The light from the cedar room flashed on, a signal that someone was trying to reach me via the scrying mirror. I set the glass down, told Blade I'd be back in a moment, and went to answer the call, shutting the door behind me.

I knew who it was before I even turned the mirror around.

"Mom, it's the middle of the night in Ireland, what are you doing up?"

She yawned, her eyes heavy, yet every strand of hair was perfectly placed. She looked radiant as always. She was a lot like Aunt Fiona in that respect.

"Hello, sweetheart. I had a bad dream and I just wanted to check that everything was all right with you."

"All good here, Mom. Go back to bed."

"Are you certain? It was a rather disturbing dream." She made a face.

I really didn't have time to discuss sleeping patterns with my mother, but I decided to humor her for a few moments.

"What was it about?" I asked.

She frowned, her green eyes crinkling at the corners. "I don't think I should tell you. It might give you nightmares."

"Lots of things give me nightmares. Most of the time, I'm awake for them."

My mother rolled her eyes.

"Tell me what it was. You never know what it could mean, but it's most likely nothing."

She considered this as I glanced behind me through the small window to make sure Blade wasn't touching anything. I was still a little ticked about that business with the sword, which, I just realized, I probably should have brought home with me to reconsecrate. The writer must have moved because I couldn't spot him. *I swear if he touches one crystal, one set of Chako sticks, or even my punching bag, I'll tranq him and dump him in the woods with the coyotes,* I thought.

Mom sighed. "I suppose you're right." She looked up at the ceiling as if searching for the right words. She settled on, "As it turns out, your head exploded."

I gulped, not prepared for that visual. "My head exploded?"

"It was most unpleasant. Shot me right out of bed."

"I'll bet it wasn't a walk in the park for me either."

Wait a minute. The skull. She must have dreamt about the skull being destroyed.

My mother saw the flicker of recognition cross my face. "Do you know what it could mean?" she asked hopefully.

I really didn't want to tell her about the skull and Blade Knight just yet, or I'd be stuck in there for hours, and I had to get the author back to Birdie's house and myself to the computer. I still needed to research that name Danu mentioned. Leanan Sidhe.

Think, Stacy. Lying was not my strong suit, as the bunny story clearly reflected. "I dropped a jack-o'-lantern on the sidewalk. It was ugly. Orange pulp everywhere."

She must have been too sleepy to question my explanation because she blinked a few times and said, "Oh. All right then. Nighty-night." She cut the call.

Blade rapped on the door. "Hey, Stacy?"

"Coming." I flipped the mirror around.

Blade said, "Well, hurry up. We have company."

Chapter 13

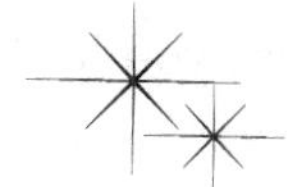

I flew out of the cedar room. "What? Who?"

Blade pointed to the laptop. I rushed over to it just in time to see a patrol car pull up. I watched in horror as Leo got out, scanned the area, and made his way toward my front door.

"Dammit! What is he doing here?"

I whirled around, did a quick body check. None of my weapons were visible.

"Uh-oh," Blade said.

Words I didn't want to hear. When you're a key member of a secret society and you're locked away in your hidden lair with a policeman in your driveway, the last thing you want to hear from the author whose parents' murder you're helping to solve is *uh-oh.*

I put a finger to my temple. "What now?"

"Isn't that your date from earlier?"

My head spun around so fast I was certain I gave myself whiplash.

"No, no, no!" I shouted at the laptop.

Blade watched the screen, studying Leo as Chance pulled into the driveway. Leo turned, waited for Chance to get out of his truck.

Blade cocked his head. "They don't look happy to see each other," he noted.

"That's because the man with the gun is my ex."

"And the guy getting out of the truck with the biceps and the work boots is the current?"

I squeezed my eyes shut and nodded. What were we going to do?

Blade said, "You know, you lead an interesting life, Stacy. Someone should write a book about you."

I popped my eyes open. "Rule number three, Blade, no books about me."

He shrugged, turned back to the monitor, and asked, "Do you have any popcorn?"

I glared at him. "So not funny." I glanced back to the screen. Leo and Chance were still talking.

Blade said, "We could just hide out in here. Pretend you're not home."

"Except Leo will check the perimeter and find the busted window." I shut the laptop. "Come on, we have some cleaning to do. Fast."

I unlocked the door and the three of us scurried through the bedroom and into the kitchen. Well, Blade and I scurried. Thor swaggered.

The broom and dustpan were in the hall closet. I tossed Blade the broom and he swept up the glass from the skull as I stooped to collect the debris.

I stood, frantically searching for a place to dump it.

"What are you doing?"

"I can't toss it in the garbage. Leo might look there."

"Why would he search your trash?"

"Because he's a cop. He does cop things like that. It's annoying."

The doorbell rang and I stood there like an idiot looking for a place to stash the broken bits.

Thor grunted, walked over to me, and gave me a pointed look. He turned and stuck his nose in the empty dog food bag sitting in the corner of the kitchen.

"Thanks," I said.

I shoved the dustpan and its contents inside, rolled the bag shut, and went to answer the door.

I gave Blade a look back and said over my shoulder, "Remember, not a word."

The author made a motion like he was zipping his mouth closed.

Chance and Leo filled up all the space on my porch. Chance looked confused. Leo looked uncomfortable.

"Well, this is a surprise," I said.

Leo said, "Sorry to barge in like this, but someone called in a disturbance." He craned his neck around my shoulder and said, "Hi there" to Blade.

I shook my head, gave my best perplexed face, and said, "No disturbance here."

Chance eyed me suspiciously. "Who's that?" He nodded toward Blade.

"He's an author."

Leo and Chance exchanged a look.

Chance said, "Aren't you going to invite us in?"

The problem with having two men you've dated standing on your porch at the same time while you lie to their faces is that they both know you're lying. And somehow, teams are chosen. Not in your favor, I might add.

"Of course," I said, reluctantly. I stepped aside and the two of them walked through the threshold.

Thor settled himself on the couch in prime viewing area of the mess that was unfolding before him. He bounced his head back and forth from Chance to Leo to Blade and me.

Then he groaned as if he just knew this wouldn't end well.

"It's freezing in here," Chance said.

Leo studied the living room for a moment then walked over to the kitchen counter. His gaze fell on the window. He approached it and stuck his head out. "That's because the window has been smashed."

Chance looked at me and said, "No disturbance, huh?" There was something different about him. His voice was deeper, his eyes darker. It flashed and then it was gone.

"Oh, that?" I pointed toward the window. "I did that."

"How?" Chance asked.

"Why?" said Leo at the same time.

One thing they didn't teach at witch boot camp was how to think on your feet. I made a mental note to write a letter to the director suggesting he add that to the curriculum as soon as I got the opportunity.

"Um" was all I said.

"Research," Blade said, stepping forward.

I stared at him, grateful that writers lie for a living. His face was statue serious. His eyes met mine briefly as he pasted on a smile.

"Miss Justice here is helping me with a story I'm writing about Amethyst. Several, actually. 'True Crimes in the Jewel of the Midwest.'"

"That's a mouthful," Chance said.

Blade said, "It's a working title."

He extended his hand to Leo, who stood closest to him. "I don't believe we've met. Blade Knight."

Leo squinted his eyes as if looking at Blade for the first time. Then his face lit up as he shook the man's hand. "Blade Knight? You write the Tracey Stone books."

"I know," Blade said, playfully.

"It's such an honor to meet you, Mr. Knight."

"Call me Blade."

Leo beamed. "Blade. I've read all your books. I especially liked the last one, *Stone Cold*."

My mouth was hanging open watching this exchange. Leo was actually gushing. He looked like a twelve-year-old who just met the Avengers. Not the cast of the movie, but the actual superheroes.

"Well, I'd be happy to sign your books if you like. I'm having a signing tomorrow night at Buxom Books."

"I'll be there," Leo said, still grinning like a teenager who just got to third base. I watched as Chance stood by, silently sizing up the writer. His gaze drifted around the cottage and fell on the broken window. I still hadn't swept up the glass from the pane.

Leo was babbling on about being Blade's biggest fan and that Kathy Bates character from *Misery* flashed in my mind.

He was saying, "And that part, where Tracey's car plunges through the icy lake, man, that was intense. That's where the title came from, right?" Leo said.

"Right," said Blade.

"I had no idea you were such an avid reader," I said to Leo.

He briefly turned to look at me as if he had completely forgotten I was there. "These books are great and the main character, Tracey Stone, she's an FBI agent who's always getting herself into these tight situations." He paused, cocked his head. "Kind of like you, Stacy."

Chance narrowed his eyes at the author.

"Like me?"

"A little," he said. "Except she's badass." Leo turned back to Blade, who looked to be growing increasingly uneasy.

I tried not to be insulted as I thought about what he had said about the car diving into an icy lake.

Because that actually did happen to me months ago. And yet, I just met the man. Unless . . .

Was there more to Blade's story than he had led me to believe?

"Wait a minute," Chance said loudly. "What kind of research?"

Blade excused himself from Leo and went to introduce himself to Chance. The men shook hands.

Chance said, "You look familiar."

"My face is on every jacket cover," Blade said.

"No. That isn't it. I feel like we've met before."

Blade said, "I don't believe so."

Chance seemed to file the inkling away and asked again, "So, the research. How does it tie in to breaking the window?"

Chance looked from me to Blade.

Blade said, "May I?"

"Be my guest," I said.

"Well, I'm sure you recall the incident involving the dead girl found at the Black Opal?" Blade said.

Leo stuffed his hands in his pockets and looked away. He hated to talk about that. He was related to the murderer.

I suddenly realized where Blade was headed with this. "That's right, a rock was thrown through my window." I regretted opening my mouth immediately after the words fell out because the tone I used was that of a game show contestant answering a question right rather than that of confirmation.

Chance cocked his head toward me. "So you reenacted that?"

"Well, I didn't mean to. I was showing Blade the size of the rock, where it was tossed from, and it just slipped."

"It slipped?"

Usually this line of questioning was Leo's territory, but Chance must have picked up that the chief was useless at this point. He was doing a damn good job at playing detective and I didn't like it one bit.

I crossed my arms. "What can I say? Maybe there was pent-up anger inside me and subconsciously I wanted to break something." This time my tone was stern.

Blade took that as a cue. "Well, I'd best be going. I'll see you tomorrow, Miss Justice." He handed me a card and Chance watched as I stuffed it in the pocket of my jeans.

"I'll walk you out," Leo said. "And if there's anything you need while you're in town, don't hesitate to call me." He stopped to pull a card from his wallet and Chance put his arm up to block his path.

"So that's it, Inspector Clouseau? You're just going to accept that answer and let him walk out of here?"

Leo's jaw hardened. "I can't arrest him for sharing a pizza with your girlfriend, Sponge Bob Square Neck."

I stepped forward. "Stop."

Chance lowered his arm and Leo glared at him. He tossed me a salute, but he didn't say another word as he left to join Blade outside.

I locked the door behind them.

When I turned back around, Chance was running his hand along where the bullet had splintered the doorframe. He looked up at me.

"I can't wait to hear the explanation for this."

Chapter 14

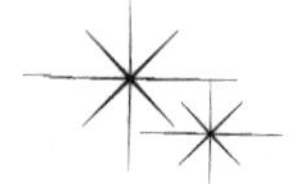

So I told him. About Blade, the real reason he was in town, about the skull and the shots. I told him everything I could, everything I was allowed to, except the one thing I really wanted to tell him. For that, I would need permission from the Council.

When I finished speaking, Chance sat back on the couch, his hand gently stroking my dog, and thought for a long time.

Finally he looked at me. "I understand that somehow you feel obligated to help this man. That there's something about your family, your witchiness, that makes you compelled to solve every murder that floats across your desk." He paused, took a sip of water.

I waited for him to say more, to yell and scream that endangering myself for a complete stranger was utterly stupid—and it was. But I wasn't just the Seeker of Justice for the Council and what they protect. It was a part of who I was now, my personal code of ethics. I had taken an oath to fight for justice and, for me, that train didn't just stop at my door, at my family's door, but for anyone who needed it.

And for those who deserved to be punished.

Instead of ordering me to stop investigating crimes that didn't concern me, Chance said in that soft, gentle way of his, "I'm really glad you told me."

He got up from the couch, came over to me, and took me in his arms. He kissed me on the lips, soft at first, but his kisses grew more demanding, more urgent, animalistic even. It was more fervent than he had ever kissed me before and I wasn't sure I liked this new technique, but I couldn't break away. It was almost as if we were both so caught up in our passion that it became a living, breathing thing. His hands wove themselves in my hair, tugging me closer.

Then they got stuck thanks to the stupid candy still lodged in my mane.

Chance pulled away as if something bit him. His hand was glued to my hair and he had to wiggle it free, taking a few strands with it.

He met my eyes and a slow grin spread across his face.

"Want some help with that, Xena?" he asked.

He had started calling me that after he discovered my arsenal. I hated it at first, but it was growing on me.

"Yes, please."

After six shampoos and some creative hairstyling on Chance's part, my hair was gunk-free and relatively intact. I made a mental note to be extra nice to Pickle the next time I saw him.

Chance was towel-drying my hair when we locked eyes in the mirror and he whispered in my ear, "Are you up for a sparring match?"

"I thought you said I needed to get a new partner."

A sexy smile curved all the way up to his eyes. "No way. I don't ever want you to get a new partner for the kind of sparring I'm talking about, baby."

I stood. "Think you can catch me?"

"I already did," he said and he was right.

He carried me into the bedroom and we made love, gently at first, but then his desire seemed to overcome him and I met it with an equal fever. He looked down at me and suddenly his eyes darkened again and he flicked his gaze away, sinking his lips, his tongue, his teeth into my neck, chest, shoulders, anywhere they could reach. Then we devoured each other as we never had before. Like we were different people, succumbing to a force greater than our own.

I watched as he drifted off to sleep and I couldn't help but wonder if I wasn't the only one who had changed.

When I woke up the next morning, both Chance and Thor were gone.

There was a pot of coffee in the kitchen with a note in front of it.

Hey, lover, let Thor out to do his business. Would have made breakfast, but I figured it would be cold by the time you got up. I covered the window up with plastic, fix it as soon as I can. Pick you up from the book signing tonight?

Love,
Chance

I had no hopes that Thor would be in the yard, but I checked anyway, and I was right, unfortunately. I drank my coffee and waited for the wrath of my cousin.

When my phone didn't ring, I did a quick workout, checked the scrying mirror for any messages, showered, and dressed in black leggings, gray boots, a tee shirt, and an oversized tunic sweater that wrapped around the waist with pockets in the front. I slipped my phone inside a pocket, an athame in my boot, and an infinity scarf around my neck. I grabbed a wool cap since it was supposed to be chillier today and headed out the door to the Geraghty House.

I crunched through the leaves, the wind circling around me, the sun beaming down, and made my way to the back door of the house that led to the kitchen.

The house was a stunning painted lady, built by my great-grandfather, that looked like a wedding cake glazed with buttercream frosting and highlighted by purple latticework and red and teal piping, all wrapped up in a wrought-iron fence.

There were thirteen rooms total, three floors, and three guest suites. The back of the house, kitty-corner to my cottage, was the innkeepers' quarters, partitioned off from the common areas and the guest rooms.

As soon as I entered the kitchen, I knew Lolly hadn't had a drop of liquor in her yet.

"Good morning, Aunt Lolly."

She looked at me, her eyes glassy, and said, "Hello. I'm sorry. There are no vacancies."

There was a frying pan on the old-fashioned stove and she was standing in front of it trying to flip a spatula with an egg. Her short copper hair was wrapped up in a bright yellow bow, blue eyeshadow was lacquered on all the way up to her eyebrows, her lipstick was everywhere but on her lips, and she was wearing what looked to be a toga pinned at the shoulder with a rhinestone broach the size of a Frisbee.

I walked over to the stove, turned the burner off, and liberated the egg from her hand. Upon further inspection, I realized it wasn't a sheet she had wrapped around her, but a tablecloth with faded sprigs of lavender splashed across it.

"Why don't you have a seat and I'll put the coffee on," I said.

Lolly nodded and I escorted her to the apothecary table in the center of the room. I pulled up a high-backed chair and she perched on it, settling her hands in her lap, blinking.

By the time the coffee was brewed, I heard steps on the back stairs that trailed to the kitchen.

I poured Lolly a healthy dose of Baileys and Folgers, set it in front of her, and turned to see Fiona glide through the doorway like a movie star at a premiere.

Aunt Fiona was the middle Geraghty sister, who had broken a lot of hearts in her day and could still turn many a head when she walked down the street. She was Marilyn Monroe, Ann-Margret, and Jessica Rabbit all in one. The woman would have given Venus herself a run for her crown. She was unattached now, as were all the Geraghty Girls. It seemed that for the women in my family, love, no matter how strong in the beginning, was ever fleeting. A fact I tried not to dwell on.

Fiona was wearing a black knit dress that hugged her curves, a gold necklace, a thick belt, and pointy polka-dotted heels. She greeted me with a kiss on the cheek, tied a frilly apron around her waist, and opened the refrigerator. She reached in and took out a potato-and-sausage breakfast casserole.

"What brings you by this morning, dear?" She peeled the Saran Wrap off the casserole, popped some toast in the toaster, and set the oven to 350 degrees.

"I need to talk to you about a few things."

I checked Lolly's coffee. It was nearly finished and from the glint in her eye, I could see that the motor was running, but the tank needed more fuel. I fixed her a second cup of Irish coffee and set it in front of her.

Fiona was drizzling maple syrup on the casserole and since Birdie hadn't come downstairs yet, I decided to ask Fiona about Thor's behavior toward Cinnamon.

When I was finished explaining his bizarre behavior, she thought about it for a moment, then waved her hand. "I wouldn't worry about it. It's natural for animals, especially one as sensitive as Thor, to guard the young. Even in the womb. I'm sure that's all it is."

I was inclined to believe her, although there was a small part of me that feared for the safety of Cin's baby. What if there was something wrong? I knew that my cousin never missed a checkup, but still, the way Thor was acting, it gave me pause for concern.

"Would it help if I had a chat with him?" Fiona asked, catching the worry on my face.

I smiled. "I would appreciate that."

She couldn't actually have full conversations with animals, but they sent her messages, images that she would then transcribe into words on paper. It couldn't hurt, I decided.

Birdie came down the stairs, dressed in wide-legged paisley pants and a loose crocheted sweater. Her signature bangles dangled as she whisked into the kitchen.

She looked up, surprise on her face. "Stacy, you're here early," she said in an upbeat voice.

She poured a cup of coffee and joined me and Lolly at the apothecary table. She put her hand on mine then instantly snapped it back.

"Something's wrong. What is it? It can't be a mission, because the Council hasn't contacted me."

Fiona had just put the casserole in the oven. She was holding a pitcher of orange juice as she turned around.

I looked to all three of them. Lolly's circuits were popping, so I got right to it.

"It wasn't the Council who contacted me," I explained. "It was Danu. She told me that you as the Mage would explain everything and I haven't had time to look into the matter myself."

"Well, go on, girl, spill it," Birdie said.

"She said, 'tell the Mage that the Leanan Sidhe has escaped. You must find and bind her.'"

Fiona dropped the pitcher of orange juice and I jumped. It splattered all over the floor and my boots.

Lolly gasped, eyes wide, mouth agape.

Birdie's face slowly twisted into an angry grimace. She stood up and pointed to both her sisters. "I was afraid of this when you cut the hair of the harlot."

Fiona winced. Lolly just looked away.

I grabbed some paper towels to quickly sop up the mess.

Their reactions all threw me for a loop. They seemed spooked by this information. And it took a lot to spook these three. Suddenly my stomach twisted in knots. Who was the Leanan Sidhe?

I dumped the broken glass and soiled paper towels into the garbage can and grabbed a sponge to wipe off my boots. They were suede, so they didn't come clean, but I managed to lessen the damage.

When I turned back around, Birdie was still steaming, Lolly looked guilty, and Fiona seemed nervous. I swiveled my head back and forth between the three of them. "Afraid of what? What is it?"

They all hunched in a huddle, whispering.

"Stop that right now! You worked long and hard to recruit me to the team, which means I'm in on all discussions. No scheming, plotting, planning, or spellcasting without me. I mean it, Birdie!"

My grandmother popped her head up and something about the look on my face made her acquiesce. "Very well."

The three sisters broke the huddle and formed a semicircle around the apothecary table.

Birdie was the one to speak. "It seems, granddaughter, that your aunts may have invoked the hundred-year curse."

I tapped my foot. "Well, that doesn't sound good."

Aunt Fiona said, "All Geraghtys pay a deep price when the curse is awakened."

"It's nearly impossible to stop," Birdie said.

"That doesn't sound any better. What price?" I asked.

"The highest price of all," Lolly answered. "Loss of our loved ones. Forever."

"You mean, as in death?" I asked.

Birdie nodded solemnly.

That wasn't an option I was willing to accept. "So what's the curse? Who's the Leanan Sidhe? And what's the plan?"

Chapter 15

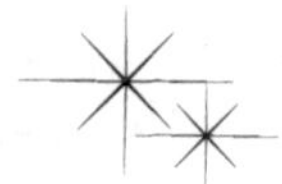

Birdie looked at me and said, "The Leanan Sidhe was once an Irish fairy-muse."

"The name translates to *fairy mistress*," Fiona added.

Birdie nodded. "That's right. Her beauty was unsurpassed by any mortal woman; her gifts, pure genius to human men."

"For whom she had an insatiable appetite," said Lolly.

Birdie continued. "Her lovers were painters, poets, sculptors, scribes, musicians, architects—anyone involved in some form of creative art. She would inspire their work through her magic, feeding their creativity, and elevating merely talented men to become masters of their craft."

"Her influence sparked some of the greatest art, literature, and music the world had ever known," said Fiona. "Gifts to humanity."

"But they came at a price," Lolly said softly.

Birdie went on to explain. "Men who were bespelled by her would fall so irretrievably in love that eventually, after weeks or months of blissful passion, the creative energy could no longer sustain them. They needed more and more of the muse herself, and that was a demand she could not meet for long, for it drained her power, her life force. Inspiration—creativity itself—was what sustained her."

Fiona said, "So she could only have them sucking that away for so long until one day, she would be forced to leave her lover."

"Which is when they would suffer an emotional pain so unbearable many would either die of a broken heart, self-destruction such as drink or drugs, or by their own hand," Lolly said.

"So where does the curse come in?" I asked.

Birdie said, "Eventually she became intoxicated by the power of her magic. It occurred to her what a waste it was that she fed these men all of her imaginative juices only for them to be discarded in death."

"So she devised a plan to siphon the energy back," said Lolly.

"How?" I asked, not really wanting to know the answer, but thinking it was important to the story.

Birdie exchanged a look with her sisters. "She would sneak into their homes after they had died and steal their bodies."

I grimaced. "Please tell me we aren't talking about necrophilia."

"No," Birdie said. "She would drain all the blood from their bodies, fill a large cauldron with it, and bathe herself."

I don't think I had ever been more horrified in my life.

Fiona said, "Sometimes she would drink it."

Correction. Now I was more horrified than I had ever been. I gagged. "Oh, so vampirism then. Much better."

Lolly said, "Really?"

"No, not really." I stood up. "This is the worst story I think you've ever told me, and I've heard quite a few humdingers." I went to the sink and washed my hands, then I stuck my head under the faucet and gargled. What I really wanted to do was boil myself and electroshock my brain to unhear that tale.

I blew out a sigh, grabbed a towel to dry my hands, and turned around. "So the curse?"

"Right," Birdie said. "You see, when the Tuatha Dé Danann discovered what she was doing to mortal men, they bound her to the Otherworld and banished her from ever making contact with our realm again."

"Only they didn't count on one of their own succumbing to her seduction. The son of a god, no less, who set her free, ages later, to once again roam the countryside seeking a lover," said Fiona.

"Except by that time, the Druids had already signed the treaty with the Tuatha Dé Danann to protect the four treasures—the spear, the cauldron, the sword, and the stone—and the Council had been formed. The two races had been working together peacefully for centuries and neither wanted to disrupt that agreement. So the Tuatha Dé Danann asked their mortal friends for help in capturing the Leanan Sidhe and they obliged."

The realization of what they were getting at was beginning to dawn on me. "So one of my ancestors agreed to be seduced by the Leanan Sidhe. And he paid with his life."

"We are sometimes forced to sacrifice ourselves for the greater good," said Birdie. "It was the only way. And when the Leanan realized she had walked into a trap, she was so incensed that she didn't even wait for him to die. She killed him herself. But before he took his last breath, she cast a curse upon her lover that his lineage would always suffer in matters of the heart. And that every hundred years, she vowed to escape and demand a blood sacrifice from his clan." Birdie looked at me. "When the first drop of his blood touched the green isle, the curse was sealed."

"So the curse is actually a double-edged sword," I said. "A blood sacrifice from a Geraghty—"

"And a heart sacrifice against the clan," Fiona said.

I looked at Lolly, whose heart had once been so shattered that the wreckage traveled all the way to her mind.

No one spoke for a long time.

I said, "So would it be strictly a lover of a Geraghty who's in danger? What about Thor? Cinnamon?"

Birdie said, "She's only known to target men. Never animals. But we think, although the curse seems to have had lasting affects on affairs of the heart for generations of Geraghty women, that the Leanan's true goal is to break a love bond, no matter what the form."

Which meant anyone I cared about was a target.

"But she's been bound, right? She hasn't escaped before? So you really don't know for certain what she'll do."

Birdie was chewing her lower lip. She shook her head, cast her eyes first to Fiona, then Lolly. "I told you both it was a bad idea to cut the hair of the harlot."

Lolly stood. "Well, it was your spell after all, Brighid."

Fiona crossed her arms and snapped, "And what would you have us do? Stacy was stuck in the Web of Wyrd. We had to pull her out somehow."

I lifted my hand. "Wait a second, what are you talking about?"

Birdie hit the button on the toaster and poured a cup of coffee. "On your birthday. When you were sucked into the realm of the Fae. I had written a fetching spell long ago and we needed the hair of a harlot to see it through to completion."

I vaguely recalled something about that, but my brain had been so scrambled when I got sucked into the Web of Wyrd—the pathway to the Otherworld—that I didn't remember much of the night I came back. "But what does that have to do with what's happening now?"

Birdie sighed and stirred her coffee. "We suspect that somehow, because the worlds had been crossed that evening, that when we cut the hair of the harlot and used the lock to cast a spell for your retrieval, perhaps we inadvertently called the muse forth."

Fiona said, "You see, dear, the Leanan needs a human form to inhabit now. She was stripped of her enchantments when last she escaped the Otherworld, so her beauty will only remain intact on this plane for twenty-four hours. After that, she'll age drastically, which would not only make it difficult to attract a man to seduce, but it would drain her energy, so bewitching won't come as easily."

Birdie said, "It would need to be someone with a free spirit, someone provocative, open to persuasion."

"Someone sexy," Fiona said.

"Attractive to men," said Lolly.

Birdie said, "Of course, you can prevent the occupation from ever happening if you find the Sidhe first."

Lolly said, "But we fear maybe the harlot would fit the profile she seeks."

Magical profiler. That was something you didn't see in the "help wanted" section too often.

I took a deep breath, groaned, and put my head in my hands. "Okay, first of all, please stop saying *harlot*. It's giving me a migraine. Second, whose hair did you cut?"

No one spoke for a few moments. Finally, Fiona said, "That nice young woman who owns the tavern across from Cinnamon's establishment."

My stomach did a flip. No. Way. They couldn't be serious. They couldn't possibly mean her.

"Monique Fontaine?" I asked, praying to the Goddess it wasn't true.

They all three nodded.

"What?" I said through gritted teeth. When they didn't answer I shouted, "What! You don't even know Monique. Why on earth would she let you cut her hair?"

"Well, we didn't ask, dear," said Lolly.

"It was a matter of life and death, you know," said Fiona.

"This is not good. Not. Good." I began pacing, chewing my nails off one by one. "If your theory is correct you could not have handpicked a better harlot, let me tell you." I stopped, threw my hands in the air. "In fact, you may as well have just strapped a big sign around her neck with blinking lights all around that says, 'Hey, vampire succubus, open vessel right here. No vacancy!'"

"Now, calm down, Stacy, I'm sure it won't be as easy as all that for the Sidhe to possess her," Birdie said.

"Are you kidding me? Monique's license plate says EASY4U! The woman writes a sex column, for the love of Danu!"

"Oh, I so enjoy her work. Best part of the paper," Fiona said.

Lolly said, "She really knows her stuff."

I glared at both of them and did a few more laps around the apothecary table. "I can't believe this, I really can't." Then a horrible thought hit me. "She's been spending time with Chance. Is he in danger?"

Birdie flicked her eyes to Fiona.

"I would suggest you limit that contact," she said.

"Oh my Goddess. This is a nightmare." I plastered my hands on top of my head and looked at the three of them. "Why didn't you just cut Fiona's hair?"

"Hey," Fiona protested.

Birdie said, "It was discussed, but she's been wed."

"Hey!" Fiona said louder.

Birdie said, "Oh please, you've enticed more men to 'be all they can be' than the Army."

Fiona stuck her tongue out at my grandmother.

"Can we focus, please, kids?" My head was bobbing from one to the other frantically. "What are we going to do? I mean, what if it's too late?"

Lolly shuffled off into the pantry.

Birdie said, "If Danu just came to you, then I doubt it will be too late. But you'll need to guard and protect the har—, er, Monique."

I narrowed my eyes. "Excuse me?"

"You'll have to ensure that the Leanan Sidhe doesn't get near her. She must not be compromised or there's no telling what could happen to the men in this town. All of them. Your grandfather, the chief, Derek, Chance, Tony. They're all at risk," Birdie said.

I shoved aside the thought of Monique seducing my grandfather. That could only be expunged on a therapist's couch after about ten years of psychoanalysis.

"But I thought you said it was just artists she targeted?" I asked. "Painters, musicians, scribes."

Scribes. Writers. Did that mean Blade was in danger too?

Fiona said, "That was before, but she hasn't fed in a while. And art comes in many forms in the modern world. Construction workers need inspiration to design their projects, scientists need inspiration to solve equations, even police officers need to get creative to solve crimes."

"Plus we don't suspect she'd be too picky after all this time," Lolly said.

"Protect Monique and we'll figure out a way to bind the muse," Birdie said.

"What's Plan B?" I asked.

Birdie frowned.

"Birdie, I'm serious. You have no idea what you are asking me to do. Please, there has to be another way. I can't stand that woman.

Besides, how am I supposed to protect her? Do I just chain her to my desk until we find the fairy mistress?"

Hmm. If I could gag her too, that wasn't a bad idea.

Lolly came back from the pantry with a cup and three straws.

Fiona squeezed my shoulder. "Just be your charming self, Stacy. I'm sure you can learn to be friends with this person. You're resourceful. You'll find a way."

"Can't I just hit her with my car?" I asked. Then I remembered I didn't have a car.

Lolly came over to her sisters, three straws sticking out of her hand.

Fiona said, "I suppose we'll need to cancel Samhain." She drew a straw.

Birdie plucked a straw too. "I'll call the coven."

I said, "And how will I know her, the Leanan Sidhe? How will I spot her? What does she look like?"

"Well, if you don't do as we say, I gather she'll look a lot like that Monique person," Birdie said.

"Very funny. Will she look human? Dark hair, light hair? What?"

"You've seen the goddesses in their true form, correct? So you know they have a regal quality about them and that they are exceptionally beautiful," Birdie said.

"But you said her beauty was stripped."

"I said her enchantments were taken from her. Those enchantments were what allowed her to appear as any normal devastatingly gorgeous human. Without them, her beauty would be in full force, which is why it will fade fast. She'll be looking for a vessel straight away. But to answer your question, she has hair as black as ebony and shiny as starlight. Eyes the color of spun gold."

Fiona said, "Buxom breasts, plump lips, and hips any man would kill to hold onto."

So I was looking for Selma Hayek. Excellent.

"Anything else?"

Birdie thought about it. "It was written in the Blessed Book that she often smells like paint and paper. Although I suspect she may smell like whoever she's targeting as her lover."

Lolly looked at her sisters. They all opened their hands. I noticed the straws were three different lengths.

"What are you doing?" I asked.

The timer on the oven dinged. I could smell that the maple sausage casserole was done.

Lolly said, "We explained this, dear. One of us needs to make a sacrifice."

As if I didn't have enough crap piled on this shit sandwich. Now, I had to worry about one of them offing themselves.

"NO. NO. NO." I snatched the straws from each of their hands, one by one.

Birdie looked at me in surprise.

"Are you crazy? This isn't the dark ages. No one is making any sacrifices." I looked out the window toward my cottage, thinking about the three men who were there last night and really hoping that not one of them—especially the one I loved—would end up bleeding to death in the cauldron of a maniac.

I faced my family. "As the Seeker it's my job to deliver justice. Let me do my job."

Birdie smiled at me. She locked hands with her sisters and they all drew me into their circle.

"Besides, I have a plan."

Chapter 16

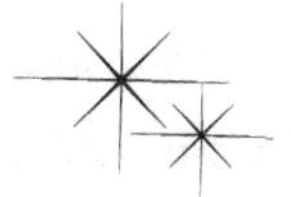

I left the Geraghty House with the keys to Birdie's car, a bottle of mead, a batch of Lolly's extra-sweet sugar cookies, plus three taffy apples. I set all of the offerings on my porch with a note of apology to Pickle and asked for his help in a very specific way that I was sure he could manage. I was hoping that would coax him back to the cottage. Maybe he could help me figure out how to capture and bind the fairy mistress.

After that, I hurried inside, grabbed the laptop and the locket. I filled the locket with ruby dust, stuffed the computer in my bag, and texted Derek to tell him I'd be in soon. I debated on the tranquilizer gun, thought it wouldn't be a bad idea, and shoved that in my bag too. Then I hopped into Birdie's Buick and drove to Cinnamon's house.

I had so much to do; my head was swimming in random thoughts. I needed to interview the valedictorians for the pre-reunion piece I wanted to write, I had to figure out how to find the Leanan Sidhe and a creative way to keep tabs on Monique, there was the matter of helping Blade determine who killed his parents and why—and more importantly, who the hell shot my window out. But all that would have to wait until I picked up my dog before Cinnamon decided to feed him a Xanax-laced steak.

When I got to Cin's house, Thor was stretched out on the front porch in front of the skeleton, ears erect, paws stretched out in front of him, lying statue-still. There was a menacing look about him as if he were the key component in the Halloween décor.

I climbed out of the car and walked over to my Great Dane.

I flipped the keys around in my hand and tapped my foot. "We talked about this, Big Man. You can't come over here uninvited or she's liable to shoot us both, as hormonal as she is right now."

Thor snorted and looked away as if I were a fly that needed shooing.

From the corner of my eye, I spotted Cinnamon's fingers separating the blinds that covered the windows of her living room. She peeked out to see who would dare park in her driveway at this ungodly hour. She made eye contact, shook her head at me, said a swear word that I lip-read, and then disappeared. I heard the faint click of a lock turning a few moments later.

"Really?" She stood there with her hands on her hips, her hair in a loose bun and her face set to annoyed.

"Hey, at least he didn't barge in this time," I said.

She stood back, swung the door open, and invited us inside.

Thor waved his snout all across my cousin as he sauntered through the doorway. I smelled bacon, coffee, and something spicy.

"Want some breakfast?" Cinnamon asked.

"Sure," I said.

We shuffled through her comfortable living room, past the flat-screen television and silver framed photographs hung at eye level of Uncle Declan, Tony, Cinnamon, her mother Angelica, me, my mom, and the Geraghty Girls, before we arrived in the kitchen.

I'd always liked Cinnamon's style. Modern, with neutral colors, clean lines, and a nod toward functionality and comfort. However, there was something different about the kitchen now. Besides the fact that there was hot food in it, I mean. Tony was the chef in the family since Cinnamon didn't have the time nor the desire for culinary exploration.

The boxy space was somehow brighter. Cheery even, though I couldn't quite put my finger on why. For anyone else, the change might seem normal. A mother-to-be nesting, preparing for the birth of her first child.

Anyone but Cinnamon, that is. For her, it seemed so out of place that it was downright disturbing.

"Coffee?" she asked, pot in her hand. She was wearing baggy sweats and a Led Zeppelin tee shirt that just barely grazed her swollen belly.

"Sure."

I watched as she reached for a mug on a low-hanging shelf. She poured the coffee, swirled some cream into it that came out of the nose of a tiny ceramic cow leaping over the moon, and handed it to me.

"Have a seat. There's a roasted red pepper, spinach, and goat cheese frittata in the oven. Should be ready soon."

A frittata? With vegetables? And goat cheese? I didn't even think Cinnamon knew what goat cheese was, let alone how to incorporate it into the first meal of the day. And she had a strict policy against eating anything green. Vegetables, Cin believed, are what real food eats.

I glanced briefly at Thor, whose eyes were struggling to stay glued to my cousin, although they occasionally betrayed their post by sliding over to the sizzling bacon in the pan. I took the mug of steaming coffee from Cinnamon, noticing that it had a crown on it, thanked her, and sat at the table.

There was something off about the table. It was softer. When I set my coffee down I realized it was because there was a tablecloth draped over it. The white cloth was covered in tiny cherries, arguably the most cheerful fruit. The Cinnamon I knew wouldn't even eat in a restaurant that had cherry table coverings, let alone be caught dead with one on her table.

What the hell was going on?

I sat down and inspected the rest of the kitchen. There was a Humpty Dumpty egg timer ticking on the stove, a salt and pepper shaker set was on the counter with the names "Hansel and Gretel" etched across the base, the curtains were printed with once-bitten apples, and the napkin holder in front of me was hand-painted with the image of Little Red Riding Hood. I turned it around to see the wolf on the other side dressed in a housecoat and bonnet, teeth dripping with venom.

Maybe Cinnamon had been featured on one of those designer remake shows and the guys who showed up to give the place a facelift were the Brothers Grimm.

I took a tentative sip of the coffee. Cinnamon's idea of coffee usually tasted like it was scraped off the bottom of the Mississippi, but this concoction was a tasty, nutmeg-infused variety.

A clock chimed and I glanced up in the direction of the noise, thinking it might be later than I thought. The clock was above the pantry, and I jumped when a mouse scurried out, tweaked its whiskers, and melted back into the base.

Okay, now I was officially creeped out. I looked at Thor, who had anchored himself in the corner, with a ringside view of the room. He flicked his eyes at me as if to say *I told you so*, then went back to studying my cousin. And the bacon.

Cinnamon was humming a tune I couldn't place as she drained the bacon on paper towels stamped with roses.

The humming was the part that lit my inner flare gun.

I once saw Cinnamon escort a man out of her bar by his nipples when he refused to stop humming. In her defense, she gave the guy three chances.

Something was terribly wrong. I decided that perhaps Thor should keep an eye and an ear on my cousin after all. I was also thankful I had engaged his audio/visual equipment last night.

Humpty Dumpty fell off the stove and cracked in half, which I assumed meant the eggs were done.

Cinnamon stooped to pick the timer up, set it back on the counter, and opened a cabinet where the plates were stashed.

"Let me help you," I said.

She waved an arm behind her. "You'll only get in my way. Sit."

I sat. When she pulled the plates from the shelf, I thanked the Goddess that they were her plain old white ones.

She set the plates on the counter next to the stove, grabbed a red oven mitt, and opened the oven door to check the egg pie. She wiggled the glass pie plate, made a slight sound of affirmation, and removed the frittata. She set it on a trivet, grabbed the salt and pepper and the plates, and plopped them in front of me.

I looked at Hansel and Gretel suspiciously, sniffing the tiny holes in their heads when Cinnamon went back for the bacon and frittata. I sneezed from inhaling the pepper.

"Gesundheit," she said absent-mindedly.

I wouldn't have been a bit surprised if Mother Goose had walked through the door right then and joined us for breakfast.

Cinnamon returned with silverware and I reached for a napkin that was also plain white, thankfully. I handed my cousin one as she cut the frittata. Over her shoulder, I noticed the light was still illuminated on the oven, indicating it was still on.

I scooted my chair back. "You forgot to turn the oven off."

Cinnamon said, "I did?"

She turned her head sideways and right before my eyes, the gas stove powered off.

Cin flicked her gaze to me for a moment as she scooped up a piece of the egg and vegetable pie. She put it on a plate and passed it to me. "It's on a timer. Shuts off automatically."

"Is that so? Then why did you use your cute little egg-man?"

Honestly, a Humpty Dumpty egg timer? Cin hated kitschy stuff like that.

She stiffened for a brief moment, then she cut herself a wedge of the pie and slid it onto her plate. "Doesn't always work. So I use backup."

"Hmm."

She was lying through her teeth.

"You've had that stove since you moved into this place. I always saw Tony shut it off manually."

Cinnamon ignored me and unwrapped the bacon. She offered me a piece, which I declined, then she tossed a few to Thor, who gobbled them up.

It wasn't a digital oven. This was an older model with dials. No way it could turn off on its own.

Cinnamon sat down in her chair and I took a bite of the frittata. It was delicious. We ate in silence for a moment and I was chewing on more than the eggs. Was it the baby that was changing her?

I've heard that pregnant women can even cause electrical surges, although I'd never seen it. Not from one who wasn't a witch anyway.

Is that what was happening? Was Cinnamon becoming a true Geraghty?

"So what's with the kitchen makeover?" I asked, sipping my coffee. "Does Martha Stewart do your decorating now?"

She glared at me. "Shut up. Tony bought this crap. I hate it."

Good. At least this woman I understood.

Cinnamon looked at our plates and snapped her fingers. "Forgot the toast."

Before I had a chance to say that I'd make some for her, the goddamn toaster popped out two perfectly golden slices of bread.

I raised my eyebrows at her. "I didn't see you put any bread in there."

"Must have been before you got here." She licked her lips.

I shook my head. "No. If that were true it would have popped up minutes ago."

She shot up out of her chair. "I'll get it."

I stood to block her path. "It's all right, let me."

She wiggled around me, faster than I thought she could move even before she got pregnant. She shoved a chair in my path and I hurdled it. We both got to the toaster at the same time.

Cinnamon grabbed the toast, whirled back to me, and stretched her hands out, dangling the two slices. "You butter them."

I stared at her for a while, trying to read her eyes, her thoughts. They were steely, just like my cousin.

"No problem. The butter's on the table," I said cheerfully.

She shifted slightly to glance at the table and I took the opportunity to scoot her out of the way.

I knew it before I saw it, but I still couldn't believe what I was looking at. What *was* I looking at? It wasn't possible. Was it?

The plug from the toaster was several inches away from the nearest outlet. I felt the small white appliance. It was warm. I held the plug in my hand and waved it at Cinnamon.

I looked my cousin square in the eye and said, "Do you want to tell me something?"

Chapter 17

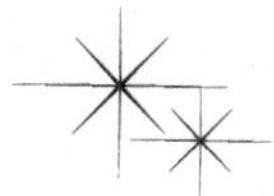

Cinnamon sighed and sank back down in her chair at the table. I went to the refrigerator to grab the butter and slathered it on each piece of toast.

My cousin dipped her head down for a minute, and when she brought it back up there was a mist in her eyes that startled me.

"I don't know what's happening to me, Stacy. I can't explain it." She grabbed another slice of bacon and bit into it, chewing slowly.

I sat down, put my hand on hers, and said gently, "Just start from the beginning."

She looked at the coffee mug in my hand. "That's decaf. It started with that. Caffeine isn't good for the baby, so I gave it up."

"Of course."

She nodded. "Then it was just little things. Reading up on how to take care of myself, you know, normal pregnant women stuff."

"And then?" I took another bite of the casserole. It really was delicious.

Cinnamon tossed her hands in the air. "And then, I don't know. Then suddenly I'm buying avocados, almond milk, and spices I've never even heard of and I'm cooking like Chef Ramsay."

"You know who Chef Ramsay is?" I asked.

She glared at me.

"Sorry."

Cinnamon stabbed at her frittata. "You see what I mean?" she said after she swallowed a mouthful. "It's freaking delicious! I didn't even use a recipe, and Stacy, I don't know how to cook." Her voice rose several notches, verging on hysteria, and I really wanted to comfort her.

"Your mother does. Maybe that's where it's coming from," I suggested.

She shook her head. "It's more than that. It's more . . . odd than that." She looked behind her as if someone were about to jump out of the pantry and yell *Boo!* "The appliances seem to have a mind of their own. Yesterday, I left a pie in the oven, forgot all about it, and fell asleep for two hours." She looked at me, her face a mixture of amusement and bewilderment. "The damn thing came out perfectly cooked, the crust flaky and golden." She tapped the tablecloth. "Cherry freaking pie. I hate cherries and they aren't even in season."

She seemed to catch herself and looked at me in wonderment. "You see? How do I know that? I'm not supposed to know stuff like that. I'm supposed to know how to make a Tequila Sunrise, where the best catfish can be caught, and how to load a shotgun."

There was definitely no explaining the appliance thing. Even that had me baffled.

I glanced around the kitchen. "And all this stuff?"

She flicked her eyes away, a hint of guilt in her voice when she spoke. "I don't remember buying any of this crap. I hate it, I really do."

"You don't remember?" This frightened me. How could she not remember?

"No," she said softly. She leaned into me and whispered, "Stacy, I think it's the baby. I think this is all because of the baby. It's like I'm possessed or something."

I didn't like where she was headed with this. Cinnamon was the most stable woman I knew and the thought of her cracking up—or worse—made my heart lurch.

"What are you saying?"

She looked around the kitchen, almost fearfully. "I'm saying that the baby is somehow controlling my actions. Does that sound crazy?"

She looked at me with those huge brown eyes that were always so in control, so void of emotion, but that now were filled with a worry I couldn't possibly fathom. I didn't want to tell her that yes, it sounded downright batshit bonkers coming from Cinnamon, but she was a Geraghty, after all. Maybe the baby *was* somehow controlling her actions, her motivations, her talents. And maybe it was natural if you were carrying a witch in your womb.

I looked around the room one last time, gobbled up the last bite of frittata, then said, "Come on, let's go in the other room."

Cinnamon sat on the sofa as I examined the living room. The pictures were the same as the last time I was here. No new faces, no new frames. The furniture was plain and comfortable, the curtains devoid of any prints, the walls pale beige, the carpet a speckled, practical earthy-toned Berber. There were no dancing tiki girls on display or nostalgic portraits of Rosie the Riveter, no gnome collections or fuzzy stuffed animals. I ducked my head in the bathroom next. A plain plaid shower curtain, two standard-issue toothbrushes, a counter-length mirror. The bedroom seemed to reflect a young married couple. Clothes tossed on the back of a chair, the bed made with a soft, blue cotton comforter. Tony's workout room was filled with weights and *Men's Health* magazines. The last room I checked was the nursery. I held my breath as I flipped the light switch.

The walls were still white. The old spare bed had been removed and there was a new white dresser with a baby-changing table next to it. No bunny-themed wallpaper and thankfully, no Chuckie dolls.

When I returned, Thor was lying at Cinnamon's feet.

"So it's only the kitchen where things . . . are different?" I asked.

My cousin nodded.

"Even the nursery is still mostly the same," I said.

Another nod from Cin.

This whole thing really didn't make much sense and I suspected maybe Cinnamon was simply fatigued, hormonal, and scared about her new addition. Perfectly normal, I would imagine.

I sat down across from her in a leather chair and clasped my hands. Leaning forward, I said, "I think you're just preparing to be a mother, Cinnamon. Decaf coffee, a scrumptious frittata, and butt-ugly kitchen accessories do not a crisis make."

She smirked. "But what about the appliances? The toast?"

That part was strange. I rolled it over in my mind for a beat. Then I thought about something. It was a far-reaching theory, but at least it would explain a few things.

"Was Thor here when you fell asleep baking that pie yesterday?" I asked.

"I think so. He was here when I woke up." Her eyes widened as if she knew where I was headed with this.

I looked at my familiar, stretched out at my cousin's feet chewing his own toenail. He was a typical Great Dane in many ways, but the truth was, Thor had talents even I wasn't aware of. It was highly likely he could have had something to do with Cinnamon not burning her house down. I certainly wouldn't put it past him and I was grateful he was here to prevent a tragedy.

Cinnamon fired a look at me, then Thor. "If you're about to tell me that the dog turned the oven off and then reheated the pie to perfection, you're nuttier than I am."

I shrugged. "Cinnamon, you are a Geraghty, like it or not, so technically anything is possible in this family. I know you've long dodged the family bullet, but maybe this time it was a direct hit."

She narrowed her eyes. "So what are you saying, Seeker?"

Cinnamon, I should point out, has known about the "prophecy" written by our great-grandmother Meagan in the Blessed Book forever. However, she didn't know that it came true.

I shrugged, thinking that if Cin did have some magic in her, maybe I wouldn't feel so alone in this. "I'm saying it could be the dog, it could be the baby, or it could be that you, my dear cousin, are a late bloomer."

Cinnamon groaned, sinking deeper into the sofa. She covered her head with a pillow. "That can't be it. It just can't."

I went over to her and rubbed her shoulder. "Look, nothing dangerous is going on, that's the important thing." I frowned. "Although I don't like that you don't remember buying that stuff. Did you drive to a store that sells the Brothers Grimm collection of freaky-ass tchotchkes?"

Her muffled voice said, "eBay." She peeked out from behind the pillow. "Are they really that bad?"

"Scary bad." I looked toward the kitchen and shuddered. "I think you should bury them in Birdie's backyard and we'll do a banishing spell so they can never harm again."

The fact that she wasn't driving at the time of her memory lapses gave me a wave of relief. Still. "I think you need to tell Tony what's going on."

Cin bolted up and in a deadly serious tone said, "No. No way. Promise me you won't tell Tony."

I didn't think that was a good idea, but neither did I think it was a good idea to upset a pregnant woman with a history of violence and newfound powers of uncontrollable electrical surges.

"Okay. For now. But at the first sign of weirdness, I'm calling you out, and Thor comes and goes as he pleases."

Thor abandoned his manicure at the sound of his name. He snuggled Cin's knee.

"Nuh-uh. He's your dog, Stacy. I have too much on my mind without worrying about that sack of gas."

"Well, then maybe Birdie and the aunts can help. Maybe they'll know what's happening. At least let me go to them."

"What? Absolutely not. Out of the question." She shook her head fiercely.

I stood up. "Look, I have to go to work. You have three choices. Tony, the Geraghty Girls, or Thor. Final offer."

She mumbled something to herself.

"What's that?"

"Fine. He can stay, but he goes home at night."

I looked at Thor. "Agreed?"

He flopped on his back and pawed the air, happy to be on assignment.

Suddenly Cinnamon said in a small voice that cracked my heart, "I miss my dad."

"I know you do, sweetie. I miss him too."

That gave me an excellent idea. Maybe it was Uncle Deck who was looking after his daughter and his granddaughter? He was always a boisterous man who loved gag gifts. Could that be what was happening? Could he be trying to reach out to his daughter through tacky kitchenware? I decided I would try to reach out to him later in the Seeker's Den. I hadn't used my gift in a few weeks. Now was as good a time as any to wake the dead. And if I could help him pay her a visit, maybe this would all go away.

Cinnamon's voice sliced through my thoughts. "Stacy, you know that book Birdie was always going on about?"

"The Blessed Book?"

She nodded, hopefully. "Do you think there's something in there about me? About this?" She rubbed her stomach.

"Maybe. I can check for you."

"Thank you."

I was about to leave when I remembered that it was her father who had believed Joseph Conrad's—now Blade Knight's—story regarding the skull. I asked Cin if she recalled anything about the case.

"That kid whose parents were killed? Oh, wow, it's so weird you brought him up. You know, he's in town. He's doing a book signing tonight. Tony and I are going."

I explained that I was working with Blade on a project.

"Yes, my dad talked about the case a lot. He always felt like he was missing a piece of the puzzle. Said if he had just gotten his hands on that . . . man, I can't remember what he called it."

She tilted her head in the air as if locating the memory.

"Skull?" I prompted.

She snapped her fingers. "Yes! He thought there was some missing skull that could have cracked the whole case wide open. It was the only case that ever stuck with him years after it happened. He only talked about it with me and I wasn't even born when that happened. Never with anyone else on the force. Not even Mama. I think he was afraid that the other cops would mock him or something. And Mama hated it when he talked about work." She thought for a moment. "You know, I may have some old notes from his private files. He was always jotting down ideas, theories, whenever a thought struck him. I can look if you want."

"Thanks. That'd be great."

Before I left, I turned off the router to the Internet to shield Cinnamon from further fairy-tale harassment, then I asked the one question that hadn't even occurred to me until that moment. I spun around, keys in my hand. "Do you know if he ever talked to Birdie about that case?"

Cinnamon shrugged. "You'd have to ask her that question."

I nodded. "I just might," I said and left.

Chapter 18

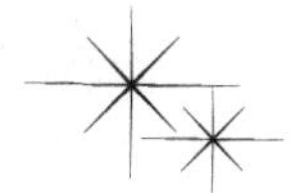

I called Tony on the way to the newspaper office and learned that my car might not be repairable, which, given all the other crap I had to worry about now, was the least of my problems.

It was nine when I got to the office. Monique's red Honda was already in the parking lot. I pulled into the slot next to it, checked for witnesses, then pulled out my athame and punctured her front left tire. It might buy me a little time at least.

Derek's office door was open so I popped in to discuss the plans I had for the day.

He was sitting at his desk, redesigning the website.

"Hey there," he said. "I'm pretty swamped trying to fit all these ads into Wednesday's edition. I was hoping you could edit Monique's column for me." His face told me he didn't have high hopes that I would agree to it.

"Sure." I sank into the brown leather chair across from him and crossed my legs.

Derek furrowed his brow. "That's it? No argument?"

I shrugged. "We're a team, right?"

"What's your angle, woman? What do you want?"

"An espresso machine."

"Done." He smiled. "I'll e-mail it to you. How's the reunion piece going?"

"I still have to do the interviews, but I have a good start on Blade Knight's profile."

"About that—I thought you could run a separate piece on Blade. Maybe cover the book signing tonight. I'll be there to shoot it."

"I can do that. Do we have enough space?"

"We'll put the signing in tomorrow's edition. Push the reunion piece back to Friday."

Our little paper only published three days a week: Wednesday, Friday, and a weekend Saturday edition for the tourists that mostly included articles from the historical archives, special events in the area, restaurant reviews, and new shops on Main Street.

"That works. I also agreed to help Blade with his project, so don't say I never do anything for you."

"Now when have I ever said that?"

I smiled, got up to leave, and told Derek I'd be in my office this morning, but in the field the rest of the afternoon.

There was a note on my office door from Gladys asking me to come see her. I plugged in my laptop, fired it up, and put the locket around my neck, tucking it under my sweater.

Monique was teetering down the hallway in thigh-high boots, her hair freshly bleached, her lipstick a glowing shade of fuchsia. She was wearing leopard-print tights, a cropped sweater that must have had industrial-strength buttons, and a red micro-miniskirt.

"Hey, I had a lot of fun with your boyfriend last night. He was a big hit with the ladies," she said in that squeaky voice that made me want to scatter mousetraps all around her.

Be cool, Stacy. Think about Chance.

I forced a smile to my lips and felt my face contort into what could only be a spot-on impression of The Joker. "I heard. About that, I thought you and I should discuss how the reunion planning is going. It would add another dimension to the piece I'm working on."

"What the hell is wrong with your face? Your Spanx too tight or something?"

My smile faded. *Maybe I should just let the Leanan Sidhe take her body. Maybe I could bind them together and send them both to Danu and Badb. Like a two-for-one package deal.*

"Pinched nerve."

"Huh. You should work out more. I do yoga." She struck a pose. I was so happy it wasn't downward-facing dog that I almost did a cartwheel right there in the hallway.

"I'm sure you do. I'll take that under advisement. So let's get together on that article."

Monique buffed her nails. "I'll see how my schedule looks. Maybe I could squeeze you in."

I wanted to say, *You mean, in between blow jobs?* But I bit my tongue. "You do that."

I brushed past her as fast as I could before I ended up slashing more than her tire. I could still feel her eyes on my back, but I was certain in that brief encounter that Monique Fontaine was still her usual nails-on-a-chalkboard, infuriating self. For now.

Gladys was working on a pagan-themed crossword puzzle when I got to the research room. She seemed to be having trouble with six down because she had penciled in letters and erased them so many times, the area was a big gray smudge. It began with an *N* and there was an *a* where she had filled *cauldron* in across and another *n* that was crossed with the word *newt.*

"Hello, Stacy."

"Hi, Gladys. What do you have for me?"

She pulled out a manila envelope. "I give these to you." She handed me the folder and picked up another one. "These, I take. Ya?"

I flipped through the folder. It contained a list of names and occupations of the valedictorians I had asked her to find. Next to the names were phone numbers, the graduation date of the students, as well as times and locations for interviews she had scheduled for today and tomorrow.

She had assigned me the author, the scientist working on a cure for Alzheimer's disease, a homemaker, and an archeologist.

"Looks good. Let me see who you'll be talking to," I said.

She reached around and grabbed the other folder. I thanked her and flipped it open. She would be interviewing a surgeon specializing in spinal cord injuries, a fashion designer whose work was all the rage in New York and London, and an animal behaviorist.

I handed the folder back to her and said. "Perfect. Send me the interviews as soon as you're done and I'll incorporate them into the piece."

Gladys beamed. "My first writing work."

"You'll do great." I pointed to her puzzle. "I can tell you six down if you want."

She nodded. "Yes, please. Is killing me."

"Necromancer." I winked and left Gladys to her puzzle and her interviews.

Back in my office, I checked my e-mail. Derek had sent me Monique's column, titled "How to Steal a Man." Except *steal* was spelled *steel*. I saved the file to my hard drive and went through the excruciating process of editing it. Then I compiled a list of questions for each interviewee, jumping on the Internet every so often to research the hot topics going on in their professions.

One of the biggest news stories in archeology recently was the discovery of what was believed to be Pluto's Gate, or, as the mainstream media insisted on calling it, the Gate to Hell. The dig took place in Turkey and the team uncovered a kind of pit emanating gases so noxious that some animals wandered too close and were killed instantly. They were in the process of covering it back up. My contact wasn't on that mission, though. In fact, I couldn't find any ground-breaking (no pun intended) stories on her at all. I wondered if perhaps she was teaching now.

The scientist was working on a cure for Alzheimer's disease, which was a subject near and dear to me since Aunt Lolly seemed to suffer from it in a very bizarre way. I found a few papers he had written on the topic, discussing the importance of stem cell research, what he believed is the genetic link, and how brain imaging could warn patients at risk. He was also working on a controversial new drug that he claimed to drastically improve, if not cure, the symptoms of sufferers.

The homemaker, I discovered, was much more than that. She had a pretty popular blog as well as a host of YouTube videos where she demonstrated step-by-step instructions on how to attain the looks of bygone eras. Her videos showcased hairstyles like 1930s pin curls, 1940s victory rolls, and 1950s Hollywood starlet styles, plus the face-painting techniques to finish the look. There were also video reviews and giveaways of what she called "new vintage" clothing, undergarments, makeup, hair products, and kitchenware.

Around noon, I saw Monique sashay past my office door. I stuffed my research notes and the folder in my bag and hurried out of the office. I lagged behind her a few steps, trying to act nonchalant, and followed her out to the parking lot.

"What the fuck!" she screamed when she saw her flat tire.

I was standing near the driver's side door of Birdie's car, about to plug the key into the lock. "Problem?" I asked.

She whirled around and glared at me. "My stupid tire is flat and I need to pick up the decorations for the reunion."

"Do you have a spare?"

She looked at me like I was the stoner of the class who only served to piss off the teacher. "Do I look like I know how to change a flat tire?"

I was careful not to smile this time. If I was going to keep tabs on Monique, I couldn't treat her too differently.

"You look like you should be selling raffle tickets at a street-walkers' convention in Nevada, but that's not the point." I tilted my head toward Birdie's car. "Come on. I'll drive you."

She gave the Buick a disgusted look, then slid her eyes to Derek's Mercedes. "Forget it. I'll just ask Derek for a lift." She turned around to walk away.

"He's swamped today. He brown-bagged it," I called.

She flipped her hair back and twisted her neck toward me. "Then I'll just borrow his car." She took a few more steps.

"Don't think so. That was a present from Daddy. Doesn't even run it through the car wash. He just buffs it with a cotton diaper."

Monique tossed her hands in the air in exasperation. "Fine."

I locked the doors after she got in, twisted the key in the ignition, and fastened my seat belt. I swung the car out of the parking lot, gaining speed to make the first light into downtown.

I said in a flat tone, "Why don't I buy us lunch? We can talk about the reunion committee."

She eyed me with the suspicion of a woman being propositioned for a ride in a dark alley. "Why are you being nice to me?"

I shrugged. "We're coworkers. I don't believe in a hostile work environment." I turned on the radio, hoping she'd shut her trap.

She snorted. "Oh, yeah? You could have fooled me. Hostile seems to run in your family. Especially that wacko cousin of yours. Of course now that she's knocked up and looks like a Teletubby, she's not such a raging bitch."

The light turned yellow and I slammed on the brake. Monique wasn't wearing her seat belt, so her head smacked the dash, leaving a good-sized welt on her noggin.

"Ow! Jesus Christ!" Monique rubbed her head and shot daggers at me with her eyes.

"Sorry."

"Where did you get your license? A gumball machine?" She reached for her seat belt and tried to tighten it over her chest. I felt like I was transporting supplies for Wilson Sporting Goods.

"I said I was sorry. Listen, I have to make a stop first, if that's all right."

"No, it's not all right. I told you I have to pick up the decorations."

"This won't take long. I said I'd feed you, so quit complaining."

I ignored Monique's brassy-pitched protests and made it to my first interview with ten minutes to spare.

Chapter 19

I parked in front of Muddy Waters Coffee House and we both got out of the car. Monique was still bitching, but she must have decided that she was hungry as soon as we walked in the door because she quit yapping long enough to order a chicken sandwich and a soda. I asked her to grab a table while I waited for our lunch, and she wandered off into the mocha-colored café looking for a spot to sit.

Iris, the gossip columnist for the paper, owned Muddy Waters. She took my order of tomato soup and tea, put a soda cup in front of me, and gave me a curious look.

"Hey, Iris. What's shaking?" I asked. "Got any dirt to report?"

"I think it just walked in the door." Iris winked and nodded toward Monique, who plopped her wool coat on a chair and wobbled off to the restroom.

Iris said, "Heard she was with your beau last night."

"Hmm. They were on the reunion committee together."

Iris tucked a pencil behind her ear and leaned over the counter. She smelled like pumpkin and her dentures clacked when she spoke. "If that man was mine, I wouldn't let him anywhere near that girl." She raised her eyebrows.

"I get your point. But I don't think I have anything to worry about."

"Well, if I hear of any hanky-panky, I'll let you know, sweetie." She patted my hand.

When Iris turned to pour my soup, I hurried to the soda fountain, extracted the locket from beneath my sweater, tapped some ruby dust into the empty cup, and filled it with ice and Diet Coke, Monique's favorite beverage. I sealed the lid on top, stuck a straw in the cup, and turned back to the counter.

Rubies were believed to shield against psychic attack and vampirism of the heart. I wasn't 100 percent certain it actually worked, or would work in this case, but Fiona, who was a love spell expert, swore by it to keep one's affections from being stolen. Technically, it was Monique's body the Leanan wanted, but I figured it couldn't hurt.

When I returned, Iris had set the soup on a tray and was reaching into the glass case for a pre-made chicken sandwich. She set that down, along with a tea bag, a mug of hot water, two napkins, and a plastic plate. I thanked her and carried everything into the dining room and set the tray down at the table where Monique had left her coat.

Monique returned from the bathroom and grabbed her sandwich without thanking me.

Be a shame if she choked on it, I thought. I dipped into my soup.

She reached for her soda and said, "So what do you want to know about the reunion stuff?"

The door chimed and in walked my first interview. Frieda Streator, class of 1986. She was wearing a faux fur coat over a black-patterned rockabilly dress, with a red patent leather belt that accented her slim waistline. Her open-toed pumps were also red patent leather, her dark hair was styled like Marilyn Monroe in *Some Like It Hot*, and she was carrying a small purse with pearl straps. She made an inquiry at the counter and Iris pointed to me.

Frieda smiled and waved. "Hello, dearie!"

Monique turned to see who I was waving at. "Who the hell is that?"

"That's my interview. Derek thought it might be good for you to sit in on an interview. You know, so you can incorporate some Q&A into your column." Blatant lie, I know, but what could I do?

Drink the damn soda, Monique.

Monique made a face. "Are you freaking kidding me? You said we were just getting lunch. You didn't say we'd be interviewing Lucille Ball."

"Shut up and be cordial," I hissed from the corner of my mouth.

I stood up and greeted Frieda. She had cold hands, a warm embrace, and a mole the size of a saucer on her right cheek.

"Jesus, that thing got a name?" Monique asked, gaping at Frieda.

I kicked her under the table.

"Ow, dammit," Monique grumbled. She reached down to rub her shin.

I smiled wide at Frieda, who was frozen for a moment. She darted her eyes away, probably mortified and looking for an escape route.

I laughed and slapped Monique on the back. Hard. "She's talking about your coat, Frieda. I'm afraid Monique's a huge animal activist. I think perhaps she thought it was real fur," I said apologetically. I gave Monique a look that stated in no uncertain terms that I would shove that sandwich down her throat if she didn't play along. "Isn't that right, Monique?"

Monique smiled adoringly and said, "Yes, that's right. My apologies. I do so love all animals." She took a big bite out of her chicken sandwich, making a huge show of what a cockamamie cover story I had just fed my interview subject.

Frieda let out a booming laugh. "No, honey, this is straight-from-the-factory fake." She rubbed her hands up and down her coat. "No harm came to any animals. Except maybe the stuffed kind." She elbowed me and winked.

I extended my arm. "Please, have a seat. Can I get you some Q&A coffee? A sandwich?"

We might have been past the awkward stage had I not said that. Frieda declined refreshments, but Monique's sandwich caught the woman's eye.

Monique flashed me a look, then set her gaze on Frieda. She pointed to her plate. "Except birds. Hate those flapping feathered bastards. Flying around the sky like they own it. Shitting everywhere. It's disgusting. Am I right?" She took another hearty bite.

Frieda just said, "Well . . ."

Because really, what else could she say?

I laughed again, knowing that Frieda was rethinking this whole interview thing, but that she was too polite to back out now.

If there had been duct tape anywhere in the vicinity of our table, I swear I would have wrapped the whole roll around that tacky blonde's head. Super Glue would have worked too, but alas, all I had was food and drink. I shoved Monique's soda in front of her, hoping she'd take the hint.

Birdie, you owe me big time.

Monique wrapped her lips around the straw and sipped her soda.

"So, Frieda, do I detect a hint of the South in your accent?"

"Why, yes, you do. After I graduated from high school, I went to Nashville. I had stars in my eyes back then," she said sheepishly.

"Didn't we all?" I leaned in toward her, giving her my full attention, hoping she'd relax and open up. I hit the audio record app on my phone and set it on the table.

Frieda's shoulders lost their sharp edge and she seemed to be realizing that I wasn't a raging lunatic like the loud-mouthed blonde. "So then after that, I wound up in Memphis."

"Oh, I hear it's just beautiful there." I tried to sound encouraging.

Her eyes brightened. "Oh, yes. Lovely place to raise a family. There's so much to do and see. My siblings and I share a vacation home here as well, so we do visit—"

Monique said, "Ugh, this is flat." She got up from her stool and yelled "Iris! The Diet is flat."

Then, to my horror, she dumped the soda down the fountain drain. So much for the ruby dust.

I sighed and turned to Frieda. "Let's hope that'll keep her busy for a while," I said.

Frieda tilted her head down. "She works for the paper?"

"She's in training. Prison release program."

"I see. Well, that's nice of you to help those people." She flicked her eyes toward Monique, who was picking something out of her teeth with a fingernail. "What was she in for?"

"Embezzlement. Hang on to your purse."

Her purse was on her lap, but now she wrapped both hands through the straps.

I nodded. "So back to Memphis. I want to hear all about that and those wonderful beauty tip videos you do. I may have to try out one of the styles sometime."

"You should! You'd look fabulous in a Lauren Bacall wave set."

I smiled. "I think the fashion reviews are fun too."

"Thank you. I do enjoy getting all glammed up, as you might have noticed." She hopped down from the high-back chair, slid her coat down her arms, still clinging to her pocketbook, and twirled. The skirt fanned out in a perfect circle, showing off Frieda's long legs.

When she sat back down, the woman seemed perfectly at ease. She talked nonstop about her life after Amethyst, chattering away about her kids, her husband, and her business.

Except I didn't hear much of it, because I was staring at her dress. More specifically, the pattern on it.

Tiny black skulls.

Chapter 20

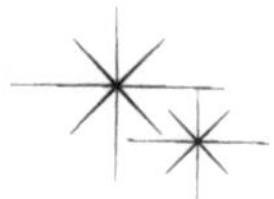

After Frieda left, we finished lunch and I paid Iris while Monique phoned Tony to ask him to replace her flat tire.

I wasn't certain if the dress with the skulls really meant anything, but it lit a spark in me. I needed to talk to Blade. He was the next interview Gladys had set up, but that wasn't for another hour, so I decided to drive Monique to get her decorations. Hopefully that would stop her squawking.

It didn't.

"Can't you drive any faster? I want to pick this crap up and get back to Down and Dirty so I can meet the liquor distributor," she said.

"Doesn't he just drop the shipments off through the back door? That's what Cinnamon arranges when she can't get to the bar."

Monique snapped. "Yes he does, but he's hot and I'm trying to get him to take me to the reunion. So get the lead out, grandma."

I wondered if the United States government paid for privatized weapons. Because I was pretty sure even the most stubborn terrorists would crack if they had to spend five minutes in a car with Monique.

I sped the car up and we arrived at the party store a few minutes later.

We both got out of the car and Monique said, "I don't need an escort."

"I thought you might need help carrying whatever crap it is that you bought."

"Huh," she said.

She walked through the door and I followed her, thinking that no other man on earth is worth all this but Chance.

The cashier rung up streamers, balloons, a large banner, a bunch of fake flowers, and several cardboard crowns like they pass out to kids at Burger King.

"What are those for?" I asked.

"For awards. Duh. You know. Most changed, most successful, who came the farthest, who got the fattest, stuff like that."

She shoved a box in my hands and we were out of there after fifteen minutes. I popped the trunk and we loaded the party supplies inside. Monique's phone made a whistling sound and she extracted it from her pocket. She tapped the screen a few times and said, "Tony says the car will be done in an hour."

"Good," I said. But I was really thinking, *Now how am I going to keep tabs on her*? I could always slip a tracking device under her bumper, but Birdie said I had to watch her like a dog watches a bone.

The next stop was Down and Dirty and the whole ride there I was trying to come up with another plan.

Monique checked the time on her phone. "He should be here any minute. Make yourself scarce. I don't want you cock-blocking me."

"Wouldn't dream of it."

I parked the car in back of the building. I watched her get out, take her keys from the side pocket of her purse, and unlock the door. I figured she couldn't get into too much trouble flirting with the delivery man.

When I heard the blood-curdling scream a few minutes later, I knew I was wrong.

I grabbed the gun out of my bag, jumped out of the car, ran to the back door, and shoved it open. Water came gushing out as soon as I did and I leapt back, tucking the gun into the waistband of my pants.

Monique was standing there, looking like she'd been attacked by the Loch Ness monster. Her hair was plastered to her head. Literally. There were bits of plaster and soggy wallpaper covering her top half. Her bottom half was standing in knee-deep water, women's toiletries floating downstream toward the front of her bar.

I looked up to find a good portion of the ceiling—and also the floor of Monique's upstairs apartment—missing. She must have dodged just in time before it collapsed. Broken tile and crumbled plaster had crushed the boxes that the liquor distributor had, unfortunately, already delivered. The smell of scotch, beer, and tequila was strong, but it was overpowered by the stench of sewage.

There was a crack above our heads, then a snap, and I looked up just in time to see a live wire disengage from what was left of the ceiling.

I reached in, grabbed Monique's arm, and yanked her out of there, then slammed the steel door shut.

As I turned around, I saw Pickle disappear behind a dumpster. He gave me a thumbs-up and I smiled, thinking he must have received my note requesting help with Monique along with the offerings and that I was now forgiven.

"It's not funny, Stacy!" Monique screeched. Her chest heaved in anger.

"Of course it's not. I'm not laughing. I'm just happy we didn't get barbecued."

Birdie always kept a towel in the back of her Buick so I went to fetch it and handed it to Monique.

"Here."

"Screw you!"

"Calm down; this is nothing that can't be fixed."

She flailed her arms. "All the liquor for the reunion was in there. What am I supposed to do now? I spent all the cash on product. Everyone's going to be pissed at me when there's no booze."

"It'll get worked out. Don't worry about it."

"Sure, easy for you to say. It's not your business on the line. This was going to be the event that gets me out of the red." She plopped herself on top of a wooden crate and started bawling.

I had no idea Down and Dirty wasn't doing well, but with the money she must have spent to get the place looking like the set of *Moulin Rouge*, I can't say I was shocked.

The towel was still in my hand, so I offered it again. This time she accepted. She wiped her head and then blew her nose in it.

"And where am I going to live?" she wailed up at me. With all the makeup she had on, her face looked like a Picasso left out in the rain.

"My mother was right. I am a loser." She sniffed.

It never occurred to me that Monique had a mother, let alone a terrible one. I had always assumed she was built in the basement of a horny teenager.

I sat down next to her. "You're not a loser, okay? Besides, you still have a job at the paper."

"Yeah. Thanks to you."

Well, not really, but okay.

Suddenly she tensed. "Thanks to you," she said slowly. She shot up off the crate and pointed. "You. This is all your fault!"

Here we go. One moment of humanity and she was back to her old self. Although she had a tiny point. But she didn't know that.

I got up too. "How is this my fault?"

She wagged her finger at me. "I'm not sure, Stacy Justice, but shit like this doesn't happen to me. It happens to you all the time, though. You're like, like . . ." She struggled to find a word.

"Kryptonite?"

She snapped her fingers. "Exactly. That's exactly what you are. And I'm not staying here another minute with you."

Monique tried to storm off, but she busted her left heel in the process and it slowed her down. Then she launched into a fresh crying jag.

I caught up to her and reached for her elbow. "Come on, let me at least drive you to your car."

She reeled on me. "Don't touch me. I mean it. I never want to see your face, your cousin's face, or this stupid town again!"

"Monique, you can't just walk all the way to Iowa with a broken shoe, smelling like tequila and urine."

"Why not?"

"Because the only action you'll get is from the hobo on Station Road and that's just because he smells the same."

She spun around, nearly lost her balance, but recovered gracelessly.

She pointed again. "That's another thing. You're always making fun of me."

"Only because you make it so easy."

Monique flipped me off then tottered back around. "I want you out of my sight." She waved a fist in the air.

I sighed. "I'm afraid I can't let that happen, Monique."

She sent me another bird and kept walking.

I pulled out my tranquilizer gun and shot her.

Chapter 21

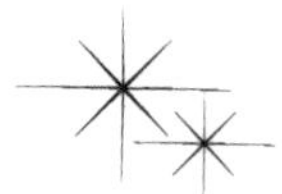

Monique landed face-first on a soiled mattress that someone had thoughtfully tossed in the alley. I plucked the dart out and called to Pickle. He helped me load her in the back of Birdie's Buick, before he disappeared again. Then it was straight to the Geraghty Girls' House.

I found an old wheelbarrow in the shed behind the house and jogged it to the car. A quick scan of the area told me no one was watching. I opened the driver's-side door, reached in, and clutched my bag. I slung it over my shoulder, shoving the tranquilizer gun back inside. Then I opened the back door of the car and dragged Monique out by her armpits. She was heavier than she looked, but that could have been because she was waterlogged. I hoisted her into the wheelbarrow just as a soft rain began to fall. I carted Monique up to the back door of the inn while the sky darkened and thunder boomed. I twisted the handle, but it was locked, so I rang the bell that only sounded in the private quarters of the house.

Birdie was the one to answer.

"Special delivery." I wheeled Monique past her and set the wheelbarrow down in the kitchen.

Her eyes widened.

"I tried, Birdie, I really did, but it got to the point where she just wasn't going to play nice."

Birdie looked at Monique, then at me. "So you killed her?"

"Of course not."

"Is she drunk?" Birdie lifted her nose, sniffed the air. "She smells like a Dublin distillery." She looked closer at Monique. "And Temple Bar at four a.m."

I decided to stifle my question in regards to Dublin's nightlife. Some things a granddaughter shouldn't know.

"She's"—I searched for a word that would make me sound more like a great Seeker and less like a sociopath—"sleeping." I grinned. "Where do you want her? Because for the rest of the day and hopefully the better part of the evening, she's your problem."

Birdie looked around the kitchen as if someone had just delivered a sack of potatoes and she didn't possibly have any room left in the cupboard for it. She made a face. "She smells bad."

"Little issue with some busted pipes in her bathroom. She'll clean up all right."

Lolly came into the room then. "One more for supper?" she said when she saw Monique slumped in the wheelbarrow, tongue dangling out of her mouth. Lolly was drinking champagne from a crystal flute, wearing glass slippers, a white leotard, and a blue veil.

"Yep. And not just tonight. I hope you have a vacancy, because it's sort of my fault that her apartment was washed away."

In my note to Pickle, I had asked him for his assistance in helping me guard Monique. I didn't anticipate that he would destroy her apartment to accomplish that goal, but I had to admit the fairy was effective.

I didn't hear Fiona come in but suddenly she was behind me. "We have one room left. That Blade Knight rented two."

"Two?" I asked. That was strange. Why would Blade need two rooms?

"Celebrities," Lolly said as if she had read my mind, and when hers was sharp, she sometimes could.

Birdie stared at Monique. "How long will she be asleep?"

"A few hours, maybe more. I figured this was the safest place to bring her. Plus, it's kind of your fault she's in this mess."

Birdie shot each of her sisters a glare, clearly indicating that this conundrum was all their doing. "Still. The state of her." She crinkled her nose.

"Yes, well, it's a messy business being a witch."

"Did you at least find the Leanan Sidhe?"

I rolled my eyes. "Sure, Birdie. I did that before lunch. It was a snap."

"There's no need to be sarcastic."

"Well, give me a bit more to go on here. It's not like I can take out a want ad for a blood-sucking sexpot with big knockers. Which reminds me. When I find her, how do I catch and bind her for transport?"

"There's a magic lasso in the upstairs chamber," Birdie said.

"Seriously?"

Birdie smiled. "No. I can be a smart-mouth too."

I high-fived her. Then I gave her my house key. "The Blessed Book is in the Seeker's Den. Since the Leanan and the curse are a part of the Geraghty history, there must be some sort of contingency plan in there if she were to escape. Hopefully, it will tell us what to do."

"I'll see what I can do, but you must bear in mind that Samhain is fast approaching."

"I know."

Samhain, when the dead pass through the veil and the fairies cross through the worlds. It was a day when anything could happen.

Lolly, always excited by any project that involved dressing someone up, accepted the challenge. She grabbed the wheelbarrow and said, "We'll take it from here, dear. You've done well."

"Great, because I have to get to my next interview." I put my hand on the door that led through to the common areas of the house.

"It's here?" Birdie asked. "Why?"

I turned to her and shrugged. "Celebrities. You want the goods, you have to go to them."

The lock clicked behind me and I passed through the hallway and one other door that fed into the parlor. There was a key under the carpet that I used to lock it behind me.

I set my bag on the piano and went to wash Monique's stink off me. When I returned, Blade Knight was standing in the living room looking as if he'd just witnessed a book burning.

"What is it?" I asked.

"We have a problem," he said.

"Well, that won't do, Blade, because I've met my problem quota for the day."

"Look at this." He reached into his jacket pocket and pulled out a piece of paper.

It was a note, the words comprised of letters cut out of magazine articles and pasted together.

It read:

Stay away from the girl and no one gets hurt.

I lifted my head to meet the author's eyes. "What girl? Who is it referring to?"

Blade tilted his head and said, "I think it means you."

I frowned. "That doesn't make sense; why would someone want you to stay away from me?"

He shrugged. "Maybe we're getting close."

"Close? We haven't even started yet." I looked at the note again. There was something familiar about it, but I couldn't quite put my finger on it. The paper? The letters? It looked just like plain white paper. But still. There was a trace of recognition in my mind as I held the paper. "Where did you find it?"

"On my car."

"And since you've pretty much talked to half the town already, anyone can know what you're driving." Not to mention there weren't too many $80,000 cars roaming around Amethyst.

He nodded.

I hated to admit it, but I felt there was no other option. "I think it's time we talked to Leo," I said.

Blade started to protest and I lifted my hand. "We need to see the police report from the day your parents were killed anyway. I think you should also show him the note, but that's up to you."

"But last night, you said—"

"I know what I said, but I can't be responsible for your safety, Blade. If anything happened to you and I could have somehow prevented it, I would feel terrible."

He sighed. "Okay. If you think that's best." He sounded doubtful.

"I do. But first, I have a couple of questions for you."

"Shoot."

"My aunts said that you rented two rooms. Why?"

"My agent's coming in tonight for the book signing."

"So the second question is why was my life the subject in *Stone Cold*?"

Blade gave me a confused look. "What are you talking about?"

"The car in the ice, Blade, that happened to me."

He still looked as if I were off my medication. Then slowly, realization spread across his face.

"That's just how fiction authors operate, Stacy. We read something, hear something on the news, see something on a television show, hell, even quirks from kids I went to grade school with—it all gets programmed into our brains and somehow, often completely subconsciously, the pieces get regurgitated into a novel."

I said, "So I'm literary vomit, then. That makes me feel better."

He walked over and grabbed my bag, handed it to me. "You're not a special snowflake. In fact . . ." He drank in the parlor with its antique furniture, flowery wallpaper, and woodworking details that weren't present in modern homes. "This house might pop up in my next novel."

"So long as I don't."

He held up two fingers. "Scout's honor."

"Why do I get the feeling you were never a Boy Scout, Blade?"

He smiled and opened the door, standing off to the side to let me pass through first. "I guess it's time to write the next chapter."

Those words triggered something in me. An ancient spark, a primal instinct. It was a niggling that wormed through my brain, my conscious, telling me that I should be picking up on a whisper planted inside me long ago. That there was a truth about Blade Knight that I had known all along, but failed to recognize. Something that, once it surfaced, would have a lasting impact on both our lives.

Only I couldn't grasp it.

But I knew one thing for certain. Our paths were destined to cross, no matter what the outcome.

Chapter 22

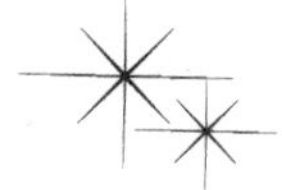

I grabbed a couple of umbrellas and Birdie's rain slicker with the triple goddess on the back and we headed out.

On the way to the police department, Cinnamon called.

"Three more packages arrived today," she said.

"Did you open them?"

"Yes. There was a Cinderella teapot, an iced tea pitcher hand-painted with Snow White and the Seven Dwarfs, and a Jack and the Beanstalk soap dispenser." Her voice had a nervous edge to it. On the one hand, I found it rather comical that my cousin was being tortured by fairy-tale characters; on the other hand, I'd never known her to be so unsettled before.

"Why don't you unpack them, put them in the kitchen, and see how you feel afterward."

Because maybe it was Uncle Deck. Maybe he was trying to buy his granddaughter a few things from beyond the grave. Although why he didn't just opt for a rubber ducky and a stuffed bear like normal people do, I wouldn't know until I tried to contact him.

"Okay. I'll try that."

"If you still feel funny, load up Thor and head to the inn. I'll be there after I take care of a few things."

"All right. Later." She hung up.

The windshield wipers on Blade's car were swooshing back and forth on high speed as the rain pelted the hood.

I sighed, worried about my cousin and, well, pretty much everyone. What if I didn't find the Leanan Sidhe? Samhain was coming up and there was a good chance that if I didn't find her by then, she'd grow stronger. Maybe stronger than I could handle. I wondered if I should call in Ivy and John to help—the other members of the Council's team of operatives. Except this wasn't a Council mission. It was a family mission. And as important as it was, there was no doubt that this thing with Blade was equally important.

Blade said, "Is someone sick?"

It took me a moment to realize what he meant and then I recalled what I had said on the phone. "My cousin. She's pregnant."

"Oh. Boy or girl?"

"They want to be surprised."

The street that led to the police station was coming up. "Turn right here."

Blade made a right and pulled into the parking lot of the police station. I put the hood of the slicker over my head and handed him one of the umbrellas.

I opened the door, stuck the umbrella out, and fanned it open.

We trotted to the steps and scaled them two at a time. The overhang on the building shielded the rain and I took a moment to shake out the umbrella before closing it.

The perky new receptionist, whose name I couldn't recall, looked happy to see someone in the station. She was a young girl with fluffy blonde hair and a dazzling smile.

"Hi, Stacy! How you doing? Don't tell me you found another dead body. Is that why you're here? Because I had October in the pool and Gus had November, but don't tell Leo, cuz we aren't supposed to be betting on dead bodies anymore. He thinks it's disrespectful, but I don't really see the big deal, I mean there ain't much else to do around here, not that I wish anyone to be harmed, but—"

"It's not about a body."

She looked disappointed.

"But I do need to talk with the chief. Is he in?"

"Sure thing. Go on back."

I started to push through the little half gate that led to Leo's office. I stopped when I realized Blade wasn't behind me.

"You coming?" I asked.

He was staring at the receptionist like a scientist examining a newly discovered gene under a microscope.

"Be right there."

I cocked my head at him.

He shrugged. "Research."

I left Blade there, walked down the short, brightly lit hallway, and turned toward Leo's office.

He was sitting at his desk, shaking his head, and mumbling to himself. His dark hair was slicked back and damp as if he'd been caught in the rain, and he was still wearing a trench coat. He looked like a character from a Raymond Chandler novel.

I knocked on the open door. "Hey there."

He glanced up, smiled. "Hey yourself." The smile faded. "Please tell me you didn't find a body. I'm having the worst day."

"Nope. Didn't find a single corpse. What's so awful about your day?" There was a wooden chair against the wall and I dragged it over and sat in it.

"For starters, I just got back from the Shelby Farm, where someone dressed up all the goats in cheap Halloween costumes."

I stifled a giggle. "What was your favorite?"

"Favorite what?"

"Costume. I'm sure one of them jumped out at you that made you say, well, that is kind of funny."

Leo tried to hide a smirk, but failed. "Cher."

"Awesome."

"Not awesome. I swear if I ever find the idiots who pull these stunts . . ." He shook his head. "Plus, the phone won't stop ringing about a kid wearing a *Star Trek* hat stealing pies, candy, flowers, and gazing balls. Gus is out taking a report right now, in fact."

Gus was Leo's deputy. He wasn't exactly Monk, so I didn't think he'd actually be able to catch Pickle, but I'd have to have a talk with the fairy anyway about true offerings and taking things that belong to others.

Leo looked up at the ceiling and muttered, his hands spread wide, "Who the hell steals gazing balls?"

The Fae do love their shiny things.

Leo finally took off his coat and draped it over the back of his chair. He sat down. "So what's up?"

"I need you to pull up a cold-case file for me. The Conrad murders. Around thirty years ago."

He narrowed his eyes, clasped his hands out in front of him. "Why?"

"Because I'd like to read the file," I said, matter-of-factly.

"Is this about the other night? Did something happen at your place?"

"Are you going to make this difficult? Because it's public record."

"Are you going to put yourself in danger again?" His voice was unflinching. "And technically, if the killer was never caught, I don't have to show it to you."

"So you are going to be difficult."

"If it means I can keep you from getting hurt, then yes." Leo sighed and ran his hands through his hair, as he often did in my presence. As if he were trying to wash me out of it. "Just tell me why you want to go digging around in a thirty-year-old murder."

"Because I asked her to," Blade said from the open doorway.

Leo practically fell out of his chair. "Mr. Knight, hello again."

"Hello, Chief."

Leo wagged a finger at the writer. "I told you to call me Leo."

"Right. Leo. I believe you also said if there was anything I needed . . . ?"

Leo fired a frustrated look at me. I sat back in the chair and folded my arms, grinning.

Leo was visibly conflicted when we left his office, but he gave us the report anyway, along with the crime scene photos. Blade gave Leo the note and told him about the shots through my window. He wasn't too happy about being lied to, but Blade was able to smooth things over with the promise of free signed copies of all his books for life. Leo said he'd be at my place as soon as he could to investigate the "vandalism."

Back at the cottage, Blade and I spread the photos out on the counter and I looked at those while Blade read the report. There were a few suspects. A handyman who had installed a deck on the back of the home, two petty criminals, and a man who Blade's father had gotten into a heated altercation with at a local sporting event. All of them had alibied out.

I said to Blade, "Did the police know if the hammer that was used belonged to your parents?"

He flipped through the pages of the report. After a minute, he shook his head. "It doesn't say. No fingerprints were found on it, though."

"So it was either wiped clean or the killer wore gloves."

"Looks that way."

"Hmm," I said.

Blade tossed me a glance "What are you thinking?"

"If I were going to kill someone in their own home, I wouldn't bring a hammer to do it, would you?"

Blade got my meaning. "No. I'd bring a gun, maybe a knife." He thought for a moment. "So it had to be in the room. It had to belong to my parents."

"Right. And your mother was an artist. Your dad was struck from behind, so maybe he was hanging a picture."

"Which means it could have been a weapon of convenience. Maybe they knew the person. Invited whoever it was in while they were in the middle of hanging some artwork." He thought for a moment, walked over to the far wall where a photo hung of my parents. He twisted his neck to face me. "Do you have a hammer?"

There was one in the junk drawer in the kitchen. I grabbed it and handed it to him.

Blade took the hammer and stood in front of the picture. "I'm about my dad's height, so if I were hanging a painting, I'd take the nail about here"—he pretended to hold a nail up—"and then swing like this." He feigned hammering a nail into the wall. "Now, the doorbell rings." He paused and looked at me.

I ran to the cottage door, opened it, and reached around to press the bell.

"Come in," Blade said, still holding the hammer.

I did.

"So maybe they talk for a while. Dad insists he doesn't have whatever the killer was looking for. The killer gets angry. Decides to try to find whatever it is, steal it, but in order to do that, my parents have to die." He looked at the wall, feigned hammering a nail. "Now step behind me and try to grab the hammer."

I tried, but I couldn't reach.

"How tall are you?"

"Five six."

"Do you have a stool?"

I dug a step stool out of the utility closet. "It's six inches," I told him.

I climbed on top and Blade did the hammering motion again. This time, I was able to grab it with inches to spare.

He said, "So he, she, whoever, grabs the hammer and strikes him in the back of the head. Then my mom probably rushes to my dad, the killer goes after her, they struggle, she tries to fight back, tables get knocked over, lamps crash to the ground, but the killer was able to overpower her."

His jaw hardened for a moment and the darkness that I had felt from him when we first met mired around him in a cloud of anger, frustration, and grief.

I gave him a moment to compose himself before I asked softly, "You okay?"

Blade looked at me, his eyes full of pain. I knew that pain all too well. Knew how it pillaged your heart, crept around your soul, lurked in the corners of your mind until, eventually, you just accept that it's eaten away the best parts of you. I ached to make it disappear for him, because no one deserved to live that way.

He attempted a smile. "Yes. I keep trying to think of this as a plot for a book I'm writing. Trying to cut my emotions from it, but it's not always easy." He walked back over to the counter and placed the hammer on top of it.

I joined him there. "I know." I looked at Blade for a long time. Finally, I put my hand on his. "I'm not going to tell you that it gets easier once you know the truth, but I can say that it shifts. The loss is still there, but a quiet peace settles in right beside it and you feel a sense of relief. Not knowing is the hardest part." I paused, then added, "We'll get them justice, Blade. I promise you that."

He turned to me then and squeezed my shoulder. "Thank you for helping me. I'm not sure I could do it on my own. It feels good to talk about it with someone who understands." Our eyes locked and my breath caught. He was standing so close, I could smell his aftershave. An ocean scent.

I thought for a moment he was going to kiss me and I froze. Instead, he pulled me in for an embrace. His cheek brushed mine and I broke away.

I cleared my throat, circled around to the refrigerator, putting the counter between us, and grabbed two waters. I slid one to Blade.

"So we're looking for someone at least five feet eight inches tall," I said, unscrewing the cap on the water bottle.

Blade adjusted his shirt and reached for his water. "Right."

I tapped the photos, trying to refocus on the task at hand, forcing myself to ignore the fact that a successful, wealthy, devastatingly handsome man just had his arms around me.

We stood in silence for a few moments, looking at the photographs. I mulled over everything I'd learned about the murders. Something about our theory gnawed at me.

I said, "But if your parents knew who it was, knew the person or persons were coming, then why go to such great lengths to hide you? Why not just stick you in your room?"

Blade took a swig of water. "Maybe they thought an argument was inevitable. Maybe whatever the killer was after was something they didn't want me to know about."

"What did your father do for a living?"

"He was a teacher at the high school and a soccer coach."

That was why Chance felt Blade was familiar. His brother was a star soccer player and every picture of the boys' sports teams hung proudly on the walls of the Stryker home. Blade must have looked like his father. I asked him if that was true and he said it was.

I pondered that for a few moments.

Blade said, "Or it could have been dangerous, could have been illegal."

I shook my head. That didn't seem to fit their lifestyle, *Breaking Bad* aside.

Then a lightbulb went off in my head like a giant flashing marquee.

"Or it could have been you."

Chapter 23

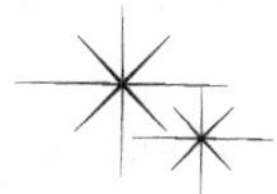

Blade appeared doubtful. "Me? I was just a kid. What would they want to do with me?"

"I'm not sure, Blade, but none of this adds up."

I didn't tell him what I was really thinking. That I had a feeling about him. Partly because I didn't want to spook him and partly because I didn't want him to get the wrong idea.

"What about the stuff that was taken? Are you sure it was only to make it look like a robbery? What about the artwork? I know you said it wasn't valuable, but is there a possibility it could have been? Or the computer? Anything on it that someone would want to kill for?"

Blade shook his head. "It was my computer that was taken. All that was on the hard drive were a bunch of stories I had written and a few games." He chugged some more water. "As for the art, I couldn't tell you. I don't even know what the paintings looked like. I always had my head stuck in a book or in a notebook."

"And the books were just commercial fiction, you said?"

"Yes. Those I remember. A few Stephen King novels, *The Maltese Falcon*, and—" He stopped short, met my eyes. His voice took on an air of excitement. "*The Book of Skulls* by Robert Silverberg."

He grabbed the report, flipped through it. "It just says *books* under items taken. I didn't even remember that until just now."

"What's the book about?"

"It's about four college students who discover an ancient manuscript called *The Book of Skulls* that promises immortality. The manuscript is guarded by an order of monks who agree to grant the young men immortality as long as they agree to a ritual."

"What's the ritual?"

"Two sacrifices for two everlasting lives."

I let that sink in for a moment. Obviously, the book itself couldn't have been what they were after, because they could have just bought a copy. But what if the manuscript it talks about was real?

I mentioned this to Blade.

"I guess it's possible, but I never heard my father talk about anything like that."

"What did your father teach?"

Blade swallowed hard. "English lit."

Could it have been a student? A fellow teacher? An old college roommate of his father's, perhaps? Or just a psycho who read this science fiction book and thought it was real? I voiced all of this to Blade. He didn't have any answers, didn't know his father's curriculum, but at least we had a start. There were two very connected pieces to the puzzle now. We just had to do a little more digging to determine if either of them actually existed, in legend or otherwise.

"Show me where you found the skull," I said, nodding toward the photographs.

He pointed out a spot in one of the pictures near where his father lay.

I studied the spot, input it into my memory, closed my eyes, and grazed my hands over the photograph.

When I was finished, after the heat of that spot he had pointed to sizzled my fingertips and the skull flashed bright, then dull, then exploded in my mind's eye, I said, "Give me a few minutes. Let me do some research."

Blade was staring at me. "What was that? What did you just do?"

"Rule number one, Blade, and since you already violated rule number two today, I suggest you don't break another." I said it playfully enough that he just rolled his eyes.

I went into the Seeker's Den and did some research on the laptop regarding *The Book of Skulls*. I discovered that the book was supposed to be made into a movie but never was, and that it had been nominated for both the Nebula and Hugo awards. Next, I Googled *black skulls* and *skulls* in general and discovered that the damn things were fairly popular, and came in a host of colors, none of which, I could discern, were worth killing for. There were clear crystal skulls that some believed to have special powers, but according to the database provided by the Council, this was pure fiction. That database also revealed that there was no ancient manuscript anywhere with the word *skull* in the title.

So what did it mean? Why would someone take the time to not only destroy the fake one, but to track Blade's movements until the opportunity to do so presented itself?

And why did the note threaten him to stay away from me? Was the killer someone I knew?

An hour had passed by the time I emerged, and I found Blade sitting on the couch, fiddling with a tablet.

He looked up. "Did you find any information about the skull?"

I shook my head. "But I might know someone who can shed some light on it."

Blade stood up. "Great. Listen, I'm having dinner with my agent before the signing, so I better get changed." He gave me a bemused smile. "Your Aunt Lolly said she wanted to approve my dinner attire before I left, so who knows how long that could take."

"Yeah, I think you may need a few extra minutes. You can leave the reports here. Maybe I'll get another chance to look them over."

He nodded, grabbed his coat, stuffed his tablet in his pocket. and headed toward the door.

He had his hand on the handle, but he hesitated, turned around. "Thanks again, Stacy. You're a remarkable woman. Chance is a lucky man."

My heart fluttered all the way up to my throat so all I could do was blink.

Blade left and I blew out a huge sigh of relief, not because I wanted him gone, but because a small part of me wanted him to stay. And I didn't know why. Nor was I particularly comfortable with the feeling.

I went back into the Seeker's Den and began the profile on Blade Knight that was due to run in tomorrow's paper. I planned to finish it after the signing so it would be ready to print. By the time I was done, Cinnamon texted that she was on her way to Birdie's house with Thor and to get my ass over there.

It was four o'clock. The signing was in a couple of hours. Birdie might know something about the black skull, maybe even shed light on what was happening in Amethyst at the time Blade's parents were killed—not to mention the fact that Cin might have brought me something from Uncle Deck's files. I decided to quickly change and head over to the Geraghty Girls' House for an intel exchange.

What I didn't expect, when I opened the door, was an unconscious fairy on my front porch.

"Pickle!"

I bent down and shook him gently at first, then much more aggressively. "Pickle, can you hear me?"

He wasn't moving. Was barely breathing.

I tried hoisting the fairy to a seated position, but he just slumped over. "No, no, no. Come on, buddy." After several shakes and a few slaps, none of which the fairy responded to, I decided I had to get him to the inn ASAP.

Luckily the rain had stopped, although the grass was wet and slick. Pickle was a lot lighter than Monique, but I still couldn't carry him. I had to drag the poor thing, my arms locked around his chest, all the way to the back door. It was open.

I gently laid the fairy on the floor and set my bag on the apothecary table just as Birdie came through the kitchen doorway that led to the common rooms.

She took one look at me, one at Pickle, and said, "Honestly, Stacy, you need to stop incapacitating people."

"No, Birdie, you don't understand. This is, I mean he's a . . . I mean . . ."

"Spit it out, girl. Who is he?"

The words spewed from my mouth like an erupted volcano. "This is Pickle. He's a Fae guide sent by Danu to escort the Leanan Sidhe back to the Otherworld and I found him on my porch like this. He's not breathing, Birdie. You have to do something."

She dropped the apples she was holding and knelt by Pickle, putting a hand to his head. "Lolly! Fiona! Come quick!"

Birdie was the Mage, but she was also a gifted healer. However, I didn't know if her gifts transferred to magical beings. I stood helplessly by, chewing my nail, staring at Pickle's impossibly pale face. He looked to be . . . fading . . . right there on the floor.

My great-aunts came rushing down the back stairs. "What's all the fuss about, Birdie?" Fiona asked, then stopped short when she laid her eyes on Pickle. "Oh my."

Birdie was examining Pickle's hands, which looked to be puffy. "Stacy, help me lift him."

I ran around toward the fairy's shoulders and hoisted him up by his armpits.

Birdie lifted his shirt and took a look at his back. There were several tiny welts spread across it.

"Oh no," Lolly whispered.

Birdie asked me how long he'd been like that and I told her it could have been up to thirty minutes, from the time Blade had left to the time I opened the door. That was my best guess.

"Then there's no time to waste. Fiona, start a sugar bath. Lolly, grab my medicine bag," my grandmother barked. "Stacy, help me carry him upstairs."

Lolly and Fiona rushed off to fulfill their duties. I grabbed Pickle's arms and Birdie lifted his feet. Together, we carried the frail Fae up the back stairs to the private quarters.

"Birdie, what's happening? What's going on?" I asked.

"Not now, Stacy," she snapped. "I need to think."

Fiona was pouring white sugar into a hot bath by the time we carried Pickle up the stairs and into the bathroom.

Lolly followed shortly after with a thick brocade bag embroidered with clovers.

"I'll need the leaves of oak, ash, and thorn, as much as you can find," Birdie said to her sister.

Lolly scurried off to collect the supplies.

Birdie held Pickle's head, splashing the water over his body as fast as her hands could move. "Fiona, help me find it."

Fiona jumped in, searching Pickle's clothing and body for something. His breathing became more shallow.

"Damn," Birdie said. "The bath isn't working."

Pickle was growing even more pale and seemed to be shriveling, shrinking even. His clothes appeared smaller, his feet retreating into the yellow legs of his now baggy pants.

"Stacy, fetch me the foxglove oil from my bag. Fiona, did you find it?"

"Not yet."

"Well, hurry. We're losing him. There may be more than one."

There was a tiny vial of oil in Birdie's bag. I snatched it and handed it to her, looking at the dying fairy, terrified that we might lose him and that it would be all my fault.

Lolly returned with the leaves Birdie had asked for. She spread them all over Pickle's still frame, gently pressing them to his skin.

Birdie lifted one of Pickle's eyelids. I gasped when I saw that his eye, once Caribbean blue, was now completely white. My grandmother put a few drops of the oil first in one eye, then the other. The rest she poured down his throat, before passing the empty vial back to me. Lolly stepped out of the way so Birdie and Fiona could better work.

"Where is it?" Birdie was frantic, her voice angry.

"I can't find it," Fiona said. She pulled off Pickle's socks, lifted his pants legs, and flipped his hat off, her hands grazing his now translucent skin as if she were applying Reiki.

"We're losing him," said Lolly.

"Not on my watch," growled Birdie. "Stacy, get me more foxglove."

"That was it. There was only one vial."

Birdie swore again, something she rarely did, and moved her hands even faster, chanting softly as she worked.

"Honey and hyssop then, Stacy."

I searched the bag, found the potion she requested, and gave it to her. This she rubbed all over Pickle's bare back.

"I need material, something dark," Birdie said.

I removed my black leather jacket and handed it to Birdie. She pressed it to Pickle's back and waited a few moments.

We all stood there, the four of us, with bated breath.

"I think something's happening," I said when I saw Pickle's leg twitch. Birdie slid her hand along the back of the fairy and I saw something lumpy pierce through the coat. She yanked her hand away as several more similarly shaped lumps popped through.

The fairy began to slowly plump back up, his legs lengthening, his color returning. After a while, he opened one weary eye and then the other. He smiled up at all of us.

Birdie breathed a huge sigh of relief and stood up. She carefully removed the jacket from Pickle's back, folded it, and handed it to Lolly, who whisked it away from the room.

Fiona tilted her head to Pickle, said a few words, and rose as well.

Birdie grabbed her bag and retreated into the hallway. I followed, with Fiona close behind. She shut the bathroom door.

Lolly joined us a few seconds later.

They all three looked at me gravely.

"What? What was that?"

"That," Birdie said, glancing behind her at the closed door, "was a fairy blast."

"Okay. What's a fairy blast?" I asked.

Fiona said, "It's like a gunshot or a bomb, small, but effective. The materials they use vary depending on the target. That was probably an acidic blast. Deadly to the Fae."

"Sometimes they use poison-tipped darts," Lolly said.

I looked from her to Fiona to Birdie.

"So what does that mean?" I asked, because I had never heard of such a thing.

Birdie sighed, crossed her arms, and pinched the bridge of her nose. When she didn't answer, I looked at Fiona.

"It means she has an army."

Chapter 24

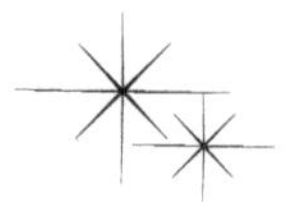

"You mean the Leanan Sidhe? You're kidding me."

"Did that look like a joke to you?" Birdie snapped.

"No, but . . . well, what do you mean by that? Are there hordes of fairy mistresses roaming around Amethyst searching for fresh blood?"

Fiona said, "Let's take this downstairs before Sleeping Beauty wakes up."

She nodded to the spare bedroom door across the hall. My guess was that's where Monique was sleeping off the sedative.

Birdie said, "I'll call the coven." She looked at me pointedly. "We're going to need them."

Lolly, Fiona, and I went downstairs into the kitchen, where Cinnamon and Thor were waiting.

Thor ran up to me and showered me with doggie licks.

"Hey, buddy. Did you have a good day with Auntie Cinnamon?" I ruffled up his ears.

Cin said, "I told you not to call me that." Then she greeted each of the aunts with a hug.

Birdie fluttered into the kitchen a few moments later, the

Blessed Book in her hands. Excellent. She had a plan. I needed a new plan right about now. Several, in fact.

Cinnamon looked at the book and said, "Um, Stacy, did you get to what we talked about?" She flashed her eyes to the book and then back to me.

"I'm sorry, I didn't have time yet, but I'll get to that, I swear."

As soon as I save Chance from a vampire, Blade from whoever wanted him to stop searching for his parents' murderer, and Pickle from the fairy cartel.

"Okay, thanks."

Cinnamon poured herself some water and Fiona asked how she was doing.

My cousin rubbed her belly. "Well, I can't see my feet, but other than that, I'm fine." She sent me a look, warning me to keep my mouth shut. I held my gaze, hoping she understood that I wouldn't tell them what was going on with her and her cargo.

At least for now. But if I felt even a smidgen of danger waft off her, all bets were off.

The bell chimed and Birdie said, "Cinnamon, dear, would you please see who's at the door?"

Cinnamon set her water down, sighed, and pointed to the book. "I get it. Official witch business. No problem."

She squeezed my shoulder on the way out of the room.

Birdie quickly locked the door behind her. She turned, had another thought, then twisted around to bolt the chain.

"Okay." She slapped her hands together. "Here's what we know." She paced the floor, her sisters' eyes upon her. "It appears the Leanan Sidhe has followers in this realm."

"How is that possible?" I asked.

Fiona said, "When the Tuatha Dé Danaan and the humans

struck a deal all that time ago, some Fae refused to leave this plane. Most agreed that it was best for all that the magical creatures melt into the Otherworld and to leave the humans this realm, but a small pocket opposed the plan."

"A war was waged. Many Fae lives were lost until, finally, Danu had had enough and left the defectors behind," Birdie said. "Of course when they heard what a paradise she had created in the Otherworld, they wanted to join her kingdom again."

"But goddesses being goddesses, Danu decided it was too late. She refused entry to any of the rebels," said Lolly, a tumbler of Jameson now in her hand.

"So you think that's who the Leanan Sidhe has recruited for her army?" I asked. "The rebels who waged a war against Danu?"

"It would appear that way," Birdie said. "The fairy blast used on Pickle could only have been constructed by an ancient Fae form."

"But why would they side with the Leanan if they want to get back to the Otherworld? Why wouldn't they try to capture her? Fight for the cause?"

Fiona said, "Never underestimate the length of a grudge held by the Irish."

Birdie explained. "Since Danu refused them entry into the Otherworld and the Leanan Sidhe herself wants to keep out of it, for it has become her prison, it would stand to reason that both the Leanan and the rebels would forge an alliance against Danu and her subjects no matter what the cause."

"But why would the fairy mistress even need an army?" I asked.

Lolly said, "The Fae don't need a reason to fight. They act on emotion. And their emotions tell them that Danu has betrayed them and that humans have ruined their realm."

"But as for the Leanan herself, I can only think of one reason she would want an army." Birdie gave me a hard look. "You."

"Me? Why?"

My grandmother smiled. "She must know of your power, your role as the Seeker. That alone would tell her she'd have a serious fight on her hands if she resisted capture."

She had that right. Because I planned to take this to hell and back and there was a good chance that one of us wouldn't come out alive.

"How many rebels are there?"

"I have no idea; all I know, all that was written in the Blessed Book, is that over time, they've shrunken to miniature size. They won't look like Pickle."

"What do they look like?"

Birdie opened the book to a page that showed various drawings of what looked to me like trolls, gnomes, and really tiny people.

I lifted my eyes to meet her. "So I'm supposed to battle the townsfolk of Lilliput?"

She shrugged. "Something like that."

"With one broken fairy."

"Well, he's fixed now, dear," Fiona said.

Good grief.

I got a text from Derek then.

Do you know where Monique is? The fire department is at her place. They just called here.

Someone must have complained about the smell, but there had been no time to deal with the wreckage at Monique's place.

I debated on what to tell him for a second, decided that I'd deal with the consequences later, and texted back: No idea.

K. See you at the signing.

It was five-thirty then and the book signing was at six.

"Okay, so were you able to find anything in the book on how to locate and bind the fairy mistress?"

Birdie said, "Nothing on how to find her, but the book had a few suggestions on how to bind."

She flipped through the book to a page she had marked. There was a slip of paper tucked inside and she handed it to me. "I wrote them down for you."

I took the piece of paper and put it in my pocket. "Thank you."

Cinnamon tried to come back through the door and I heard an "oof."

"Hey, Birdie. There's a horde of women out here with broomsticks and suitcases."

"The coven!" Fiona clapped her hands.

Reinforcements, I thought. Thank the Goddess.

Lolly and Fiona opened the door and Birdie was about to rush out behind them.

"Birdie, wait," I said. "I need to talk to you about something."

Birdie hung back and looked at me. "What is it?"

Cinnamon slipped around the corner and into the restroom.

"It's about Blade Knight. His real name is Joseph Conrad." I waited for a sign of recognition, but none came.

"Well, many writers use pen names."

"That name doesn't ring a bell for you? Uncle Deck never talked about him with you?"

Birdie rolled her eyes. "Your uncle didn't talk about much with me. It was your grandfather who he confided in."

I chewed my lip.

Birdie touched my arm. "What's bothering you, Stacy? Have you gotten a signal from the man? Is something amiss?"

I unloaded the entire story on her. When I was finished, I asked, "So is there anything in the Council archives, anything in history, about an ancient script or an artifact, regarding skulls, that you learned about?"

Birdie tapped her lip, flipping through her mental files. "Not that I can recall. But I'll call the Council tonight. Perhaps Tallulah or one of the other board members has some information."

I thanked Birdie just as Cinnamon came back through the door, carrying the excited chatter of a room full of women with her.

She thumbed behind her. "Who's the weirdo in the *Star Trek* hat? He licked my hand, so I punched him, and he burst into tears. He's rolling around on the carpet like a newborn who can't turn over."

"I'll fix this," Birdie said to me. She left to greet her guests, and Cinnamon sat down at the table, flipping through the Blessed Book.

Thor parked in front of the refrigerator and howled.

I went to sift through it, looking for something to feed him, and asked Cin if she had found her father's files.

"Stacy, I tore that house apart, but it's the damndest thing, I couldn't find them. I don't know if we lost them in the move or what. I'm sorry. Is it important?"

"Don't worry about it."

I found some leftover meatloaf, heated it up, and fed it to Thor along with some green beans and olive oil.

When I turned around, Cinnamon was still turning the pages, a look of concern on her face.

"Don't suppose you have time to go through this now?" she asked miserably.

The locket was tucked beneath my sweater. The Seeker before me had told me that it would "do anything I wanted it to do."

Well, at that moment, I wanted it to help my cousin. I sat down next to her at the apothecary table.

"I can, but you have to promise not to freak out at what I'm about to do," I said.

Cin rolled her eyes. "Twenty-six years in this family, girl, nothing shocks me."

"Okay." I removed the locket and held it tightly in both hands. Eyes squeezed shut, I concentrated on the power of the talisman, sent it an image of Cinnamon, then dangled it by the chain from my left hand and floated it over the book.

The coppery piece twirled, twisted, and twined itself around my hand, then floated over the book in an infinity pattern, gaining speed with each loop until finally, it came to rest. I clicked open the clasp and pointed the face of the piece down at the closed leather cover. The tome rustled, its spine blew out puffs of smoke, until eventually, the pages flipped and fluttered back and forth before settling on a passage near the end of the book.

I tucked the locket away and Cinnamon and I both bent over the page.

In Meagan's swirling script, the passage read:

The Seeker shall never be alone in the New World, for another child will join her. Together, the pair will battle inner and outer demons, loss, and tragedies great and small. This child, born of two ancient families, will carry a great burden. For the child holds the key to—

I flipped the page to find a list of herbal remedies, recipes, and crystal enchantment spells.

Cinnamon flipped the page back and forth.

"That's it? What's the burden? What's the key? And what does it unlock? And is the child me or the baby?" Cin asked, frantically.

I scratched my head, flipping back and forth between the pages.

Then I stopped, ran my fingers along where the pages met.

"There's a page missing." I looked at Cinnamon. "Someone cut it out."

Chapter 25

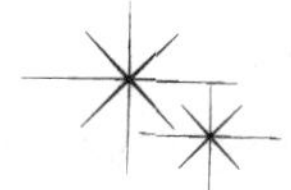

I heard a loud, screeching voice coming from the back hallway. "Where the hell am I? And why the hell am I dressed like this?"

Cinnamon fired a look at me. "Please tell me that's a guest who's lost her way."

"Afraid not. Witchy business. I can't explain it all right now, but I have to keep an eye on Monique. She's in danger."

Cin narrowed her eyes. "She's going to be in danger if she pushes my buttons." She closed the book and shoved it in a cabinet. "What kind of danger?"

"The kind that would lead to trouble for all of us if I don't stop it."

"Yeah, well, good luck with that." She started to walk out of the kitchen.

I grabbed her by her shirt and said, "Don't leave me with her. I need to think of something to tell her so she stays here. Besides, I ruined her apartment and her business and I kind of feel bad about that."

Cin turned around, a smirk on her face. "You did what?"

"Oh, didn't I mention that part? Her place is trashed. Pipes exploded. It was ugly. So she's staying here."

"Jesus, that sounds about as fun as a dinner with a cannibal." My cousin smiled and said, "I hope Ben Smalls is her insurance agent."

Ben Smalls was the beady-eyed little weasel who had accused my cousin of burning her bar down for the insurance money last February.

"Bite your tongue, because he'd have to come here, and I don't want to see that smarmy toad."

Monique eventually found her way down the back steps. Her hair was twisted into a lovely chignon, her makeup was done simply, with just a streak of eyeliner and a swipe of mascara, and she was wearing a Grace Kelly–style swing dress with black flats. She actually looked quite nice.

She stopped when she saw us. "Of course. Laverne and Shirley. I should have known."

Cinnamon and I exchanged a glance, trying to figure out which one of us was Laverne and which one was Shirley.

"Hey, Monique. How are you feeling?" I asked.

"Like I partied with Charlie Sheen. What the hell happened?"

She rubbed her head where it had hit the steering wheel earlier today. Aunt Lolly had done a beautiful job covering up the bruise.

"A pipe burst in your place. Don't you remember?" I asked, trying to gauge what she recalled.

"Dammit. That's right. But why am I here?" She eyed me suspiciously.

I said, "You needed a place to stay, so my grandmother offered you a room. Free of charge."

She looked around the kitchen. "This is the guesthouse?"

"Yes."

She shook her head. "Oh no. No way. I'm not staying here. I've heard the rumors. Those women are lunatics."

She searched the room. "Where are my clothes? Where's my phone? I need to call Tony to see if my car is fixed."

Cinnamon piped up. "He was pretty swamped today. Won't be fixed until tomorrow, maybe the next day." She pressed her lips together, clearly trying not to laugh.

"It's a flat tire, how freaking long can it take?" Monique's agitation was pulsating through the pearly white buttons of her frock.

Cinnamon just shrugged. "I don't know what to tell you."

"Fine," Monique grumbled. "Where's the land line?"

"They don't have one," I said.

She rolled her eyes. "Of course they don't. What about your phone?" she asked me.

"Battery's dead."

Monique tapped her foot, her mouth straining. Like she was trying not to spit on me. "Whatever."

She started for the back door and I snapped my fingers. Thor trotted over to it and stood in front of the door, staring at Monique.

"Out of my way, Marmaduke," she said.

Thor, who absolutely hated to be called Marmaduke, growled. Monique backed up.

"Where are you going to go?" I asked. The woman didn't have any friends that I knew of. Just barflies looking for cheap drinks and free Viagra on Thursdays.

"I'll call Derek. I can stay at his place."

"He's having it fumigated. Termites," I said.

She glared at me. "Then I'll stay at a hotel."

Cinnamon said, "They're all booked. Halloween, the reunion. Busy week."

Birdie came through the door, Lolly and Fiona behind her.

"Oh, excellent, you're awake," Birdie said.

Fiona asked Monique, "How are you feeling, dear?"

Monique licked her lips. Her left leg started to tremble and her eyes darted this way and that like a rat trapped in a spiraling drain. "I'm fine." She inched back toward the counter.

"So then, Stacy explained everything to you?" Birdie asked.

"Um, Birdie—"

Monique shot me a nervous look. "Explained what?" Another step back.

"About the vampire." Birdie looked at me. "Didn't you tell her?" As if it would be as easy as explaining a grocery list.

Lolly said, "You were right, Stacy, she cleaned up just fine." Lolly had donned her ritual cape. She had the hood up and everything.

Fiona smiled warmly at my coworker. "You look beautiful, dear."

Monique swung her head around, spotted the butcher block, and grabbed a carving knife. "Look, I don't know what's going on here with the Addams Family, but I'm out of here. You people are batshit crazy." She waved the knife around.

"Nice going, Birdie," I said.

"Well, I thought you would have explained things."

Thor took a step forward, lowered his head, and let out the low growl of a mama bear protecting her cub. His hackles were standing up so high, he seemed to grow another foot taller.

"Monique, for God's sake, put the knife down," Cinnamon snapped.

Monique was crouched forward in a wrestling stance, her eyes darting wildly from one to the other of us.

"You better put it down, Monique," I said. "Thor doesn't take kindly to threats. Just relax. I'll explain everything."

"No!" she shouted, hysteria starting to settle in. Her eyes took on the look of a rabid raccoon and she grabbed another knife. "Just let me go."

There were two options at this point. I decided to take the one least likely to get anyone hurt.

"Fine, Monique. Have it your way. Thor, heel," I said.

The dog gave me a look like, *You sure? Because I think I can take her.*

I nodded and he trotted over to me.

"Okay. Now all of you take a step back," Monique ordered.

We did.

She headed for the back door.

"Um, Monique, you want to leave the knives here, please?" I asked.

She turned, backing out of the kitchen slowly, and put the knives on the pie safe next to the door.

"So long, psychos, I'm history."

Monique spun around and grabbed the handle, yanking the door open.

I reached for the tranq gun in my back pocket and shot her again.

"I told you earlier I couldn't let you do that, Monique," I said.

Birdie rolled her eyes. "Honestly, Stacy, you're going to give the girl brain damage."

Cinnamon walked over to Monique, who was crumpled on the floor. She looked at her nemesis, then back at our grandmother. "Might be an improvement."

Chapter 26

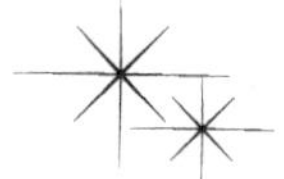

Fifteen minutes later, Cinnamon, Thor, and I were driving to the book signing.

I gave her a sideways glance. "So, I guess you're wondering what that was all about."

She slid her eyes to me. "Not even a little bit."

"Okay then."I scratched my neck. "This damn thing is itchy."

Lolly had insisted I wear some sort of protection out in public, lest I be captured by tiny bandits and strapped to railroad tracks. She decided that her faux fur coat, circa 1970, was the way to go and she sprayed some special potion on it as an added precaution. So now I looked like Bigfoot.

Cinnamon wrinkled up her nose. "It kind of smells too."

I sniffed the sleeve and coughed. "I know. I think it's been doused with a combination of catnip and cow dung."

There was no parking anywhere near the store, so we pulled the car around to the next block and backtracked up to Main Street.

Thor hung back to water a fire hydrant while Cinnamon and I walked into the bookstore. Birdie made me leave my tranquilizer gun at home, but I still had a few tricks up my sleeve so I wasn't completely unarmed. I didn't know if whoever shot my window out would be here, but I had a pretty good idea that someone was watching Blade closely and I wanted to be prepared for anything.

The place was packed, standing room only, and Blade had already begun his reading. Cinnamon spotted Tony and waved to him. He rushed over to us and kissed his wife and handed her a fast-food bag.

"I love you!" Cinnamon said and snatched the bag.

"I saved seats for you two," Tony said.

Tony was a sweet guy and I was glad to call him my cousin-in-law. He had the typical Italian skin, dark hair, and dreamy eyes a girl could fall in love with. He also had the patience of a saint, which had served him well these last few months and, I hoped, would sustain him for the next few.

"Thanks, Tony, but I'm going to stay in back and find a spot for my laptop. I'm covering this for work so I have some notes to take." I patted my bag.

"Okay, see you at the Opal after?"

There was a cocktail reception at my cousin's bar and grill following the signing, compliments of Blade's publisher.

"Yep. I'll be there."

I found a place in the corner with a sturdy table, shoved a couple of books aside, and set my computer on top of it. I fired it up and entered my password.

As the file that I began earlier opened, I assessed the audience. Leo was standing off to the side, trying to look threatening, but I could tell he was hanging on Blade's every word. I recognized the archeologist and the scientist I was scheduled to interview tomorrow from the research I had done. They were seated toward the back, side by side, and I briefly wondered if they knew each other. The archeologist was a weathered-looking woman with a face aged by sun, sand, and wind. Her white hair was pulled back in a tight ponytail and she was wearing jeans and a cargo-style jacket with zippers and pockets covering every inch of it. The scientist was a thin, balding man in his fifties with wire-rimmed glasses and gaunt cheeks. His tee shirt had the face of Einstein on it and he was wearing plaid pants. Chance was nowhere to be found, but I spotted Frieda there in the front row. She seemed intensely interested in Blade's reading. His book was nestled in her lap and she kept opening and closing the covers, the pages cascading like a paper fan.

Several townspeople and old classmates of mine were also scattered about the room, as well as some business owners, the mayor, Derek, and Gladys. I made a mental note to pull Gladys aside afterwards and ask how her interviews had gone.

I typed a few notes in the Word file about who was in the audience, the passage Blade was reading, the book's title and cost, and where it could be purchased.

When I was finished saving the file, I looked back toward Blade. There was a large spider weaving a web along the base of the podium where Blade was speaking. When I had seen the sign before, in my office, I had assumed that it was Blade Knight who was the uninvited guest. Now I knew better. He was the target. I studied the audience, centered myself, and tried to capture a signal from someone, calling on my spirit guides to aid me.

One word whispered in my head.

Reunion.

Could that be it? Was the killer someone who went to school in Amethyst? A student of Blade's father? Or a soccer player? A teacher?

Something flashed out of the corner of my eye, and I whipped my head sideways to catch it. A nanosecond later, and I would have missed it. There, next to the latest Barry Eisler and Janet Evanovich novels, was a display case featuring a family of gnomes. Except one of them, wearing a faded green hat, blinked.

I stood stark still, pretending to read the titles in the bookshelf next to him. There was a slight flutter in his hands and I brought my arm up quickly. My face shielded from a potential fairy blast, I pulled an aspirin-tipped nail file from the coat sleeve, and, in one swift motion, launched it at the sucker.

It was a direct hit in his pointy little head. He toppled over instantly, stiff as a statue. A few people glanced over toward the direction of what sounded like a plastic cup hitting a wooden table.

Blade, ever the professional, did not flinch.

Aspirin, I had been informed by Fiona, was safe for humans, but hell on fairies.

I sent Birdie a text. Cleanup on aisle four.

That was the code she told me to send if I needed one of the coven members to collect any casualties of war.

Three tiny pebble-like things rolled around the carpet near my right foot. Ammunition for a fairy blast, I supposed. I ground them into dust.

It seemed like all was clear until two thick hands came up from behind me and slapped over my eyes.

I was about to pull my Taser out when a voice I hadn't heard in years said, "Guess who?"

"Oh my God," I squealed softly and turned around to see Chance's brother, Caleb, standing in front of me.

I pulled him off to the side away from the crowd then hugged him tight and stood back to look at him. He was twelve years older than Chance, but other than a few more lines and a touch of gray in his hair, he was the spitting image of his brother.

"What the hell are you wearing, Red? Is that a bear carcass, because it smells like one." He smiled.

Caleb was the prankster in the family. The man would do anything for a joke. He used to work at a pizza place and whenever Birdie would order one, he'd shape it into a witch's hat. She complained every time, but I think she secretly loved it. I'd always adored him.

"A gift from Lolly," I said.

Caleb held his hand up. "Say no more, sister, say no more."

"What are you doing here?" I asked.

Caleb worked in New York for a television studio.

He shrugged. "The reunion. I haven't been to one in a while, figured I may as well make an appearance, see some old friends, visit the folks and that knucklehead you're dating." He glanced around the room. "By the way, where is he?"

"Working late, I guess. He's supposed to meet me, though, so he should be here soon."

Caleb nodded and a serious look spread across his face. "Good, because I need to talk to you anyway."

I raised my eyebrows. "Oh? What about?" I didn't like the tone in his voice.

"About Chance. Mom said he's been acting strange. She wants you to come by the house to talk. Plus she misses you. Hasn't seen you in what, a week or so?" He grinned, stuffed his hands in his pockets.

Now I felt guilty. It had probably been close to a month since I'd last visited Chance's parents.

"Longer than that, I'm afraid, but I haven't noticed a change in Chance. Did she say specifically what was strange about the way he's been acting?"

"No, but you know Mom. She's not happy unless she's worrying about something."

"I'll stop by tomorrow." I pointed to Blade, who was now taking questions from the audience. "Are you a fan?"

Caleb looked over to the author. "I've read a few of his books. The studio is in talks with his agent about a network series based on the Tracey Stone character."

This was new information, although I doubted it was relevant to the murders. Speaking of which. "So you know who he is then?"

Caleb cocked his head. "What do you mean?"

"You played soccer, right? His father was a coach and a teacher. Conrad."

Caleb's head snapped toward Blade. "I knew he looked familiar. That's Joseph Conrad?"

"Yes. Did you know him?"

"I knew who he was, but he was a few years younger than me." His face darkened. "A shame what happened to his parents. Coach Conrad was a great guy. Everyone loved him."

"So he didn't have any enemies then? No one you could think of who wanted to kill him?"

Caleb gave me a funny look. "What gave you that idea? I thought it was just a break-in gone bad."

"Maybe, maybe not," I said.

"Are you working on a story? Digging up old ghosts?"

"Something like that." I looked at Caleb. "What were the rumors going around at the time? Anything you can remember?"

Caleb scratched his chin, thinking for a moment. He shrugged. "Just the usual, I guess. Some people thought it was a couple of kids looking for drug money, others thought maybe they were in a cult." He rolled his finger in circles around his head as if to say the ones who thought that were cuckoo for Cocoa Puffs. Then something sparked in his brain and he shook his head as if waving the thought away.

"What?"

"Nothing. It's stupid."

"No, tell me, anything that can help."

Caleb scratched his chin as he thought back to his youth. "A few weeks before he died, the coach started carrying around a book all the time. He would read it on the bus to and from games and you couldn't talk to him when he was reading."

"That's not so unusual. He was an English teacher."

Caleb furrowed his brow. "It was more than that. He was always scribbling in it, taking notes, highlighting passages. I mean, the book wasn't that thick. A guy like him could have finished it in a few days." He gave me a curious look. "It was like he was studying it."

"Maybe he wanted to incorporate it into the curriculum?" I said.

Caleb shook his head. "No way. Not in this town. The school board would never allow a book like that in the reading list."

"What was the book?" I asked, although I had a pretty good idea what it was.

"Skull something or other."

"*The Book of Skulls*?"

Caleb said, "That's the one."

The bookstore door chimed and I looked over to see Chance walk in, accompanied by Thor. Thor trotted over to me, a toy in his mouth.

Caleb scratched Thor's ear. "Hey, big guy, I've heard a lot about you."

He reached down to take the toy from the Great Dane's mouth but Thor held on tight. The dog shook his head back and forth and the legs dangling from Thor's jaw slapped his shoulders. There was a squeak followed by a yelp.

I looked closer at Thor.

In his mouth was another member of the Leanan Sidhe's army. A troll, injured, but still alive.

"Good boy," I said. Then I leaned in and told him to take our POW to the Geraghty House.

He trotted back to the door and a woman browsing the new releases let him out. When she turned, I caught her profile and recognized her as one of Birdie's coven members. I nodded toward the gnome. She winked, walked over to the shelf, and discreetly collected the fallen soldier.

Chance walked up to me then, scooped me in his arms, and kissed me. "Did you lose a bet?" he asked, pointing to the coat.

Caleb said, "Lolly."

Chance smiled. "Got it."

He greeted his brother just as Blade Knight walked over to say hello. "Did you get everything you need for the article?"

"Yep, all good."

He lowered his voice. "Can I speak with you a moment?"

Chance stepped in between Blade and me, put his hand on the author's chest, and said, "Can it wait, Shakespeare? I haven't seen my lady all day."

He emphasized the word *my* and looked at Blade like he wanted to clock him.

I shot Caleb a look and he raised his eyebrows.

This was new. Chance had never shown signs of jealousy before. He was radiating so much heat, I thought his ears would start smoking any moment.

And it made me wonder. What if his mother was right?

Chapter 27

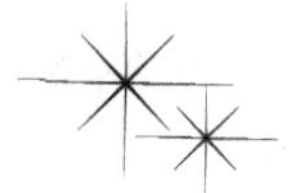

Blade gave Chance a steady look. "Sure. It can wait." He nodded at me and said, "Hope to see you all at the cocktail party. Drinks are on me."

This seemed to incense Chance even further. His jaw was so taut, it looked to be wired shut.

"Are you okay?" I asked him.

"I don't like the way he looks at you."

Caleb politely excused himself, but he hung close by, keeping an eye on his brother.

I decided that no good could come of discussing what just happened, so I changed the subject. "How was work?'

"Not bad. Bid on a couple of new jobs, and a project I thought we'd lost came through. Then I met with the reunion committee. Monique never showed, which was weird. She seemed all gung-ho about it yesterday." He grabbed my hands. "I don't want to talk about any of that, though. Let's get out of here and you can tell me what you did today."

"I can't. I still have to discuss a few things with Derek and Gladys and I told Cin I'd meet her at the Opal."

"Okay." He looked disappointed. Then he glanced over to where Blade was signing books. "This might take a while. Want to go for a walk?"

"Sure." I e-mailed Derek the file, shut down my laptop, and walked over to where Tony and Cinnamon were standing in line, waiting for Blade to sign their books. I asked Tony to hang on to my bag and told them I'd see them at the Black Opal. I let Gladys and Derek know too.

The temperature had dropped outside and I was almost glad Lolly had insisted on dressing me in this monstrosity of a coat.

Chance took my hand and we walked along Main Street, admiring the Halloween decorations. Some shop owners went the traditional route with carved pumpkins, plastic witches, and scarecrows flanking the entryways. Others were more macabre, arranging entire scenes in their storefront windows. We made a game out of guessing which movie or book had inspired the displays. There was a mannequin in a hockey mask, brandishing a knife, that had to be Jason from the *Halloween* movies. Another, in a dirty red and green sweater, with a charred face, was Freddy Krueger. There was a simple display of Poe surrounded by ravens, the distinctive mask used by the killer in the *Scream* movies, and beyond that, the hideous-looking puppet from the *Saw* movies perched on a tricycle.

We turned the corner and continued walking down a quiet street, the game over. "I was thinking it might be nice to have dinner with your parents tomorrow. I haven't seen them in a while."

Chance slid his eyes to me. "I don't know if I can. I'm pretty swamped and they like to eat early."

"Well, maybe I'll stop over there at lunchtime. I'll bring some sandwiches." I studied his face, searching for a reaction. Did he not want me to talk to his mother? Was something going on with him?

Chance gave me an easy smile. "That would be nice. I think my mom would like that. She's been acting nutty lately since my dad retired."

Chance's mother was a warm woman who made a killer lasagna and liked to crochet. She was a stay-at-home mom who loved her sons to the ends of the earth and always kept a teakettle on the stove. His dad was recently retired from the construction business that Chance was now the owner of, although he didn't come by it easily. He'd been working with his father since the age of twelve and had saved every penny to buy the business from him. They were a typical Midwestern, middle-class family, and both parents taught their sons the value of a dollar and a woman.

"I would imagine he gets in her hair. She's not used to having him around so much."

Chance laughed. "Want to know a secret?"

A small twinge pinched my stomach at the word *secret*, for I knew many. When this was over, after the Leanan was banished and the murders solved, I vowed to tell him mine, Council be damned.

"Your dad's taken up ballroom dancing?"

"Better. I'm pretty sure my mom breaks things around the house just so he has something to fix."

"Clever woman."

"The only kind I like." He reached for my elbow. "Watch your step." He brushed some broken glass out of the way with his foot.

As he did so, I felt a tingle dance up and down my spine and something hit the back of my coat and bounced to the ground. A tiny arrow.

I grabbed the corncob holders from my jacket pocket, whirled around, and fired at the puppet from the *Saw* display. He gave a slight cry and fell to the pavement. Two lithe hands reached out from the shadows and yanked him back by his ankles into a dark alley.

Chance was just kicking the rest of the glass out of the way when I pivoted back around. He offered me his arm and I took it.

We walked a little bit more in silence, listening to the crickets. Someone was making popcorn in an apartment above a shop and, farther down, the sounds of a piano drifted out into the street.

"We should probably head back," I said.

Chance pulled me toward him tightly. He put both hands on my cheeks, looking at me with the intensity of a man just back from war. He sunk his lips into mine, and we kissed under a cloudy night sky.

His hands unbuttoned my coat and he slid them around me, pulling me closer still. "Not yet. I need you all to myself a little longer."

I responded to his kisses enthusiastically, my heart beating faster, my breath coming in short gasps. Chance moaned and unbuttoned my pants. His hand slipped around, cupping my backside, and my pants almost fell to the ground.

I grabbed them with my left hand. "What are you doing?"

He grinned at me, his eyes dark, devilish. "Come on." He glanced around. "No one's looking," he said in a husky voice.

"I don't think so."

I started to button my jeans, but he pulled me back to him by the waistband, turning with me until I was up against the wall. He kissed me again. Hotter, deeper, his tongue probing my mouth and I felt my arms circle his neck against my wishes. He stuck his hand up my shirt and cupped my breast, then yanked my pants down with the other hand.

The shock of the cold air brought me to my senses.

"Chance, stop it."

I pulled my pants up and got them buttoned again.

He grabbed me one last time. "I need you, baby." His eyes were unfocused, glassy.

That's when I slapped him across the face. "I said no!"

Chance stepped back, confused. He rubbed his cheek where my handprint had formed.

Then he looked at me, completely horrified. "I, I . . . I'm so sorry." His voice cracked and he took a step backwards. He stared down at his hands a moment as if they had betrayed him. As if he didn't recognize them.

"Chance, it's okay."

He swallowed hard, ran his hands through his hair, and I thought I saw tears well up in his eyes. "No it's not. I have to go."

He turned.

"Wait! Chance, wait!"

I started toward him and he stopped, but he didn't turn around. "I have to go, Stacy. Can you get back okay?"

We were only two blocks from the bookstore. "Yes." This time it was my voice that cracked.

He nodded and disappeared around the corner.

Behind me, a voice said, "He's been tainted."

I whipped around to see the young witch from Birdie's coven and the bookstore; she was carrying a sack that was kicking.

"No," I said forcefully. "You're wrong. He's just under stress." He couldn't have been compromised. Monique was safe inside Birdie's house.

Unless we were wrong. Unless the fairy mistress had found another host. But who?

I looked at the witch.

"He's strong. He wouldn't let it happen."

She looked doubtful but she didn't say anything. She just turned and took her sack of trolls with her.

I stood there, alone, on a dark street beneath a shallow moon, more determined than ever to find the bitch who had destroyed love for generations of Geraghtys and run her out of my town.

And if that didn't work, I'd kill her.

Chapter 28

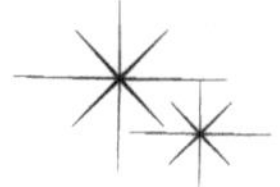

Back on Main Street, I saw people walking out of the bookstore and toward the Black Opal, so I made a left and went there first.

I hung the coat up because it was starting to make me sweat and I didn't want the stink tattooed on my skin.

A young bartender walked over to me and took my drink order just as Cinnamon sat down next to me.

"Hey, where's Chance?" she asked. Tony handed me my bag and then went behind the bar to assist with the cocktail orders.

"He was tired. Had a long day."

The bartender, who smelled faintly of motor oil, handed me a glass of Merlot. She smiled at me and I couldn't help but notice she was stunning. Long jet black hair, amber eyes, and pinup-girl curves.

"Thank you." I studied her with the intensity of a boxer sizing up his opponent.

Cinnamon said, "Hey, Daphne, this is my cousin, Stacy."

"Nice to meet you," she said cheerfully.

"Likewise."

Cinnamon told Daphne to start a tab for the crowd and she turned around to ring up the wine.

I watched the long-haired bartender walk over to Tony. She touched his arm as she talked to him, pointed to a few things, and when he shifted over to stock the beer cooler, I couldn't help but notice she let her eyes linger on him a little too long.

The woman certainly fit the description that Birdie and the aunts had given me of the Leanan Sidhe. Perhaps she wanted a host who looked like herself? That, coupled with the fact that the bartender smelled like motor oil—because they insisted the fairy mistress would smell like her target—and seemed a bit too interested in Tony gave me pause.

"Who is she?" I asked my cousin.

"She's new in town. From Las Vegas."

"Las Vegas? What's she doing here?"

Cinnamon shrugged. "I'm not sure. She said her parents were raised here, but they're gone now. Said she's helping out an aunt who's ill. She fills in here sometimes, but she's mostly been at the garage helping Tony."

I raised my eyebrows. "You're going to let that around your husband?" I sipped my wine. It was peppery and warm.

Cin rolled her eyes. "I don't think I need to worry about that." She slid her eyes in the direction of where Daphne had been standing.

When I traced her gaze, I caught Daphne staring straight at me. She quickly averted her eyes and busied herself lining up glasses and filling them with ice.

Cin let out a snort. "She plays for the other team. And I think she likes you."

Or that's her cover, I thought, deciding that it might be a good idea to keep an eye on Daphne. And possibly Tony for any changes.

"I hope you put that on my tab." Blade sidled up next to me and ordered a scotch on the rocks from Daphne.

Cinnamon slid off her stool. "Don't worry, Knight. Drinks are on you." She disappeared into the bathroom.

"Well, actually, they're on my publisher." He smiled and scanned the room. "Where's the boyfriend?"

"He went home."

He cocked a brow. "Nothing I said, I hope?"

I gave Blade a wry smile. "Actually yes, he hated the reading."

"Touché." He clinked my glass.

"So what did you want to talk about?" I asked.

He leaned in and said, "I asked Leo if he could track down the original suspects listed in the report. He said he'd get on that tomorrow. I was wondering if you'd go to my parents' house with me."

"Why?" I took another sip of my wine.

"You know, do that voodoo that you do so well."

I rolled my eyes. "Okay. I have two interviews in the morning. I'll text you when I'm done. In the meantime, I found out a few things. I'll fill you in on the details later, but I want you to work the room and tell whoever will listen that your next project is a retelling of Silverberg's *Book of Skulls*."

"Why?"

"I have a hunch."

Blade said, "Okay. Come on, I want you to meet my agent."

I followed Blade to the far side of the bar. Frieda was standing near Lolly's coat, admiring the plushness of it.

She stopped me. "Hi, Stacy. This is yours, right? I thought I saw you wearing it in the bookstore."

"Actually it belongs to my aunt." I motioned to Blade that I'd be right there.

"May I?" she asked, her voice giddy.

"Knock yourself out."

She tried on the coat that thousands of stuffed animals must have given their lives for, admiring the stitching.

Gladys came up to me then, a screwdriver in her hand. She pointed out her interview subjects and I told her I'd love to meet them after I met Blade's agent.

I wove through the tables and found my way to the corner where Blade stood, and a few other people were gathered.

"Stacy, this is Yvonne, my agent."

She was in her late forties, with a sleek haircut and hungry eyes. She looked every bit the New Yorker in a navy coatdress tailored to fit her thin hips, boots that cost more than my mortgage, and a bag that likely hadn't fallen off the back of a truck. She smelled like old money and new books.

I stuck my hand out. "It's a pleasure to meet you."

Yvonne declined my hand and said, "I'm afraid I have a terrible cold. Wouldn't want to pass it on to the woman who's working with my star author. Have to keep you both healthy so he can pump out the next book." She smiled warmly, then held a tissue to her red nose.

Someone asked what he was working on next and Blade, true to what we had discussed, began gushing about a retelling of *The Book of Skulls*.

Yvonne snapped her head around so fast, I was afraid she popped something out of place.

She seemed to debate calling Blade out right there, thought better of it, and instead turned to me. "I thought he was doing a true-crime piece about small towns in the Midwest. I thought that's why he was here talking to you."

I shrugged. "Authors."

She gave Blade an odd look, then excused herself. I watched her walk to the bar and order something.

Caleb approached me then. "Where's my brother?"

"He went home. Do you think you could check on him? He seemed . . . upset."

"Why? Because of this clown?"

"I honestly don't know," I said. And I didn't. Maybe Chance was stressed out from working too much. I hoped that's all it was anyway.

Caleb must have seen something in my face because he kissed my cheek and said, "I'll take care of it."

"I appreciate that, Caleb."

He winked, grabbed his coat, and left.

Derek was sitting at the bar next to Gladys. She was talking to a tall woman with bobbed hair angled at her chin, dressed in a very complicated collection of scarves, jewelry, leggings, a skirt, and a sequined tank top with a sweater and a shawl. I could only assume it was the fashion designer. She looked to be in her fifties, judging from the lines on her ringed hand, but either Botox or time had been kind to her.

I squeezed into an open spot next to Derek, who was flirting with the bartender as effectively as a guy with a lazy eye who lives with his parents.

"Hey, Romeo. How's it going?"

I turned my back to the bar and plopped my elbows on it. Daphne asked if I needed anything and I declined. She frowned and whisked away to serve another patron.

"Why do you always do that?" Derek asked.

"Do what?"

"Crunch my mojo."

"Well, the way Cin tells it, your mojo is wasted on tall, dark, and luscious."

"Why? Boyfriend?"

"Nope. Let's just say she butters her bread on the other side of the toast."

Derek frowned. "No. Really?"

"That's the word on the street."

He sulked into his beer and I told him the article was in his in-box.

Gladys said, "Stacy. Please to meet Lucinda. She is fashion design lady." I walked over to them. Lucinda took one look at my attire and said, "Honey, you need to come to New York and let me dress you." She flicked her eyes toward the coat rack. "And burn that piece of shag carpet the minute you get home."

I instantly disliked Lucinda.

"I'll get right on that."

She turned her head to lift her martini and I caught a glimpse of her earrings. Black skulls. She was certainly old enough to have known Blade's parents. I was just about to ask her if she knew the author when a text from Birdie chirped on my phone.

Come home immediately. We have word from the Council. Blade Knight is not who he appears to be.

I looked at Blade, who caught my eye and winked. Yvonne was standing next to him drinking a mug of steaming something, talking to the scientist I was supposed to interview tomorrow.

"Hey, guys, I have to leave," I said to Derek and Gladys. To Lucinda, I said, "Nice to meet you." She nodded as if the pleasure was all mine.

I made a mental note to pump Gladys for all the information I could about Lucinda before I left the Black Opal.

As I walked out, I felt two pairs of eyes boring through my back.

Chapter 29

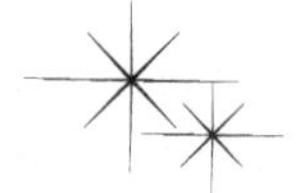

I jogged up the hill toward the Geraghty Girls' House, wondering what Birdie could have meant by that message. I kept my eye out for wayward fairies the entire way, making sure the coat was buttoned all the way up to my throat.

A block before I reached the house, I tripped over some sort of vine in the middle of the street.

Except it wasn't a vine. It was a trap.

I heard snickering and smelled chocolate chip cookies before I saw him. I reached inside the inner pocket of the coat where Lolly had said there was an athame, but before I could get my hands on it, the sneaky little toad lassoed my legs. I crashed to the pavement and caught a glimpse of him as I squirmed there on the street like a worm after a hard rain. He looked like he should have been on a cereal box instead of trying to hog-tie a human four times his size. I reached out with my right hand and grabbed the rope. The damn thing was sizzling hot and it seared my flesh.

"Agh!" I yelled.

Captain Butt Munch snickered.

I assessed my surroundings as he dragged me to a nearby tree. His home, I assumed. There was a garden shovel and a rake that someone had left near their garage, but I was way too far to reach either of them.

He pulled me farther through the lawn and I was clutching clumps of dirt and grass, trying to secure a hold on something, anything. At one point, the rogue fairy dragged me close enough to grab a good-sized rock. I hurled it at him. Missed.

Then he lassoed my right arm.

Frantic now, I kicked and screamed, shouting every enchantment I could think of for banishment, but none worked.

The little bastard was freakishly strong and he kept chugging along like a redneck at a tractor pull.

Then, I saw my chance. A metal garden stake was inches away from my left hand. I yanked it out quickly, but he was faster and captured my last free limb.

We were getting closer to the tree and I desperately searched for something, anything, that would get me out of this mess.

I saw nothing.

He stood in front of the maple, me on my back, helpless as an infant, and waved his hands around. The tree trunk yawned open, revealing a bright light. I couldn't see anything inside of it. All I could think was, *So this is how it ends? Lassoed by a Kellogg's character and buried in a tree trunk. Awesome.*

Then, just as he turned to yank me through to the other side of whatever the hell was beyond the tree, Pickle plummeted from the sky and knocked my attacker unconscious.

The fairy was camouflaged in sunset-colored fall leaves. He must have been hiding in the treetop. He shot me a grin, then got busy securing the enemy in a gunnysack. He walked over, took out a blade, and severed the ties around my legs and arms. Then he licked my hand.

"Happy to see you too, my friend," I said, scrambling to my feet. "Happy to see you too."

Birdie opened the door back at the inn. "Well, it's about time you got here," she said.

"Sorry. I was tied up."

I didn't know where Pickle had gotten off to, but he wasn't behind me when Birdie shut the door.

I hung up the coat and went to use the restroom, realizing I hadn't eaten dinner yet. With everything that had happened earlier, I wasn't even sure there was dinner. My stomach growled angrily and I went back into the parlor to ask Birdie if there was any food.

"Yes, yes, upstairs in the Magic Chamber. Come now, there's much to do."

She grabbed my hand and I yowled.

"I burned my hand, Birdie."

She examined it, said there was ointment in her medicine bag, and rushed upstairs. I followed.

There was another door at the top of the front stairs that separated the private quarters from the guest suites. Birdie unlocked it, grabbed some salve from the medicine bag that was still in the bathroom, handed it to me, then hurried down the hall.

I followed her through the door at the end of the hallway that led to the chamber room. We had to crawl down a narrow passageway first, but we reached it in moments. There was another door and Birdie simply waved a hand to open it.

The full coven was there, donned in ritual garb, and Birdie took her seat at the helm of the round table. The massive table was etched with scenes and symbols of our Celtic heritage, highlighted with glittering gold filigree. There were thirteen red velvet chairs situated around it, and in all but one sat a witch of varying age and ethnicity.

I smeared the ointment on the burn, then grabbed some olive tapenade, three tea sandwiches, and some cranberry juice.

My grandmother held a gavel in her hand as she instructed me to sit. She smacked the gavel on the table and called the meeting to order. She was wearing her special pentagram necklace and it jingled as she took her seat. It had been crafted for occasions just like these, with a thick pewter base, pyrite on each point, and a huge black obsidian in the center—all of which aid in fighting dark magic.

"What I am about to say does not leave this room," she began. "Each of you will be sworn to uphold the Celtic laws of a program that has been in place for more than a millennium."

The women chattered in hushed whispers among themselves, anxious for what Birdie was about to say. Lolly passed around the Blessed Book and each woman took a moment to swear secrecy and alliance.

"Birdie, do you think this is a good idea?" My eyes darted around the room. While I knew most of the women and Birdie certainly trusted them, in our line of work one couldn't be too careful. You never knew when a friend would turn foe. There were several attractive women in this room who would certainly serve the Leanan's purposes.

She looked at me, her eyes fierce. "Desperate times call for desperate measures."

The Council must have given her some sort of temporary pass to include the coven in this mission. Whatever it was.

My knee was shaking. There was a lot to do and I wished she'd just get on with it.

Fiona turned on the laptop I bought them and pulled up an Internet page. I was so proud. They'd come such a long way technologically speaking since the last time I had sat in this room.

She clicked to the website of the Royal Irish Academy and I sat up a little straighter in my seat. Now they really had my attention. I nibbled at my dinner, waiting for the briefing.

Fiona maneuvered the mouse and clicked on another page. The image on the screen was that of an ancient text written in old script.

"This is the *Book of Dun Cow*. It was written in the years 1090 to 1106. The primary scribe was Mael Muire. It is the oldest surviving record of Irish literature. The manuscript contains, among other things, the first known recording of the Otherworld fantasies and the introduction of Queen Maeve, who was instrumental in negotiating the peace treaty between the Tuatha Dé Danann and the Druids."

I heard a loud snore and looked to find Thor napping beneath the table.

Birdie continued. "So as you can see, the book is part fantasy, part reality. Much of the text was destroyed in the Viking wars, but for the most part, our ancestors had been able to determine fact from fiction. Except for one story."

Birdie nodded to Fiona, who clicked the mouse again. A ravaged page popped up on the screen.

"This is the last page of the book. The title reads: 'The Places Where the Heads of the Ulster Champions Are Buried.' It was never completed. For years, the Council has debated on whether this story was fact or fiction. It was suggested that perhaps it could be a blending of the two."

Heads. Skulls.

I wiped my mouth with a napkin. "So are you saying that the science fiction novel, *The Book of Skulls*, is connected to this story?" I took a sip of the juice.

She rolled her eyes. "Please. They don't make scribes like they used to. I'm saying that this is a fictionalized version of a true story. A key, if you will, that was to reveal the location of one skull that isn't a human skull at all, but the legendary—and elusive—obsidian skull."

Gasps from across the room. Whispers of *It really exists* and *I heard one archeologist has been searching for it for decades* and *My art history teacher talked about it* and *My mother told me about it* were scattered across the room. The witch who had collected the gnome and told me Chance had been tainted stared at me. Her makeup-free face was stuck on a look of shock. She scratched her freckled nose, slid her eyes away from me, and tucked a stray dark hair beneath her hood.

I swung my head from one woman to the next.

"What's the obsidian skull?"

"It was rumored to be the only art the Leanan Sidhe ever fashioned herself. The source of all creativity for humankind. The reason that so many of her lovers went from starving artists to wealthy masters of their crafts. It is the tangible form of the Midas touch. Whoever possesses it would have access either directly or indirectly to an endless pool of valuable creativity. And we believe she may want it back."

"So if we find it, maybe we can flush her out," I said.

Fiona said, "It's our best shot. But she must never lay her hands on it. Because if she destroys it—"

"All art is lost," I concluded.

Fiona nodded gravely.

The room was silent as every woman absorbed the information.

I asked, "But I don't understand what this has to do with Blade."

Birdie said, "We think his parents knew where the skull was located and they were killed because of it."

Fiona said, "Thirty years ago, a Council member was sent to search for the skull. He checked in, said he had information on its location, and linked it to the Conrads, but he was never heard from again."

I looked at Birdie.

"It was before I became a Council board member."

I stood up, pacing the room. So maybe that's what happened. Maybe Blade's parents tried to pass off a fake and that's why the killer became so angry.

But then why destroy the fake? Why risk shooting through my window to do so?

"But wait a minute, if the story was never completed and that was the key to the skull's whereabouts, then how could anyone have discovered its location?"

"We believe perhaps the father had written a code of his own. Had continued the story of the original scribe. We'll never know for certain, but the link may have been a lineage back to the original author of the 'Heads of the Ulster Champions.'"

I shook my head. "Blade's father was a teacher and his mother was an artist. Plus, I highly doubt they would have risked their lives and their son's life. Not to mention, why wouldn't they give the location of the skull to the Council member to protect?"

"We haven't determined why that would be. Unless perhaps they intended to use the skull for their own purposes."

Again, I disputed that. "They bought art at garage sales. They lived on a teacher's salary. Don't you think if they had that kind of intention they would have banked on the power of the skull? Cashed in somehow on its creative energy. His mother could have made a fortune selling her own art if that was their plan."

Birdie began pacing with me, reaching for another avenue.

"Perhaps the Council member was rogue?" Fiona offered.

Birdie looked at her. "Impossible. He was meticulous. Checked in every step of the way throughout the entire mission. He said he had discovered an ancestral link to the original scribe. The Council assumed that link was the Conrads."

I racked my brain to come up with a solution. What had Caleb said about Blade's father? He wasn't just reading *The Book of Skulls*, he was studying it. Highlighting the book, making notes in the margins. He was looking for clues. So maybe someone had tailed the Council member. Someone else must have known that somehow the Conrads were the key to finding the skull.

No. Coach Conrad wasn't hiding the Leanan's creation. He was looking for it himself to protect his family. Someone else knew about the skull. If the Council member had linked it to the Conrads, then someone else could have as well. And that person may have thought the Conrads were indeed hiding it, but I didn't believe that.

I mentioned this to Birdie.

"I suppose it's possible."

Fiona said, "Maybe the Council member didn't get a chance to tell the board everything he knew when last he checked in. Maybe there was more to the story."

I stopped short and Birdie bumped into me.

"What did you say, Fiona?" I asked.

Fiona repeated her remark.

More to the story. Could that be it? Was it possible that all of this was connected? Was Blade more important to this whole thing than any of us had realized?

I looked at Lolly. "Lolly, is there anything in the Blessed Book about a scribe in the New World? Anything about the Seeker encountering one?"

My hands started sweating as I waited for Lolly to search.

A few of the witches widened their eyes at the word *Seeker*.

"You didn't tell them that part?" I asked my grandmother.

She gave me an annoyed look.

If I was right, then everything—Blade showing up when he did, the newspaper clippings about me, the strange feelings I had when I was near him, him seeking my help—would make sense.

It wasn't long before Lolly found a passage and read aloud. "The Seeker shall cross paths with the first Scribe of the New Age. Quill and sword must unite to protect a legend long ago lost."

"So what does that mean?" Birdie asked.

I took a deep breath and grabbed my grandmother's shoulders.

"It means that Blade is the Scribe. It means his parents didn't know where the skull was. It means that the Council member who tracked the lineage of the original Scribe was right. He just had the wrong Conrad."

Birdie's eyes widened. "It means no one could find the skull because thirty years ago, the rest of the story hadn't been written."

Chapter 30

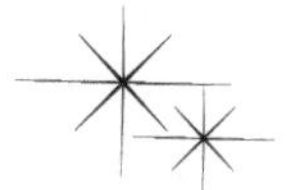

Blade Knight had gifted his entire collection of Tracey Stone books to the library at the inn. He had signed each and every one of them, and Birdie and the aunts agreed that his personal stamp on the page might give us an advantage in searching out clues in the text. Clues we hoped would lead us to the obsidian skull, and in turn, the Leanan Sidhe. Since the Council member who had tracked the Conrad family all those years ago believed there was a lineage link to the original scribe who had begun the story in the *Book of Dun Cow*, it made sense that Blade was the one to finish it.

I found it interesting that Blade had told me about the writer's subconscious and how it leaked into his work.

He didn't know the half of it. Scribes are gifted at birth with storytelling, but more importantly, they hold the keys to history. Those keys—or rather clues—were embedded in their work completely unbeknownst to the author.

Like a perpetual state of automatic writing.

Birdie, the aunts, and I were all convinced that Blade's books held the key to the location of the skull—and possibly other treasures we had yet to learn about. And that my great-grandmother Meagan's vision was dead-on accurate.

Now, we just had to pick apart the story and piece it together again.

"So here we are, ladies. Everyone grab a book." Fiona said.

I reached for *Stone Cold* and went to grab a seat, but Birdie stopped me.

"Stacy, a word, please."

She pulled me aside to the hallway that separated the library from the parlor.

"It has come to my attention that perhaps Chance has fallen under the Leanan Sidhe's spell."

I shot a look at the witch who had approached me on the street earlier. She was probably only twenty-two or twenty-three years old, but I expected more from an initiated coven member. I could handle my own messes; I didn't need a neophyte tattling on me to my grandmother. The young witch felt my eyes on her and turned, smiling. The smile fell from her thin lips when she caught my glare.

"Now don't go blaming poor Shannon. She was only doing what I asked of her."

My glare quickly shifted to Birdie. "What you asked of her? What are you talking about?"

Birdie's voice was irritatingly calm. "You have quite a task to fulfill, not to mention an army of angry Fae on your tail. You cannot possibly do this all by yourself. I've asked everyone to keep their eyes and ears open and report back to me any unusual behavior."

"It's under control, Birdie. Chance is fine."

I wasn't 100 percent certain about that, but I was certain I could find a better way to protect him myself than having complete strangers follow him around town. I could bind him if I had to. Weave a protection spell all around him. That would be better, because who knew if Birdie's coven members could be trusted? These were woman I had only met a handful of times if at all.

No way was I going to trust Chance's safety to anyone but me.

"We're all in this together, Stacy," my grandmother said. "You need to learn to work with a team when it's required."

"I don't need a team when it comes to Chance."

She lowered her voice. "Then be prepared to lose him." She carried her book into the parlor and sat down to read, without giving me another look.

Maybe she was right, maybe I did need help, but it wouldn't come from someone I hardly knew.

I texted Caleb and asked how Chance was doing. He texted back that Chance was fine. He had just gotten home and they were having a beer.

So where had he been these last couple of hours?

I sighed, grabbed the book, and found my own spot in the parlor.

Every witch was using her own method for ferreting out information from the books. Some were using scrying mirrors, others crystal balls; one woman had a turquoise necklace around her neck to aid intuitive powers. I was using the locket.

No one was actually reading the books. We were all skimming the pages, using our instincts, spirit guides, and internal messaging systems to highlight passages that jumped out at us. At someone's suggestion, Lolly had rolled a large whiteboard into the room and, every once in a while, a witch would jump up from her seat and jot down a line that seemed important.

An hour later, Shannon scooted over to me. "I hear *Stone Cold* is about you."

I didn't look at her as I said, "You heard wrong."

She tried another approach. "Did you find anything good?"

"I guess we'll have to wait and see when we piece it together."

She folded her legs beneath her. "So that's the locket, huh? The Seeker's locket? Wow, it must be so cool to have that title."

I marked my page and shut the book. "I'm trying to work, Shannon. Don't you have work to do?"

She gave a nervous laugh. "Oh, I finished mine. You want me to finish yours?"

What was with this girl?

"No." There was an edge to my voice I couldn't control.

Shannon inched closer to me and I suddenly yearned for a flyswatter.

"Look, I'm sorry about, um, the thing. I didn't mean to get you in trouble." Her green eyes seemed sincere and I felt like an ass all of a sudden.

"I'm a grown woman, Shannon. You didn't get me in trouble with my grandmother."

"Oh." She flicked her eyes to Birdie, who looked up as Pickle bounced in the room. "Because she kind of scares me."

I looked at Birdie too. Her reading glasses were perched on her nose.

"Yeah. She has that effect on people."

"Not you, though. You're strong. Stronger than all of us." Shannon looked behind her quickly. Birdie was reading a note Pickle had handed to her. The girl's voice was barely a whisper when she spoke. "Maybe even stronger than her."

"I doubt that." I looked at Shannon. "I forgive you, okay? Let's forget it."

Shannon bobbed her head up and down like a puppy. "Cool."

Then Birdie said, "The rebels have been taken care of. Now who would like to check on Sleeping Beauty?"

That reminded me. I wondered how Cinnamon was doing.

Shannon shot her hand up. "I will!"

She galloped up the stairs two at a time, her cape in her hands.

"Brownnoser," I muttered.

The witch sitting next to me snickered.

From across the room, Birdie sighed loudly. "Yes." Her eyes trained on me. "She's like the granddaughter I never had."

I rolled my eyes and went back to the book. There were only a few pages left and I found nothing in them.

I closed the book and stood up to stretch.

Lolly and Fiona were arranging the clues on the board. Several other witches got up to assist. I heard them chattering away, arguing about where the puzzle pieces fit, as I twisted my back and stretched my legs. Birdie played ringmaster until they had a sensible text to work with.

They all took a step back just as a car door slammed. I rushed over to peek out the window. When I saw Blade's car I chained the door.

"He's back," I said.

"Well, that's unfortunate. Because something's missing. And we've been over every line of all these texts."

"Something's missing all right," Shannon said from the top of the stairs. We all looked over to her. "Monique."

Chapter 31

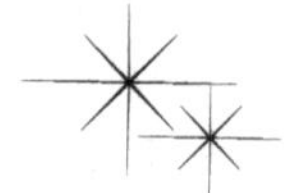

"Fiona," Birdie said.

"I'm on it," said Fiona.

I gave Birdie a curious look.

"She put a tracking spell on the harlot. She won't be hard to find."

Two of the witches turned the board around as I heard a key slide into the lock. I scanned the room.

"The tools," I hissed.

The witches got busy putting all their talismans away and hurriedly took their seats, books in hand, looking like some sort of book club from an Alice Hoffman novel.

The bell rang and I went to unlock the door.

Blade and his agent, Yvonne, entered the parlor.

The author said, "That was strange. My key didn't work."

"Hmm" was my response.

Blade looked around the room at all the women holding his novels. "What do we have here? A new fan club?"

"Something like that," I said.

Yvonne said, "Wow. Well, you have the author at your disposal. Any questions?"

The women all looked at each other as Blade stood there expectantly.

"Guess not," I said.

"I have a question," Shannon said from the top of the stairs. "What happens next?"

Blade's eyes trailed to the landing.

"Well, young lady, I guess you'll have to wait and see."

She descended the steps slowly, swinging her hips back and forth. Her voice took on a sultry tone that would impress even Fiona. "Oh, come on. I'm sure you have an unpublished manuscript on your *hard* drive."

Oh, brother. This was too much. He'd never fall for it.

Blade said, "Well . . ."

Yvonne looked at him as if the cheese had slid off his cracker. She parked a hand on her hip. "Well, what?"

He shrugged. "They're my fans. What could it hurt?"

Yvonne slapped him upside the head. "It could hurt sales, you nitwit." She coughed.

"We won't leak it, if that's what you're worried about," Shannon purred. She danced her fingers up Blade's arm.

"See. They won't leak it," Blade said to Yvonne.

The agent pulled her author aside and said through gritted teeth, "Do you honestly want to show these people your WIP before your beta readers even see it? Hell, I haven't even read it. What if it sucks?"

Blade looked hurt. Shannon swooped in to massage his ego.

"Oh, I doubt that very much. Blade's a master at his craft," she said.

Blade tightened his collar. "She has faith in me."

Yvonne sneezed and threw up her hands. "I give up. I'm going to bed. Do what you want."

Blade watched as Yvonne ascended the stairs. When she was gone, he turned to the group with the enthusiasm of a kid who just popped his first wheelie. "Be right back."

We all watched Blade bound up the stairs and turn the corner.

Birdie said, "Shannon, that was impressive."

Shannon clapped her hands and looked at me.

"I would have thought of it eventually," I said.

Birdie jabbed my ribs with her elbow.

"Just kidding. Good job with the author."

Shannon's face lit up.

"Bad job losing Monique," I said.

Her face deflated.

Birdie gave me a hard look.

"Hey, I'm just using your tough-love approach, Birdie."

The woman never let me slide on a mistake. Never.

"That's because I expect more out of you." She smirked.

"Stop doing that. Stop reading my mind."

It was nearly eleven o'clock when Blade came back down the stairs. I had a big day tomorrow, so I said good night to everyone, called to Thor, and left out the back door with my bag slung over my shoulder.

The night sky was clouded and dark, but there was a light on in the kitchen of my cottage, only it wasn't the one I had left on. I pulled my Taser out and motioned to Thor. He slinked around to the side of the door and waited for my signal.

I tested the knob. The door was unlocked. Another thing I hadn't done. Didn't ever do.

Slowly, I pushed the door, Taser in hand, Thor at the ready.

The cottage was quiet.

Then I heard movement. I kicked the door as hard as I could and hit something on the other side.

"Ouch! Son of a . . ."

"Chance?"

I pocketed the Taser and peeked around the door. My man was holding his nose with both hands. A slow trickle of blood dripped down, splashing his tee shirt with red splotches.

"Oh, no. I'm so sorry!"

I ran into the bathroom for a towel and dampened it. Ran back out and tried to gently dab Chance's wound.

He held up his hand. "It's okay, Barbarella. I got it."

He sat down on the couch and tried to stop the bleeding.

Thor walked over and put his head in Chance's lap, explaining that he had nothing to do with it. He was just following orders.

"What are you doing here?" I asked.

"Fixing your window." He pulled the towel away. "You're welcome."

"I'll get some ice."

I put a handful of ice in another towel and handed it to him.

He thanked me and put it to his nose.

"I'm really sorry. I didn't see your truck. I thought maybe someone broke in."

"I had a couple of beers with Caleb, so I walked. Dropped the window off earlier today. I wanted to surprise you." He gave a wry smile. "Surprise."

"That was really sweet. Thank you."

We sat in silence for a moment. After a while, he pulled the towel away. "Look, Stacy, I'm sorry."

"No, don't even mention it. We both got carried away."

He shook his head. "No. It's really not okay. I've been stressed out and I'm not myself and I acted like a jackass."

"Hey, everyone does once in a while. What's got you stressed? What did you do today?"

He gave me a funny look. "I told you. Just work. That committee. Oh, and I gave a girl a ride who was stranded."

I wanted to ask, *What projects? Where are you working? Who's on the committee?* But I thought that would be too much too fast. So I worked backwards.

"Oh? What girl?"

"I think she said her name was Daphne. Works at Tony's auto shop."

Bingo. That tartlet just made the top of my list. Lesbian, my ass.

"So the committee is going well?"

"That's done. Next time I see those guys will be at the reunion."

Guys? Did that mean men, or was he speaking figuratively?

"So who all was on it?"

"I think the only one you know is Monique. The rest were earlier classes."

I nodded. "So. What about the projects?"

He shrugged. "Couple of remodels. Everybody wants everything done yesterday."

"Anyone I know?"

He looked at me and his eyes darkened. "What's with the third degree?"

"Nothing." I smiled. "Just making conversation."

He patted my knee and stood. "Well, I'm beat. I'll see you later."

I stood too.

Don't go, don't go, don't go.

"Why don't you stay?"

Don't go, don't go, don't go.

He smiled at me and squeezed my shoulder. "I need to sleep in my own bed. Plus, you've got a lot going on with that author."

"I'll always make time for you," I said, stepping closer.

"Maybe we should take a little time for ourselves."

"If that's what you want."

Say no, say no, say no.

"Yes. Just for a few days. I just really need some downtime."

"Okay," I said, choking back a tear.

He put his finger under my chin and lifted it up. I met his eyes.

"Hey, I just need rest, that's all. Don't go all girly on me and read too much into it. Okay?"

I smiled. "Okay."

He grabbed his coat. "Besides. It'll give you more time to work on kicking down doors."

I gave a small laugh.

"I'll pick you up for the reunion."

He kissed my cheek and left.

And for the second time that week, I was sure I was losing the only man I ever loved. The only man I ever needed.

"Come back to me, Chance," I whispered.

Chapter 32

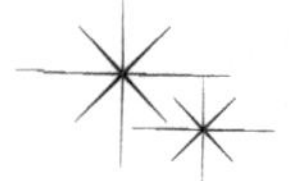

Before I went to bed, I tried to contact Cinnamon's father, but nothing, not even the locket, worked to call him forward. There was just too much on my mind to focus properly, so I shut the light off in the Seeker's Den.

As I did so, the scrying mirror chimed and I hurried to answer the call.

It was my mother on the line. Again.

She fizzled into view and I read the worry on her face immediately. "Honey, I heard about what's happening. Are you all right?"

It made me wonder if she had known. If that's what had been bothering her these past few weeks.

"I'm fine, Mom. Everything's under control and Birdie called in the cavalry."

This seemed to relieve her a little bit.

"I'm glad to hear that. Listen, sweetheart, I'll be out of town for a few days so I won't be in contact."

I was glad to hear that. Not that I didn't enjoy talking to her, but my plate was so full, it was about to crack.

"All right. Anything important?"

She flicked her eyes away as if she was looking at someone else in the room. "No. Just a getaway for two."

"Well, you and Pearce have fun."

Pearce was my mother's boyfriend. He had protected her all those years she was locked away for her crime, and they had fallen hopelessly in love.

We said our good-byes and disconnected the call. I locked up the den and the cottage and fell into bed utterly exhausted.

The alarm sounded far too early for my liking the next morning, but I had a breakfast meeting with the archeologist and I didn't want to be late.

I borrowed Birdie's car again and dropped Thor off at Cinnamon's place and he did a perimeter check of her house. Then he stationed himself on her porch, his jaw tight as if he were the secret service. His surveillance equipment was charged and ready to go, and the backup solar chip in his collar would keep it that way. All he needed was a pair of shades.

I passed Monique's bar on the way to Muddy Waters and saw the owner of the building, Mr. Huckleberry, talking to the chief from the fire department and a man I recognized as a local plumber. Most of the buildings on Main Street weren't actually owned by the proprietors. They simply rented the space. Still, I hoped Monique had a solid insurance policy for both her apartment and Down and Dirty. I also hoped Fiona had found her and that she wasn't at the police station right now telling Leo my family had kidnapped her. At some point, I'd have to figure out a way to convince Monique that we were just trying to protect her and hopefully she would offer a reasonable explanation for her absence.

More likely, we were all going to jail, but I pushed that problem to the end of the list.

I ordered a coffee from Iris and grabbed a banana muffin, found a table near the window, and slung my bag over the back of the chair. I was a few minutes early so I pulled the phone out of my bag and opened the recording application. Then I scanned the notes that Gladys had provided.

A blast of cold air blew by me and I looked toward the door, surprised to see both the archeologist, Roberta Rubinski, class of 1970, and the scientist, Donald Yearwood, class of 1969, enter the shop.

They placed an order with Iris and when Roberta turned to give the place a once-over, I waved.

She nodded and both of them joined me. As soon as they arrived at the table, I realized two things. They were older than I had originally thought and they were a couple.

I shook Roberta's hand and instantly a sharp pain pierced my head. Images of the dead, one after the other, stormed through my brain. Bloodied murder victims, rotting corpses, ancient soldiers spun through my mind like a kaleidoscope of the macabre. And skulls. Lots and lots of skulls flipped through my third eye, all different shapes and sizes. But the smell—the rancid odor of musty tombs, decaying flesh, and bile—nearly made me vomit.

I dropped her hand, and leaned on the chair to steady myself.

"Are you all right?" she asked.

"I'm fine. Just a little dizzy. Probably because I haven't eaten."

"Or it could be a brain tumor," said Donald helpfully.

Roberta rolled her eyes. "You think everyone has a brain tumor."

He shrugged. "It's what I study. Brains."

"Why don't we have a seat," I said.

I waited for the nausea to pass before I sipped my coffee. What *was* that?

"Do you mind if I record our conversation?" I asked.

Neither one protested.

I looked at Roberta, my mind coming back into focus. Was the episode due to her profession? Or something more?

"So, I didn't realize that you were together. Are you married?" They didn't share the same last name, so I wasn't certain.

Roberta scoffed. "Marriage was designed to beat women into submission, trade them like cattle, and keep them chained to a life of servitude."

"Roberta is a feminist," Donald said. He took a sip of tea.

Roberta gave her partner a scathing look. "I am no such thing." To me she said, "I don't believe in labels. I'm simply a woman of strength and independence. And I loathe that word." She took a drink of her coffee. "It's just a polite way to say *bitch*. Don't you agree?"

"Oh yes," I said, because I didn't want to get on Roberta's bad side. "So tell me about your work. What got you interested in archeology?"

Donald took his jacket off and I noticed the tee shirt he was wearing today had a portrait symbolizing the evolution of man.

"My first year in college, I read a book that changed my life. The characters went on this great adventure and I knew that's what I wanted to do with my life."

Now Donald scoffed. "Adventure, my foot." He turned to me and said, "She dug up dead people for a few years then took a cushy position at a university."

Roberta tightened her ponytail. "That's only because I had to support your endless years of schooling."

Donald pushed his glasses up the bridge of his nose. "At least my work is important. At least it helps people. What does your work do? They can't get any deader, dear."

This wasn't going well. I tried to interrupt, but Roberta was on a warpath.

She puffed up in her chair. "That may be so, *sweetheart*, but at least in my work, people learn something about our culture, human history, the sacrifices made, and the treasures left behind. We can't move forward without first examining the past. Otherwise, we're destined to repeat the mistakes of our ancestors." She looked at me. "Am I right?"

"Quit badgering the girl," Donald said.

"Why don't you tell me about your work, Donald?"

He launched into a ten-minute speech about his research in seeking a cure for Alzheimer's disease, half of which I couldn't understand.

"That's fascinating. So do you feel as if you're close?" Maybe it would help Aunt Lolly, although I suspected her brand of dementia was a flavor all its own.

Roberta tossed her head back and laughed. "Close? Hardly. All he has to show for the past thirty years is a box of dead mice."

Donald seethed at his life partner. "You based your entire career on a book you didn't even understand the meaning of. That book wasn't an adventure. It was a horror story."

I made a feeble attempt to put this train wreck back on track. "So how did you two get together?" Because honestly, I couldn't see it. They acted as if they hated each other. How does that happen? And why stay together?

Roberta said, "He was a mistake I made one drunken night at the University of Illinois and I still can't shake him. He's like a flea that can't be killed."

"Sure I can, but I'd take you with me. Just like the book. A murder-suicide. What do you say? Shall we put us out of our misery?"

"That's the most romantic thing you've ever said, Donald."

Was she serious? She hadn't said it sarcastically, so I couldn't be sure.

Donald's voice softened. "See, I listen to you."

"Did I miss something?" These two were certifiable.

Roberta sighed. "He's referring to our first date. He asked what I was reading."

"And she told me the whole plot." Donald took Roberta's hand.

"And what was it called?" I asked.

"*The Book of Skulls*," they both said.

Chapter 33

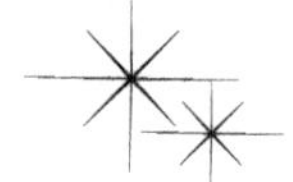

I texted Blade and asked him to meet me back at the inn. He said he was having breakfast with his agent, and that he was stopping by the police department to find out what Leo had learned about the original suspects in the case. It was nine o'clock in the morning and he said he could be there in an hour.

There was a lot to discuss. I didn't know where Blade's father had gone to college, but I learned that the couple from crazytown went to the University of Illinois. I also wanted to find out who at the bar last night seemed interested in his new novel idea.

Birdie was convinced that the 1978 novel by Silverberg had no link to the Leanan's obsidian skull, but what if she was wrong? What if there was a connection? Blade's father had seemed to believe so. Or was he just desperate for answers after the man from the Council had paid him a visit? It made me wonder too when he had first read it. Did he also discover the book in college? And if so, was it assigned for the classroom? Or just a recommendation from a friend?

I sent Blade another text with Roberta's name and date of birth and told him to pass it on to Leo as a possible suspect. Then I swung the car around and headed toward Tony's auto shop.

Monique's car was still there, the flat tire fixed. I wondered if she was back at the inn now.

I pulled the car over to the next street, keeping an eye out for insurgents, and parked.

I crept through the weeded lot next door, saw my hunk of metal still crippled, and circled around to the back window. Peeking through the dirty glass, I saw Tony firmly lodged beneath a Toyota.

Perfect. I duckwalked around the side of the building until I got to the corner. I craned my neck around and spotted Daphne bent over the hood of a Mustang.

I was just about to pull out the binding spell from the back pocket of my jeans when my stupid phone rang.

I whipped it out and shut the ringer off, then turned the phone off completely, but it was too late.

She turned her head to the side and when she saw me, she stood up so fast she banged it on the hood of the car.

"Oof," she said, rubbing her head.

The bartender stepped away from the car and said, "Oh, hi."

It was cold outside and her cheeks flushed. She shuffled from one foot to the other, nervously.

Good. You should be scared, I thought.

"Hi," I said.

I walked toward her slowly, wishing I had my sword, but it was still back at the office, still unconsecrated.

"Stacy, right?"

As if you didn't know.

"That's correct."

She said, "You have the red Fiat?"

I nodded.

"I don't think your car is repairable. Tough break."

"Yeah, tough break."

She gave an uneasy laugh and pointed to the garage. "Tony's in there if you want to talk to him."

"Actually, I came to talk to you."

"Oh?"

Daphne smiled at me and something shifted within her. She seemed to relax a bit. She wiped her hands on a towel and stuffed it in her back pocket.

"I heard your car broke down yesterday. A man gave you a lift?"

She shrugged. "I know, ironic, right? A mechanic who can't fix her own car. What are the odds?"

"Not very good."

"So how'd you hear about that?"

"Small town."

She stepped toward me.

"So what, you want to be my chauffeur?" Her eyes glinted in the morning sunlight, sparkling almost. Like fool's gold.

"Actually, yes."

I'll drive your ass right back to the Otherworld, you bloodthirsty ghoul.

She looked at her watch. "Well, I take my lunch at noon. You can show me around town."

I glanced back toward the garage. "Tony doesn't seem to need any help. How about we go for a drive now?"

She glanced around the parking lot. "I guess I could take a break."

We were both playing the game, both dancing around the fact that what we wanted were two very different things. For a moment I hesitated, wondering what she might have up her sleeve. Wondering where her army was or if we had captured them all. Wondering too how powerful she was. She didn't seem too leery of me anymore. In fact, she seemed downright delighted.

But she didn't know one crucial component of what made me tick. That I would do anything for the people I loved.

"After you." I motioned toward the street and we walked to the car. I opened her door and she hesitated before she climbed in. Her eyes stared into mine. "I guess you work fast."

"Fast and efficient, that's me."

"We'll see about that," said the Leanan, wickedly.

We pulled up to the inn a few moments later.

She looked out the window at the house and whistled. "Nice place. The Geraghtys have done well."

I followed her up the steps to the inn, keeping a close eye on her, while scanning the yard for soldiers.

On the porch, she turned and said, "Let's not go in just yet."

"Why not?"

She lifted her head to the sky and raised her arms. "It's nice out here." Her voice deepened and she stared me down. "I like to play outside. Don't you like to play outside?"

She trailed her fingers along a pumpkin that sat on the porch railing, then she fluttered them through her thick black hair. Her powers were connected to her sexuality and I could feel her stirring them up.

But I wasn't going to fall for her tricks. I held my eyes steady, waiting for her to make a move. She took two steps toward me and I tensed. "Or we could go in, but I have to warn you." She ran a fingernail along my cheek, and whispered in my ear, "It might get messy."

She lunged at me suddenly, her mouth going for my neck. I pulled out the tranquilizer gun and shot her.

She collapsed on the porch in a heap.

"My darts are effective," I said, stepping over her.

Chapter 34

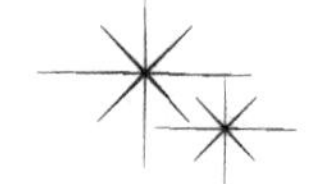

I rang the bell and Birdie answered the door.

"I found her," I said.

She looked down and frowned. "That's not Monique."

"I know that's not Monique—wait—you haven't found Monique yet?"

Birdie shook her head.

"Well, never mind about that, I think this is the Leanan Sidhe."

Her eyes widened and she called for help. Shannon was at the door in a flash and we carried the fairy mistress inside.

"Upstairs," Birdie barked.

We carted the body upstairs to the Magic Chamber.

"So you're certain it's she? You did the test?" Birdie asked.

I frowned. "What test?"

Birdie gave me a look of utter disappointment. "You didn't even read the notes I gave you on how to test and bind her, did you?"

Damn. I hadn't had time to even look at it before my phone rang. "No, sorry."

Shannon widened her eyes. Probably thinking I was in trouble. Which I was, but I didn't have time for a lecture. I had to meet Blade.

"Can you test her? I don't have time."

Birdie rolled her eyes. "Fine, but I'll specifically need you to do the binding. Pickle was clear on that."

I looked at Pickle, who was stuffing a hot fudge sundae in his face as ice cream dribbled all down his chin. He grinned and waved at me.

I waved back. "Did he say something to you? Because I've never heard him speak. Only scream and cry."

Birdie said, "Of course not. The Fae don't speak our language."

"Of course not." I told her I'd return as soon as I could and went to hunt for Blade, but before I did, she confiscated my tranquilizer gun. Again.

Yvonne was in the library, flipping through a book.

"Hi," I said.

She practically jumped out of her shoes. "Oh, you startled me."

I apologized and asked where I could find Blade. She said he was in his room and I went to go knock on his door.

"Come in."

Blade was sitting at a desk, red pen in his hand, flipping through a manuscript.

Which reminded me. I had forgotten to ask Birdie if the coven had uncovered a code in Blade's books that might tell us where the obsidian skull was located. Even if I was right about Daphne being the Leanan Sidhe and we didn't need it any longer to find her, it was still important that the Council be informed of the skull's whereabouts so they could properly protect it.

The author looked over at me and smiled. "Hey, if it isn't the president of my new fan club."

"How'd it go last night after I left?"

"Pretty good. They're fast readers, I tell you."

I smiled, thinking I should have also asked Birdie if I was supposed to explain to Blade who he really was. Probably not, though. That was a job for a Council member.

"Have a seat," Blade said.

There was a comfortable chair near the desk and I pulled it closer and sat down.

"So the new-book idea about the skulls. Anyone seem overly interested in it?"

Blade said, "Quite a few people, actually. It went over so well, in fact, I might just do it."

"So no one stood out at the bar last night? You didn't get a feeling about anyone in particular?"

"I don't get feelings. That's your job. Although there was one woman who bought all of my books and had me sign them." He looked at me. "She seemed pretty interested."

"Who was that?"

"Her name was Lucinda something."

I remembered the skull earrings that Lucinda had worn yesterday. Maybe she was just into skulls. Or maybe she was involved. I pulled the notes out from my bag and jotted down her full name and birth date. I passed it to Blade and decided to talk to Gladys about her. See what she found out in her interview.

"Call Leo and ask him to check her out."

"Why can't you do it?"

"That's a question, Blade. Besides, Leo's smitten with you."

He gave me a sly smile. "I think he's smitten with you."

I stood up. "Come on. You can tell me what Leo found out on the way to your parents' old house."

In his car, Blade explained that Leo was still looking into Roberta, but that the two petty thieves at the time still had rock-hard alibis. One was in the hospital with a broken leg and the other was getting married in front of fifty witnesses.

"What about the handyman?"

"You know, it's the strangest thing. It's like the guy never existed. Leo couldn't find anything on him. Not even a Facebook page."

That was strange.

"Do you remember what he looked like?"

"Not really. Just sort of average looking. Medium height, medium build."

Blade slowed the car down and pulled up in front of a dilapidated ranch with broken shutters, paint so chipped that the wood was showing through, and a cracked concrete sidewalk.

"I do remember he had a funny accent."

We got out of the car and went to the door. It was open. Wide open.

I tensed, reached in my back pocket for my tranquilizer gun, but I remembered Birdie had confiscated it again.

Blade said, "The house has been abandoned since the murders."

That might explain the door if it wasn't for the spider's web across the threshold.

As soon as I walked in, I knew. I felt it right down to my bones.

"Someone's been here recently."

Chapter 35

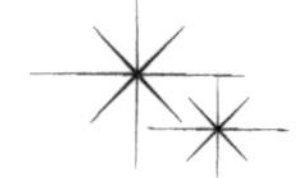

"Do you still have the Taser I gave you?" I whispered.

Blade pulled the phone-shaped gun from his jacket and waved it.

I took mine out of my bag and set the bag down on the floor.

We crept through the house, Blade behind me. The living room held nothing but discarded beer bottles and a couch that looked like it had been run over by a truck. The paint on the walls was chipped, some parts of the plaster were exposed, and there was a splatter that could have been spaghetti sauce, but was more likely old blood, high up on the far right side of the room. The carpet—once likely a beige shag—was soiled with mud and ground leaves. There was an odor of rot permeating the space that could only come from violence and lost hope.

I tiptoed down a hallway that led to a bathroom. Rusty stains encircled the toilet and the mirror had been broken. The shower curtain was missing and the bathtub was filled with discarded pizza boxes, beer cans, soda cans, and empty cigarette packs. The room after that was what must have been Blade's childhood room. There were books strewn all across the floor, some ripped apart, some shredded. In the center was a dirty mattress that covered a metal twin bed.

No one was there.

There were only two rooms left to inspect, Blade's parents' room and the kitchen. The floral wallpaper was torn in several places in his parents' old bedroom. A curved bed frame with no mattress sat next to an antique oak dresser with a mirror that had lost its silver. The dresser drawers were missing and the top was covered in water stains. Rectangular shapes lighter than the rest of the printed wallpaper sprinkled the walls as if phantom artwork were still hanging there, waiting for someone to admire it.

The whole house felt heavy, distressed even. As if it were waiting for someone to appreciate it again. To relieve its pain.

A crash came from the kitchen that startled Blade. He grabbed my shirt and dropped his Taser.

I looked back at him and whispered, "You're a crime writer. Buck up."

"I write about crimes. I don't fight them," he said.

Slowly, we wound our way down the hall and toward the kitchen. I pressed my back to the wall, listening. There was a loud screech and I charged in, Taser ready.

That's when a raccoon launched himself at my chest and I dropped my Taser.

He was clawing and scratching and biting me. "Get him off!" I screamed while simultaneously running around the room like a maniac.

Blade grabbed a broken broom and said, "Hold still!"

But I couldn't. The damn rodent clawed right through my coat to my rib cage and was furiously eating what was left of my outerwear.

Blade swiped the broom, but only managed to smack me in the head.

"Shoot him!" I screamed, still running around, bumping into random appliances.

He grabbed the Taser and aimed.

"Don't miss!" I yelled.

"Hold still!"

He fired and both the raccoon and I crumpled to the floor, twitching.

I wasn't sure what disgusted me more, the filthy floor I was flopping around on or the wild animal that had tried to eat me.

A few minutes later, Blade was helping me to my feet.

"Are you okay?"

I growled at him. "Oh, sure. I always love a good electric jolt to get my juices going. In fact, just this morning I stuck my tongue in a light socket."

"I'm sorry."

I heard voices in the living room and there was a pounding noise. I put my finger to my lips and went to check it out, grabbing my weapon.

I was stunned at the scene playing out before me.

The entire living room was pristine, as if it had gone from black-and-white to Technicolor.

A man was hammering a painting on the wall. He turned and called out, "Does this look good?" He was the spitting image of the author.

A woman, who I assumed to be Blade's mother, came into the room, a towel in her hand. "Perfect."

She kissed him and the doorbell rang.

The man looked at his wife and said, "Remember what we talked about. They don't know what it actually looks like. Just give them that skull like the man told us to do and this will all be over."

She nodded and walked over to the coffee table. The black skull Blade had brought to my house was perched on it.

Blade's father muttered, "Never should have gone to that damn reunion."

The woman went to open the door, but when I shifted to see who was there, the room faded back to its state of disrepair.

Blade was talking and shaking me. "Hey, you okay? Stacy? What is it? Did you see something?"

I snapped back from the vision. "You can stop shaking me now."

Blade let go of me then stood there expectantly.

I had never seen such a vivid vision before. Could it have been the Taser? Did it ignite my gift into overdrive?

"I saw your parents. It happened just like you said it did."

Blade grew excited. "Did you see who did it? Did you see the killer?"

I shook my head sadly. "I'm sorry."

"It's okay. You did your best." He gave me a reassuring smile.

"There was something, though. He said 'they.' So there could have been more than one person."

Which shot the Bickersons to the top of the list.

"He mentioned a reunion too. Do you recall your parents attending a reunion before they died?"

"No, I don't. But they went out a lot. They had a weekly date night."

"What about the novel? Did he ever tell you when he first read it?"

"In college. Said it changed his life."

"That's what Roberta said, the archeologist."

I quickly told Blade about the legendary obsidian skull, what it represented, and that it was in fact a real artifact. I mentioned that his parents had tried to pass off the glass one as the real deal, thinking whoever killed them wouldn't be able to tell the difference. I didn't tell him, however, that it was sculpted by a succubus. That was Birdie's department.

"An archeologist would be just the type of person who knows about legends of ancient artifacts," Blade said.

I asked Blade what college his father had attended. It was the same one where Roberta and Donald had gone.

"But why shoot the fake?" he asked.

"Probably because whoever killed your parents had their fingerprints all over it."

"Which means they must have a record. Otherwise it wouldn't have mattered."

"Unless they worked in government." Then a thought occurred to me. "What about your father's college roommate? Any idea who he might have been?"

"No. And I don't even know how I would find that information."

"That's okay. I might be able to with that voodoo that I do." I smiled at him.

Blade looked at me for a long time. "You really are something, Stacy Justice. I hope your boyfriend knows that."

"He knows."

Blade sighed, ran his fingers through his hair. "So if the skull is real, if it actually exists, do you think they came back here looking for it?"

"That's my guess. Someone was here. I can feel it."

Unless it was the Leanan Sidhe. She could have been the one looking for it.

"So that means it was never found." He looked around the place. "Any ideas where to start?"

"I'm glad you asked."

Blade raised one eyebrow at me.

"Mr. Knight," I said, "I think it's time we have a chat with my grandmother."

Chapter 36

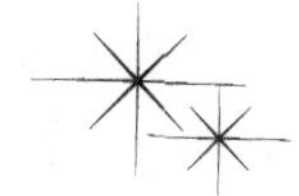

We drove back to the inn and I texted Birdie from the driveway and asked her to meet us in the parlor.

She took one look at my bloody shredded coat and said, "Good Goddess, girl, what happened to you?"

I looked down at it too, praying that damn raccoon didn't have rabies.

"I don't want to talk about it."

I pulled her off to the side and asked about the Leanan.

"We need her awake to perform the test, so we're not certain if it's her yet," she said.

Blade was standing off to the side, admiring the piano. He stepped over to the whiteboard and flipped it over, inspecting the notes.

"Why didn't you put the board away last night?" I asked in a low voice.

Birdie frowned. "I thought Lolly did."

"Hey, what's this?" Blade asked, reading the notes. "These look like lines from my books." He read a few of them aloud.

"Birdie," I whispered. "It's time. You need to tell him."

Yvonne came down the stairs then. "Thought I'd do a little

shopping. Maybe pick up a Halloween costume," she said. She flicked her eyes to Blade and the board, giving them both a curious glance. Then she grabbed a Kleenex and blew her nose. "What's all that?" She pointed to the board and walked over to it.

Birdie said, "We take our book club very seriously."

Yvonne was reading through the passages we had jotted down the night before. "Apparently," she said.

Birdie walked over and erased everything.

Yvonne gave my grandmother a dumbfounded look.

"We'll be playing a parlor game later. No cheating." She wagged her finger at Blade's agent.

Yvonne said, "Great, I love games." She shot Blade a *these people are nuts* look.

"Mr. Knight, would you be so kind as to help me open a jar in the kitchen?"

"Sure thing," Blade said.

He followed my grandmother through the dividing door. Birdie paused and said, "Come along, Stacy."

Yvonne studied me with suspicion. "Must be a hell of a jar," she said.

To Blade, she called, "See you tonight for dinner."

I followed my grandmother and Blade down the hall, locking the door behind me.

"It's on the counter, there, Blade," Birdie said.

The author went to inspect the applesauce jar.

Birdie pulled me into the pantry and handed me a piece of paper.

"We're still missing a piece of the puzzle. I've recorded everything we found, but I need you to study this, see if you can think of anything. Any other works he may have written that would lead us to the skull."

I tucked the piece of paper into my pocket. "Will do."

"Now scoot. I'll handle this."

"Roger that."

I left out the back door, glad I wasn't going to be there when Blade heard the whopper of all tales. He seemed open enough to believe that there was something supernatural within me. But it was one thing to believe that about other people. It was an entirely different ball game when it's you who has the gift. I should know. I'd spent years shunning mine.

Outside, I called Chance's mother and asked if she was busy for lunch. She said she'd just made some butternut squash soup and garlic bread, and invited me to come over at noon. I tried to call Chance too, to let him know I was going to visit his parents, but he didn't answer, so I left a message.

There was enough time to shower and change so I quickly did that, strapping on a belt that hid a few tools of my trade, grabbed my bag, and left.

It was sunny and warmer by then, but since I had no idea how many more Fae were lurking around the corner, I decided I'd be safer in Birdie's car.

The Strykers lived a few blocks down the hill from the Geraghty house. I parked in the driveway and jogged up the walkway. There was a flock of crows circling the house, cawing. The front porch was decorated with corn stalks neatly tied in pumpkin-printed ribbon, a basket of gourds, and a "Happy Halloween" wreath hung on the front door.

Mrs. Stryker opened the door and pulled me into a bear hug. "I feel as if I haven't seen you in ages, Stacy."

She had hair the color of sunshine and eyes that invited you into her heart. She was wearing a creamy wool sweater and olive yoga pants.

"I know, I'm sorry I haven't been here in a while."

She waved her hand. "Well, you're here now. Come on into the kitchen." She started toward the kitchen, but paused at the stairwell. "Caleb! Jack! Stacy's here. Come have some lunch."

I heard battle cries coming from the upstairs guest room that was once Caleb's old room. They must have been playing a video game.

Mrs. Stryker went to the stove and I asked her if she needed some help. She told me to sit, that she didn't have nearly enough kids to dote on anymore and to leave everything up to her.

Her kitchen smelled like autumn. The aroma of nutmeg, cinnamon, and brown sugar blended with the pungent scent of garlic and butter. It made me think of campfires and ghost stories.

Caleb and Mr. Stryker appeared a few minutes later and Chance's mother filled up four soup bowls and set them in front of each of us. She filled a large basket with garlic bread and brought that over along with a spinach salad and hot tea.

"So Stacy, how's work going?" Mr. Stryker asked. He was an imposing man with a fondness for bacon and flannel shirts. His hands were calloused from years of lifting lumber, but his eyes were soft.

"Jack, I'm sure Stacy doesn't want to talk about work." Mrs. Stryker sat down next to her husband and spread a napkin across her lap.

She was right. I didn't.

"It's going fine." I grabbed a piece of garlic bread and set it next to my soup bowl.

"Caleb tells us that famous author in town is staying at your grandmother's house," Mrs. Stryker said. She poured herself a cup of green tea.

I looked at Caleb.

"I was talking to his agent. Still trying to negotiate the pilot."

"Any luck?" I asked.

Caleb rolled his eyes. "She's a shark, that one. Been in the business a long time. Took it over from her father, who was also a pain in the ass."

Mrs. Stryker said, "Caleb, language."

"Sorry, Mom."

We chitchatted about the weather, the Halloween parade, and the reunion as we ate our lunch.

"Will you be at the reunion?" I asked.

Mrs. Stryker sighed. "If I could get Jack off the couch to go anywhere, it would be a miracle."

"Hey, I like my retirement. I worked hard all my life. A man deserves the right to sit on his duff in his golden years."

"I just hope you have better luck with Chance when he retires," Mrs. Stryker said.

I nearly choked on my bread. Mrs. Stryker was forever asking when Chance and I would get married. Now she had jumped from marriage to thirty years down the road.

"Geez, Mom," Caleb said.

"What?" she asked.

Mr. Stryker said, "Well, the boy works hard. He'll earn his retirement too." He flashed his eyes to Caleb.

Caleb got up from the table and rinsed out his soup bowl. "I work hard too, Dad. Just because I don't swing a hammer doesn't mean I don't work hard."

He kissed his mother on the cheek.

"Come on, old man, you owe me a rematch."

Mr. Stryker grunted as he rose from his chair. "You ready for another ass-whupping?"

"Language, Jack," Mrs. Stryker said.

The men left the room and it was just the two of us. Mrs. Stryker waited until she heard footsteps on the stairs before she spoke.

"Honey, I'm worried about Chance." Her voice was thin, drawn, and I wanted to hug her and tell her that everything would be all right, that I would never let anything happen to the man we both loved, but I couldn't make a promise I wasn't certain I could keep.

"Caleb mentioned that. What has you concerned?"

She twisted her napkin in her hands, wringing it back and forth. "I can't put my finger on it, but he seems distant lately. And he's impatient whenever I phone him, if he picks it up at all." She set the napkin down and put her hand on mine. "Are you two having trouble?"

I was prepared for that question, but I still didn't know how to answer it.

"We had a fight, but we're working it out."

She raised her eyebrows. "Oh. What about?"

I rearranged the salt and pepper shakers as I spoke. "It was nothing really. Just that we're both really busy and we don't spend enough time together."

Chance's mother sat back in her chair. She seemed a little relieved. She stared at me for a while, then leaned in and said, "I think I understand. It's a sex thing. Is that it?"

If there was any liquid in my mouth, I would have spit it all over her. That was the last thing I expected her to say.

"Er . . . um . . ."

"It's all right, sweetie. I'm perfectly aware that even though you aren't married you are having sex with my son."

Dear Goddess, kill me now.

"Have you tried toys?"

I sprung up out of my seat so fast, the chair toppled over. I picked it up and smacked my head on the underside of the table in the process.

"There's nothing wrong with spicing things up, Stacy. No need to be embarrassed. We're both adults."

Okay, Danu, if you won't kill me, at least strike me deaf so I don't have to listen to sex tips from my boyfriend's mother.

"It's not that, honest. It's just a time thing." I put my soup bowl in the sink.

"Well, you know, Chance's father and I go to Sybaris sometimes. It's really romantic."

Lalalalalalalalalala!

"I'll look into that. Thanks for lunch. Gotta go."

I practically sprinted to the car.

Caleb caught up with me outside.

"Hey, you got a minute?" he asked.

So close. "Sure."

He stuffed his hands in his pockets and glanced back toward the door. When he spoke his voice was low. "Did my brother stay at your place last night?"

A tingle ran up and down my spine like a thousand spiders crawling inside my skin.

"No."

He swore, then met my eyes.

"He didn't come home last night."

Chapter 37

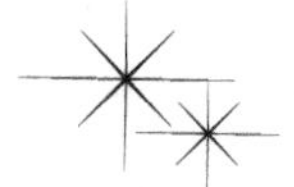

Caleb explained that he was staying at Chance's place, not his parents' house.

I took a deep breath. "Look, Caleb. Your mother is right. There is something going on with Chance."

I decided then and there that Birdie was right too. I did need a team. And I had to recruit Caleb to keep Chance safe.

He looked concerned now. "What is it? Drugs?"

"No, nothing like that." I racked my brain for a plausible explanation that wouldn't land Chance in rehab.

"Gambling?"

"No, that's not it."

His cloud of anger swept over his face. "Is it another woman?"

"Yes! That's it."

"That son of a bitch. I'll kill him."

"No, don't kill him. In fact, don't say anything." *Think, Stacy.* "Um, you see, we decided to see other people."

He looked surprised. "You did?"

"Yes, you know. Before we settle down, we thought maybe it would be best. Plus we've been arguing so we thought time apart might do us good. Absence makes the heart grow fonder, they say."

Caleb smiled. "So you're getting married?"

"Well, no, maybe, you know, someday."

"I don't understand." Then something seemed to click and he said, "So are you seeing someone else already? Is that why he's acting like a jackass?"

If I said yes, Caleb wouldn't agree to what I was about to ask him to do.

"No, but I think Chance might be and I think she's trouble."

"Well, who is it?"

"I don't know. Maybe you could find out."

"Sure, I'll ask him."

Uh-oh. I couldn't have that conversation taking place because then Chance would wonder why I had lied to his brother.

"Please don't do that. He'd be furious if he knew I told you about our . . . problems."

"So what do you want me to do, follow him?" He laughed.

I didn't answer. Just stared at him.

He stopped laughing. "You're kidding."

"Just until the reunion on Friday. We made plans and I'm going to tell him I don't want to do this anymore."

Caleb crossed his arms. "You two are crazy, you know that. You're perfect for each other. I don't know why you'd risk throwing that away."

Caleb was divorced. He had married a woman right after high school who cheated on him. Now he writes a hefty alimony check every month.

"I'm trying not to," I said.

Caleb sighed. "Okay. You got it." He smirked and tagged my arm. "Sis."

As I climbed into the car, I felt a little bit better that Caleb had agreed to spy on his brother, although I couldn't help but worry that Chance hadn't been home last night. Where had he been?

I tried to call him again, but the phone went straight to voice mail. Why hadn't I put a tracking spell on him?

Leo called on my way to the newspaper office. I decided to call him back when I got there. I wanted to pick up my sword and consecrate it before the reunion, because I had a pretty good idea that Samhain was going to be D-day.

Derek was in his office so I popped in there and told him that I would try to get him the reunion piece today or tomorrow. He didn't ask me about Monique since she was only in the office on Mondays and Fridays. Then I went to speak with Gladys about her interviews.

She said she e-mailed me the notes already. But there was one person I wanted details on.

"How did it go with Lucinda?" I asked her.

"Very good. She is nice lady," Gladys said.

"Anything unusual about her?"

"She dress nice," Gladys said.

I thought she dressed like a carnival ride, but to each his own.

"Do you know where she went to college?"

Gladys shuffled through some notes. "University at Illinois."

Another one. I guess it wasn't that unusual since these were all graduates of Amethyst and a lot of people went to college in their own states. Still. Illinois had quite a few universities, so the fact that this particular one kept popping up sent off warning signals in my head.

"Did she happen to mention anything about a favorite book?"

Gladys thought for a minute. "No. She likes the Mr. Knight books."

I thanked Gladys and went into my office to do some work for a few hours. I e-mailed Derek the piece for Friday because I wanted to clear my plate for tomorrow, and I told him I'd be taking the day off.

It was dark by the time I left and I had completely forgotten to return Leo's call. I sat in the car and dialed his private number.

"Hey," he said.

"Hey yourself."

"I wanted to get into your place to check out the incident."

"I'm headed home now. Did you find anything out on the two names Blade sent you?"

He told me that Lucinda had been arrested for assault a few times. Something about a fur fashion show and an altercation at a nightclub years ago. The archeologist had been arrested at a few protest rallies, but nothing violent.

I thanked him, hung up the phone, and twisted the key in the ignition. It wasn't until I was crawling up the hill toward the inn that I spotted the spiderweb on the visor.

Uninvited guest.

Before I could slam on the brakes, two meaty hands lurched at my throat.

The car swerved as the hands found their way around my eyes. I tried to peel them off of me, but they had a good grip.

I heard honking and screeching of tires.

My athame was in my boot so I reached for it and slashed blindly at my attacker. There was a wail and the hands lost their grip. I whipped the wheel around and did a U-turn right on Crescent Street, narrowly missing a passing truck. A thump came from the backseat along with several grunts and snorts. When I twisted my neck around,

I saw that it was a woodland sprite. Olive skin, bulging eyes, and a drool problem worse than Thor's. They could only emerge at night, were allergic to sunlight and something else I couldn't recall.

What was it? There were a few potions in my bag that Lolly had prepared for me, but I wasn't sure which one would do the trick in this instance.

I slammed on the brakes, then accelerated to buy some time, weaving the car all over the road. Through the rearview mirror, I could see the little cow pattie bounce around the backseat like a bowling ball.

Then I remembered.

Mirrors. Woodland sprites couldn't gaze upon their own reflection.

I ripped the rearview mirror off the windshield and when he came at me again—or maybe it was a she, I had no idea—I flashed it in the creature's eyes.

The sprite screamed as if it'd been dropped in a pot of boiling water. I held the mirror on it while I stopped the car, popped the trunk, and catapulted over the seat. There, I trained the mirror directly at its two yellow eyes while it continued to screech and squirm. The smell of burning wood and musty leaves littered the car as I picked it up by the scruff of its mossy shirt. The thing was still smoldering when I tossed it in the trunk.

Leo was waiting for me when I got to the house. I pulled into Birdie's driveway, texted her that there was a present waiting for her in the trunk of her car, and went to meet the chief.

Leo had a funny look on his face when I got there.

"What?" I asked.

"You look like you've been wrestling with a pig."

That's because I have, I thought.

"I fell," I said lamely.

Since I wasn't the most graceful ballerina in the troupe, he accepted that explanation. As soon as I opened the door to the cottage, my phone rang.

It was Cinnamon. "Did you forget something?"

Right. Thor. "Sorry. I'll come and get him."

"It's okay. I'm on my way to open the bar now. Apparently Daphne never showed up. Tony said she bailed out of work too. Neither one of us can reach her. I tell you, the way things are going, I just want to shut the place down for a while. And with the receipts from last night's soiree, I probably could."

"So do it."

She paused. "I got another package today."

"What was it?"

"A Rapunzel mop."

"Come over."

She said she would and we hung up.

Leo looked at me. "I won't be too long."

I asked Leo to lock up, washed my face, and changed my clothes for the third time that day, then I went over to the Geraghty House.

Cinnamon was just pulling up into the driveway when I got there. She wobbled out of the car, opened the back door, and Thor came charging at me.

He jumped up and gave me a hug. "Missed you too, buddy."

"That was fast," I said to Cinnamon.

"Daphne finally showed up. She said she'd been sick as a dog all day, but she was feeling better and wanted to work."

I was really sorry to hear that. Because that meant I was wrong. She wasn't the Leanan Sidhe. I wondered if the coven had performed a false-memory spell to make her forget what had happened. I hoped so anyway.

"She kept babbling on about you too. I think she's got the hots for you." Cinnamon shrugged her purse up her shoulder.

Now I felt really guilty. The poor girl probably thought I was hitting on her. I hoped that spell reached far enough back that she forgot I was ever at Tony's shop.

But I had an even bigger problem than leading on the bartender. I had no idea who the Leanan Sidhe was.

And Monique was still missing.

Chapter 38

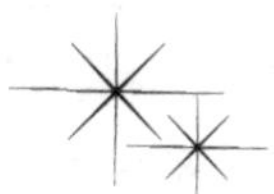

I retrieved the sword from Birdie's car, thinking I'd be able to consecrate it faster with a full coven around me.

The front door of the inn was unlocked. Thor trotted inside and howled to Fiona that he was hungry.

She got up to feed him and I said I'd take care of it, but she turned to me and said she needed to have a "talk" with him anyway. She nodded toward Cinnamon. I stuck the sword in the umbrella rack.

The rest of the coven, as well as Birdie, Lolly, and Blade, were all sitting in the parlor. Blade kept looking around the room, grinning like a loon, as if he'd won the mother of all lotteries.

Cinnamon shuffled off to the kitchen behind Fiona, saying she was hungry too, and I went to join my new team for a debriefing.

"Hey," Blade said. "I had the best day."

"I'm sure you did."

I glanced upstairs.

"Yvonne's still shopping. She's picking me up for dinner in a couple of hours," Blade said.

"So what have we got?" I asked.

Birdie started to answer, but Blade interrupted. "We think whoever killed my parents must have killed the Council member who tracked the skull to them."

I raised my eyebrows at him.

"Oh, yeah. I know all about the Council. I've been anointed as the Scribe." Emphasis on *anointed.*

"Congratulations, Blade," I said.

Birdie rolled her eyes.

Lolly stood. She was wearing a glittering gold ball gown and a grapevine crown. Grapes still attached. She walked over to the whiteboard and flipped it around, sucking down a mimosa.

I said to Birdie, "So I guess Daphne wasn't the Leanan."

"The Leanan? Who's that?" Blade set his gaze on me. "You mean Daphne, the bartender from last night? What's a Leanan?"

Birdie shot me a *shut up* look. I guess that part of the story was above his pay grade.

"Never mind. Do we know where the skull is?" I asked.

Lolly was aiming a long pointer at the whiteboard. She touched the tip to the phrases the coven and I had extracted from his books the night before, and Blade read them aloud.

"The skull was shiny, as if it had been picked clean," Blade read. "That was from *Hollow Stone,*" he said with a look back to his audience.

"We don't need all the details, Mr. Knight," Birdie said.

Blade gave a sheepish smile.

Lolly pointed to the next line.

The author stood. "It was a dark, damp place, like a thousand rains had washed out all the color."

The stick jumped down.

"There, hidden beneath old rubble, was the key to his past."

Lolly pointed again to the board and Blade stepped forward. “Secrets lie in the echoes. If you listen carefully, you can hear the truth whistle through the walls.”

The next line he read was, “It was the source of all his passion.”

Lolly looked at me as Blade spoke the phrase after that. “It wasn’t until he met her that he knew a piece of him was missing.”

Blade glanced my way too and I shuffled uncomfortably.

The last line Blade read was this: “The river was shallow that day and even the fish looked forlorn.”

And that was all.

Heads swung my way. I walked over to the board and touched it, closed my eyes, then pulled the locket out and asked it a silent, penetrating question.

I didn’t open it. Not yet.

The talisman vibrated softly in my hand as my fingers trailed the length of the board. The locket moved faster and faster as my hands moved, building into a frenzy of jerks and pulls until I arrived at the end of all the passages. Then it stopped.

“We’re still missing something,” I said when the locket came to a limp rest.

Birdie frowned. “Blade, is there something else you’ve written in this series? A short story, perhaps?”

He shook his head. “You’ve seen everything. I have other novels, though.”

“No.” Birdie shook her head. “It would somehow be connected to these works. I can feel it.”

“Unless—” I looked at Blade. “You told me that when you left home, when you went into foster care, you took one book with you from place to place. Surely that must have inspired you.”

Blade locked eyes with me. "Every writer is inspired by something."

I gave him a look of annoyance. "What was the book, Blade?"

"*Huckleberry Finn.*"

I read each passage carefully again. "That's it." I pointed to the last line. "The river was shallow that day and even the fish looked forlorn." I looked at Blade.

"*Huckleberry Finn* takes place mostly on the Mississippi," said the author.

"The river line refers to the location of the last clue," I said. "Do we have *Huckleberry Finn*?"

"We have it in the library," Birdie said.

Shannon jumped up. "I'll get it."

Her movements were swift and she had Mark Twain's tome in my hands in seconds. I set the book down on the piano, closed my eyes, and opened the locket. I pointed it facedown over the closed cover, conjuring an image of a skull in my mind's eye.

There was a whooshing sound and I opened my eyes as the spine of the book cracked open. The pages flipped back and forth for several moments until finally coming to a rest.

Everyone had gathered around me. I shut the locket and let it dance around until I saw a passage of text shoot out at me as if in 3-D.

I read it aloud. "There warn't anybody at the church, except maybe a hog or two, for there warn't any lock on the door, and hogs like a puncheon floor in summer-time because it's cool."

I looked at Birdie. "A church. It's in a church."

Blade said, "The book is also about freedom and race relations."

Birdie snapped her fingers. "The old underground Baptist church."

Blade asked what that was and Birdie explained that it was the first African-American Baptist church in the state.

"Amethyst, being so close to the Mississippi, was a prime stop on the Underground Railroad," I explained.

Lolly said, "Sadly, the church was burned to the ground years ago. All that remains is the foundation and pieces of rubble."

Blade looked at me and said, "Let's go get it."

"Easy, cowboy. I'm not sure you're equipped to handle this rodeo," I said.

Cinnamon returned from the kitchen and asked, "Hey, has anyone seen Monique? Someone from the reunion committee called me. Said she's supposed to have all the booze and the decorations."

Fiona and Thor were behind her. Thor plopped himself on a plush rug near the fireplace and settled in for a nap. Shannon went to sit by him. As she stroked his fur, I couldn't help but think this girl was after my job.

"The decorations are in the back closet," Fiona said. "I took them out of Birdie's car."

"Thanks, Fiona. I forgot all about that," I said.

She patted my arm, then smoothed a rogue hair on my head.

"Well, I can give you an update on the booze. It was destroyed when her pipe burst. She said she used up all the funds too," I said.

"I knew she'd cock it up," Cinnamon said. "At least there will be food."

The Pearl Palace restaurant was catering the event.

Blade said, "You can't have a reunion without liquor." He looked at me. "What do you say we make a deal?"

I crossed my arms. "What kind of a deal?"

"Include me in the mission and I'll spring for an open bar."

Cinnamon pursed her lips, looking from me to Blade.

I looked at Birdie.

"It's up to you, Seeker," she said.

"What do you say, Seeker of Justice? The Mage is cool with it," Blade said.

Apparently, he had been granted the security clearance to know who Birdie and I were. I guess he just couldn't know about the Otherworld.

Cinnamon looked confused, but decided she didn't want any part of whatever it was we were talking about. She sank into a chair and kicked her shoes off.

"You can't have an open bar without bartenders." I smiled at Birdie and the aunts. Blade watched as the three of them crouched into a huddle.

Birdie popped her head up. "Done."

Good. Because I had a sneaky suspicion that something awful was going to happen that night and I could use all the help I could get.

Chapter 39

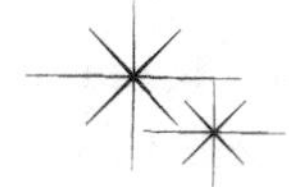

It took two hours to consecrate my sword, but I was confident that it was back to full throttle, and I warned Blade that if he touched it, I would shank him. It was resting in front of the life-sized portrait of the Goddess Danu.

Birdie thought it was best to retrieve the skull in daylight, as there would be less of a chance of the Leanan's army attacking then. We didn't know if there were any soldiers left, but I agreed that it was a good idea to wait for daybreak. She chose three witches to accompany our mission, one of which (of course) was Shannon.

The author went to dinner with his agent, and I spent a good deal of time trying to contact Chance until, eventually, Caleb texted me and said he was at home sleeping.

I was relieved to know that he was safe. For now.

Cinnamon went home to Tony, and Thor and I were about to call it a night as well when Fiona pulled me aside to tell me that she believed Thor was indeed just protecting the baby.

One more thing I didn't have to worry about.

With all of that out of the way, I finally was able to concentrate on studying the binding spells and tricks that Birdie had outlined for me. I read through her notes back in the cottage, but none of them seemed particularly effective. Which was understandable. We were sailing on unknown waters. No one had battled the Leanan since the last Geraghty she had cursed.

And that didn't end well.

I spent the rest of the evening and well into the night poring over the Blessed Book, my reference materials, herbal grimoires, crystal enchantment texts, and the Council's database.

There were a few promising options that I jotted down, along with some curse-reversal spells I cooked up on my own, but the truth was, until I was in her presence, until I understood her power, I had no clue how to fight her.

And if all else failed, there was always the locket. It had served me well since I had been gifted it, and I had to believe it would aid me in this quest. I had to. Lives depended on it. Humanity and all that was beauty in the world depended on it.

I fell asleep in the Seeker's Den, dreaming of ancient battles, evil fairies, and Geraghtys long deceased.

The next morning I woke up groggy and unfocused, like I had already waged war. My muscles ached, my head throbbed, and there was a pounding at my door.

Thor was sleeping on my exercise mat. He groaned and rolled over.

I looked at the clock and was surprised to see that it read ten-thirty.

When I answered the door, Blade Knight was standing on my porch in a pair of jeans and a hoodie, two coffees in hand, accompanied by a box of Milk-Bones.

"Good morning," he said.

"Hi, Blade."

I left the door open and shuffled into the bathroom.

When I came out, Thor was on his back and Blade was feeding him treats. The author handed me a coffee and I thanked him.

"Just let me change and we can get going."

I threw on a long-sleeved tee shirt, jeans, an old sweatshirt, rubber boots, and a baseball cap. There were gardening gloves in the shed out back, so I ran to grab those, and the lot of us piled into Blade's car, while Thor trotted off to Cinnamon's place.

Birdie had warned us not to touch the skull with our bare hands. Since it wasn't a manmade artifact, she was afraid of what human contact might do to it, so I, Blade, Shannon, and two other witches about my age were all wearing gloves when we arrived at the site of the old church.

Lolly and Fiona had given Blade a velvet-lined safe to cart the skull home safely. It was agreed that after we found it, I would keep it locked up in the Seeker's Den until a Council member could arrive to retrieve it.

Blade pulled some shovels out of the trunk of his car and he, the coven members, and I hiked through a small forest, past faded oaks, coppery maples, and crimson ash trees, until we came upon the site of the old Baptist church.

All that remained of the house of worship was a boxy rock-wall foundation sunken into the earth. The edges were charred in spots and tendrils of ivy curled around the cold stone, while moss and brambles carpeted the parts of the dirt floor that weren't covered in debris. There was an old brass cup perched on one of the corner stones as if someone had performed a ritual recently, and along the outer bank of the far wall was a rotting tree stump littered with walnut husks. The music of a nearby stream was all but drowned out by the chatter of excited birds preparing for their autumn journey. A few steps away, two squirrels chased each other around an old tire.

I watched them for a moment until the woman next to me blew out a shaky sigh.

The witch was an African-American woman with tightly cropped hair and I wondered what she was feeling in that moment, standing on the ruins of what her people had worked hard to build. Ignorance and fear are the food of hatred and, right now, we were looking at the devastating destruction that human beings do to one another when common sense is discarded for intolerance.

She looked at me, shovel in hand, and said, "Let's do this."

We all climbed into the pit, kicking boards and cola cans out of the way, moving rocks and fallen limbs. Above, a ray of sunlight punctured the tree canopy, providing a soft glow of light and welcomed warmth.

The five of us dug for hours. Our feet were caked with mud, our backs aching. We had made a fair dent in the rubbish pile, but there was still only a small area of the floor that was uncovered.

Shannon said, "Stacy, can you try to use the locket?"

I didn't like to use the locket outdoors, especially in the daytime. While the sun could often cleanse a crystal, charging it with power, I was afraid of what it would do to this delicate heirloom. Because, like artwork, ancient talismans have been known to be washed by the sun, draining them of their energy.

But, as Birdie said, desperate times.

I pulled the locket out from beneath my tee shirt, wiping the sweat from my brow. As I had done yesterday with the Mark Twain novel, I centered myself, concentrating on the image of a black skull. I walked to the center of the church's foundation, removed the locket, and held it briefly to my third eye. Then I unclasped it, dangled it in my hand, and watched it spin.

It sputtered around for just a second and then stopped. I tried again, but the piece didn't seem to be picking up on anything.

"It's not working," I said.

"So we keep digging," said Blade.

The African-American woman said, "I have a better idea."

She pulled out a Tibetan skull amulet that was often used by voodoo practitioners to remove revenge spells and curses.

I smiled at her. "Do your thing."

I stepped away from the center of the church and the woman took my place. She held her arms up high, chanting in a language I didn't understand. The skull danced in her hand, spinning in a wide circle. She walked with it, carefully moving around the space, stepping over rocks, discarded liquor bottles, and fruit crates until the skull finally tightened its circle near a spot in the corner of the foundation. Then it spun into a frenzy.

"Here," she said.

Blade got busy tossing out rotted wood, broken glass, and piles of rocks. After a while, he said, "I see something. It's shiny."

We all knelt down, dusting away the dirt with our hands, until eventually a set of glimmering black teeth appeared.

Chapter 40

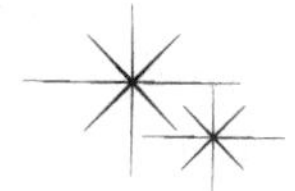

It was dark by the time we had carefully dug up and dusted off the skull and placed it in the safe.

Shannon offered to hold it on her lap on the way back to the Geraghty House. She had called Birdie earlier to tell her we had found the obsidian skull and now she was texting that we were on our way home.

I texted Caleb and asked about Chance. Caleb said his brother was working late and that he had just texted to say he had left the construction site to head home and hook up with Caleb for dinner.

I hadn't eaten all day, so I was thrilled to smell baked ham and sweet potatoes when we got back to the Geraghty House. Lolly was playing a Billie Holiday tune on the piano and Fiona was singing. We all kicked off our muddy shoes and left them on the porch.

Blade and the three witches went to wash up while I wandered into the kitchen to find Birdie. She was setting the table in the dining room, her carnelian hair pinned in a loose bun. She was wearing a long, flowing Indian-style dress with gold embroidery and green beading.

I grabbed some glasses and helped her set the table.

"So now what do we do?" I asked.

"Now we wait." She grabbed some silverware from a drawer in the buffet. "She'll know it's been moved. She'll come looking for it. When she does, you'll be ready."

I wasn't so sure about that.

"What if she casts another curse? What then?"

Birdie set the salt and pepper shakers on the table and I opened the cabinet on the far side of the room to fetch the napkins.

"She can't curse the same family twice, and besides, we have Danu on our side."

That reminded me. I needed to get my sword and my costume for tomorrow. I didn't need to go to a store or a rental shop. I just raided Lolly's wardrobe.

"Any word on Monique?"

Birdie sighed. "I don't understand why your aunt's tracking spell didn't work. But to answer your question, no. We haven't located her."

That made me nervous. If it wasn't Daphne, who else besides Monique would the Leanan Sidhe use as a vessel?

Blade came into the dinning room.

He clasped his hands together. "Well, that's one mystery solved. One to go."

"Will you be joining us for dinner, Mr. Knight?" Birdie asked.

"No, I'll be having dinner with my agent." He looked at me. "Do you want to get together tonight and go over the reports again?"

I agreed to that and we made plans to meet at the cottage after dinner.

The happy chatter of twelve witches filled the dining room as they discussed their victory and indulged in wine, glazed ham, sweet potato casserole, and green beans. Pickle was perched on a chair in the corner eating a bag of marshmallows, grinning at me.

As I looked around the room, I knew one thing for certain. We weren't out of the woods yet. Not by a long shot.

When I got up to clear my plate, I caught Shannon staring at me.

Everyone escorted me back to the cottage, despite my protests. Shannon volunteered to stay with me until Blade arrived, but I sent her back with the others. The girl was really a pest and I needed to be alone with my thoughts for a few minutes before launching into yet another investigative search.

I leaned the sword against the porch railing and dug my key out. The small safe with the obsidian skull was sitting next to that as I unlocked the door.

Behind me, I heard a branch crack.

I grabbed the sword and whirled around, lunging at a figure in the dark.

It was Adia, the woman who had found the skull.

"Whoa, easy." She held up her hands. "I come in peace."

I blew out a sigh and lowered the sword. "Sorry. You startled me."

"I should know better than to sneak up on a Seeker." She pulled something out of her coat pocket. "I thought maybe you could use this." It was the Tibetan skull necklace.

"Oh, no, I couldn't. It's your talisman."

She reached her arms up and draped it around my neck. "Nonsense. We're sisters now. What's mine is yours."

I felt myself choke up. I didn't know what to say. "Thank you."

She dug into her other pocket and extracted another necklace. It was a Buddhist dharma wheel. The symbol represents discipline, wisdom, and concentration.

"This is from Shannon. She asked me to give it to you."

I opened my hand and she dropped it in. The piece was heavy, comprised of brass, copper, and pewter.

"The power of three," Adia said.

She turned to go and I called out, "Tell Shannon thank you for me." Maybe the kid wasn't so bad after all.

I draped the dharma around my neck and Adia waved. The weight of all three talismans dangling down my chest lent a certain comfort.

A short while later, Blade showed up and we spread the reports and the notes from Leo across the counter.

We discussed the fact that the University of Illinois seemed to be the common thread to everyone who was interested in *The Book of Skulls*, including Blade's father. Was there a connection between the book and the obsidian skull? Neither one of us was certain, but the fact that his father had studied it and it was taken by whoever killed him made it important to at least consider.

"What about a professor?" I asked. "A history teacher or maybe an English lit teacher? Since it seems the obsidian skull legend is known in some circles, there could be a connection leading to the college."

Blade grabbed his tablet and searched for a list of professors from the years 1970 through 1974, but there wasn't any information going that far back.

"What about the book? You read it. Was there any mention of an obsidian skull in Silverberg's novel?"

"No, but it could have been coded." Blade thought for a moment. "When you had the vision, my father said *they*, right?"

"Right."

"And there was mention of a reunion."

I nodded.

"So maybe *they* were members of a fraternity he belonged to?"

"It's possible. Do you know if he was involved in anything like that?"

The author shook his head. "Not that I can recall. Although he did have an unusual ring I found in his dresser once. I was looking for money to buy a book."

"What was it?"

Blade looked at me. "A skull with crossbones."

"Skull and bones, skull and bones." I rapped my fingers on the counter. *Why did that sound familiar?*

Blade said, "Wait a minute. There was a secret fraternity at Yale called Skull and Bones."

He tapped his tablet a few times and discovered a Wikipedia page on the secret society. Its members included presidents, senators, judges, historians, lawyers, CEOs of Fortune 500 companies, presidents of universities, and other influential people.

"It says they stopped publishing their member rosters in 1971," Blade said.

"So maybe there was a branch chapter at the University of Illinois."

We searched for a few hours, but found nothing indicating that. And of course, given the nature of secret societies, we wouldn't.

Late in the evening Blade said, "Well, I'm beat." He got up and stretched. "I'll see you tomorrow."

I walked him to the door and he turned to me, his face inches from mine. "So I guess we really are a team now."

"I guess so."

He lingered at the door a little longer as if he wanted to say something more. Then he thought better of it and said, "Good night, Stacy."

"Good night, Blade."

I watched him leave just as Chance's truck drove by.

It didn't stop.

Chapter 41

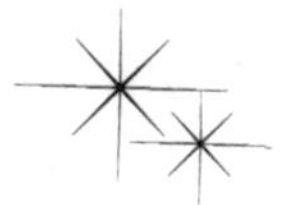

Chance's phone went straight to voice mail again. I texted Cinnamon and said I was sorry that I didn't have a chance to pick up Thor and asked if he could stay the night. She wasn't too happy about it, but she agreed to the arrangement.

I climbed into bed alone.

After work the next day, I spent a good hour getting ready for the reunion. The Batgirl costume I had borrowed from Lolly was perfect for hiding all of my weapons, although Birdie still had my tranquilizer gun. I paced back and forth in the Seeker's Den, studying the binding spells and practicing calling Pickle. The poor thing was dizzy after the third time I called him, so I stopped. I performed a sacred spell, asking the ancestors to aid me in my quest tonight, and waited for Chance to pick me up.

When he didn't show, I became alarmed. I called Caleb, who assured me that Chance was just working late, and that he could pick me up.

But if that was the case, why didn't Chance call me?

Chance's brother got to my house a little after 8:00 p.m. He was dressed as a vampire and it sent a shiver down my spine.

I climbed into the front seat of the car, shifting my sword so it fell in my lap.

Caleb gave me a funny look. "What's with the sword? Aren't you supposed to be Batgirl?"

"Batgirl 2.0. She comes with a sword."

Caleb shrugged and threw the car into reverse. As it crested the hill that led to the venue, he gave me a sideways glance. "I haven't seen him with anybody. I don't think you have anything to worry about."

If only. I smiled at him and said, "I appreciate that. I just wish he would have called me."

Where the hell are you, Chance? The skull was in my possession, locked safely back in the Seeker's Den, but still, the fairy mistress hadn't come forth to claim it.

Why not?

Unless it wasn't the skull she was after at all. What if Birdie was wrong and all she wanted was to fulfill the curse and destroy another Geraghty?

Or someone a Geraghty loved.

Then a disturbing thought flashed in my mind like a warning bell. It was the night of Samhain. The Leanan might not need a body now. She could just be wearing a disguise. A costume. Because really, since the curse had never been invoked before, how did Birdie know for certain that she would age on this plane? How would anyone know what could really happen?

Caleb dropped me off at the entrance and I entered the building alone. I scanned the room. It was a packed house. Scores of people in costumes were mingling, drinks in hand, chatting up old friends, while the DJ played an Elvis song. It looked like some classmates had opted for a group theme. There were characters from *The Wizard of Oz*, the crew of *Star Trek*, a group of greasers, women in poodle skirts and saddle shoes, and a team of Disney characters.

A pregnant woman dressed as an angel said to me, "Quite a turnout."

I smiled at her. "Yes it is."

Her skin was glowing from some sort of translucent powder and she had the bluest eyes I had ever seen. Her hands were resting comfortably on her rotund belly.

"When are you due?" I asked.

She looked down, a trace of sadness on her face. "Oh, not for a while."

Odd. She looked to me like she might need a midwife any moment now.

The woman met my gaze. Her voice was soft when she spoke. "It's amazing how strong babies are even in the womb. Almost as if they know more than we do. When to eat, when to sleep, when to be born."

"Children are magical," I said.

"Indeed. It's a shame we ever grow up. Peter Pan had it right." She glanced around the room, then back at me. "That's what babies are for anyway, to remind us that we're all born magical. To teach us lessons. It's just that so few adults listen to the messages children try to tell us."

She excused herself then and melted into the crowd. I watched as a feather floated off her left wing and drifted to the floor.

I wove through the crowd to the back of the room where the bar was situated. Lolly was dressed as Cinderella, Birdie as a flapper, and Fiona was a sexy cop. Fiona's section of the bar was six deep with men begging to be arrested.

Birdie caught my eye and waved me over.

"Anything?" she said.

I struggled for a signal, a warning sign that there was danger present, but I felt nothing.

"No."

"Be alert," she said and poured a glass of wine for Mickey Mouse.

Lolly was lining up shots, taking one herself now and then, and tweaking them, it seemed, to suit her customers. I watched as she took a pinch of this or that from a tray behind the bar and sprinkled Goddess knows what into various customers' cocktails. It wasn't long before James Dean asked Marilyn Monroe to dance, a zombie bride was chewing out a pirate, and a black-and-white-striped inmate was hugging a tearful chambermaid.

Blade and Yvonne came over to me. He was Sherlock Holmes and she was Little Red Riding Hood.

"Great costume," Blade said to me.

Yvonne let out a squeaky sneeze and grabbed a tissue from her basket.

"Thanks. You guys look great too," I said.

Blade gave Yvonne a disappointed look. "I wanted her to be Watson. You know, since she's been my partner in crime all these years."

The agent rolled her eyes. "What woman wants to dress up as Watson?"

She scooted up to the bar and ordered a hot toddy.

Blade said quietly, "She's just jealous because I've been working so closely with you lately. She likes to think of herself as my right-hand woman."

"I wouldn't dream of taking her place," I said.

Blade glanced around the room. "Where's your date?"

"He'll be here. He's working late." I hope.

He made a tsk noise. "Foolish man, leaving a woman like you all alone, surrounded by scoundrels and dressed in tights."

I ignored that comment and asked if he was any closer to solving his personal mystery.

He shrugged. "I guess I know the why. I may never know the who."

I spotted Roberta and Donald near the edge of the bar. "My money's on them."

Blade traced my gaze. "Shall we?" he said, offering his arm.

I nodded and we approached the couple I was certain would be voted Most Likely to Kill Each Other.

Or someone else.

"Ah, Mr. Knight," Roberta said. "We were just discussing the influence of modern literature on popular culture."

Donald said, "I think it rots brains." He sipped his scotch. "No offense."

"None taken." Blade flicked his eyes to me.

"And I think it inspires creativity in all its forms," Roberta said.

Creativity. This time I shot Blade a look. Imaginative thinking could come in very handy for an archeologist. A significant find could lead to a substantial windfall, fame, recognition.

"After all, it was modern fiction that inspired my chosen profession," Roberta said.

"Oh?" asked Blade.

"Yes. Roberta was telling me just yesterday that it was a novel she read in college that prompted her to enter the field of archeology," I said.

"It's called *The Book of Skulls*. Perhaps you've read it?" Roberta asked.

Blade widened his eyes. "As a matter of fact, I have."

"Nonfiction," Donald said. "That's what I prefer. Knowledge."

Roberta ignored him and continued talking about the book.

Blade asked what prompted her to read it. She flicked her eyes to Donald for just a moment, but I caught it, and Blade did too. We exchanged a glance.

"I cannot recall," she said.

Someone called my name and I turned to see Cinnamon dressed as a nun. She waved.

I excused myself and fought through the crowd to get to her. Tony joined us, dressed as a priest, and handed his wife a glass of cranberry juice.

"Nice costumes," I said.

Cinnamon rubbed her swollen belly. "You think?"

"A pregnant nun and a priest? I love it." I sipped on a soda. "Where's Thor?"

"I left him over by the buffet table. He was eyeing a tray of chicken wings and I couldn't get him to budge."

"Anything new?" I asked, referring to her shopping spree.

"A Peter Pan lunch pail," she said.

"That's funny. Someone just mentioned Peter Pan to me," I said.

Tony grinned and put his arm around Cinnamon. "I think she's becoming domesticated. I'm all for it."

Cinnamon punched him in the gut.

"Oh come on, the kitchen's full of fairy-tale stuff. It's adorable."

Cinnamon was about to hit him again, but she doubled over instead.

Tony grabbed her arm. "You okay, honey?"

Cin said, "I'm fine. The baby just kicked me, that's all. Wasn't expecting it." She stood back up.

Tony put his hand on her belly. "Maybe there's a future football player in there." He frowned. "Guess I missed it."

Cinnamon smiled. "I'm sure it'll happen again." She raised her glass and pointed. "Someone's coming over."

Lucinda was dressed in a gossamer gown with wings attached to the back. She was accompanied by one of the men on Chance's crew.

"Glad to see you burned that coat," Lucinda said.

Wes, the man who worked with Chance, said, "I see you've met my mother, Stacy."

"Yes, we've met. You're much better dressed today, Miss Justice," said Lucinda.

"Thank you. And is this one of your creations?" I motioned to the dress.

Lucinda twirled. She wasn't wearing skull earrings today. She was wearing tiny fairies in her ears. "From my Shakespeare collection."

Cinnamon asked, "And who are you supposed to be?"

"Why, the fairy queen, of course."

Cinnamon bent over again, clutching her stomach. "Man, it's like the kid's playing soccer in there."

I smiled at Lucinda. "Maybe Shakespeare knew something we didn't. Maybe fairies do exist."

"Yow!" Cinnamon clutched her stomach.

"Are you sure you're okay?" I asked.

Tony said, "You want something to eat?"

"I'm fine. The baby's just kicking up a storm right now, that's all."

Wes said, "Did Chance get here yet? He was supposed to come when he was finished with that kitchen remodel."

Cinnamon clutched her stomach again. This time she had to hold on to Tony.

I stared at her for a moment, wondering why the baby was so active right now and hoping that it wasn't something serious.

Then the angel from earlier floated by us. Literally. She was drifting through the crowd, her feet inches from the floor, staring into my eyes. Her words sang through my head. *It's just that so few adults listen to the messages children try to tell us.* The angel—or rather, as I just realized, the spirit guide—disappeared into the wall.

My mind raced, thinking about all that had transpired these last few days. Was the baby trying to tell us something? Everything that my cousin had bought for the kitchen, completely unbeknownst to her—was it the baby making those purchases, as Cinnamon had suspected? Hadn't it all started happening around the time the Leanan Sidhe escaped?

Was the child remodeling Cin's kitchen? I swung my head to Wes, who was chatting with Tony. All the items purchased from eBay—the napkin holder, the clock, the mop, the teapot, the lunch pail—-all of them were fairy-tale themed. *Fairy* themed.

I stared at Lucinda, dressed as a fairy, and thought of the baby kicking.

The appliances that seemed to work on their own.

Thor shadowing her, *them.*

All of it was anchored to the kitchen.

And Chance was working late. On a kitchen remodel.

Cinnamon wasn't developing powers. And it wasn't her father speaking to her.

It was the baby speaking *through* her. Trying to send us a message.

I ushered Cinnamon away from the group, placed both hands on her belly, and spoke to the baby.

"Fairy."

My cousin yelped.

"Kitchen remodel."

She cried out again. "What are you doing?"

"Chance."

This time I actually saw the foot imprint.

I kissed my cousin's belly and said, "I'm going to buy you a pony, kid." To Cinnamon, I said, "You're not crazy. And you're not a witch. Give me the keys to your car."

She snorted. "I would be crazy if I gave you the keys to my car."

"Fairy."

She shrieked at another kick and pulled her keys out of her pocket. "Fine. Just knock that off."

I kissed her, then ran up to Wes. "Where's the job?"

"What job?"

"The job, the kitchen remodel."

Cinnamon howled again.

Wes stammered out the address and I raced out of that place so fast, I didn't see who was following me.

Chapter 42

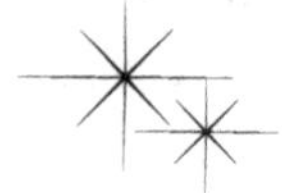

The clouds had parted and the Blood Moon sizzled high in the sky as I sped to the cottage. I ran inside, unlocked the safe where the skull was hidden, slipped on some oven mitts, and shoved the skull in a sack.

This was my insurance. I wasn't certain if the fairy mistress wanted the skull, but obsidian itself has powerful properties. It can banish demons, open portals to the Otherworld, and, of course, its most prominent feature—one that made so much more sense now—was that it served to remind us that birth and death were always present.

It was the best weapon I had to save Chance.

What I didn't expect was Shannon waiting for me on my front porch as I headed out into the night.

"What are you doing?" She eyed me suspiciously.

"Don't have time to chat, Shannon. Gotta run."

She stepped in front of me to block my way.

"Get out of my way, kid. I don't want to hurt you."

"What's in the bag?" She reached for it and I yanked it away.

"None of your business."

"Do you have the skull in there?" Her eyes widened, then grew fierce. "Give it to me."

"Shannon, get out of my way."

She pulled out my tranquilizer gun and said, "I can't let you take it."

Good grief, this kid was getting on my nerves.

"Put the gun down, Shannon. I don't want to hurt you."

I stepped forward.

"You can't take the skull. Birdie said it would be too dangerous."

"I have news for you. Birdie doesn't know everything. Now put down my goddamn gun before you make me do something I'll regret."

Her hand was steady. I braced myself as she weighed her options.

"We'll all go. Let me call the coven," she said.

"There's no time!"

"You can't have the skull."

"There are two options here. Either you step away and let me go or . . ."

"Or what?"

She either wanted my job or she was working with the fairy mistress. Neither option appealed to me, so I did the only thing I could do. I set the bag down and nudged it toward her.

"There. Okay? Are you happy? You can have the skull, but I need to go." I raised my hands in defeat.

She gave me a wicked smile. "That wasn't so hard. Some Seeker."

When she bent to reach for the sack, I whipped the nunchucks off my belt and fired them at her left hand. The tranquilizer gun skidded across the porch and into the bushes and the girl scrambled to retrieve it. I kicked the backside of her knees and she went down like a heap of bricks. I didn't say another word as I grabbed the skull, jumped in the car, and rushed to save my love.

Thankfully it was late and there were no trick-or-treaters on the streets anymore as I made my way to the address Wes had given me. I cut my lights a block down from the house where Chance was working, and rolled to a stop. Crickets chirruped through the open window of Cinnamon's car and somewhere a bullfrog croaked, but other than that the street was quiet.

Chance's truck was in the driveway. I didn't see any of the Leanan's army. Maybe we had captured them all. I grabbed the sack with the skull in it, put a hand on my sword, and stepped out of the car.

I was about to shut the door when I heard a chipmunk-like noise and something hit the back of my head. Stars swirled in my mind as I lost consciousness and crashed to the pavement.

Two things occurred to me when I awoke. There were feet on the other side of the open car door and the skull was missing.

Holding my breath, I catapulted my legs forward and kicked the heavy door with all my might, knocking whoever was on the other side to the ground. There was a high-pitched screech as I rolled beneath the door before it swung back at me. I picked a woman up by the scruff of her neck and said, "What are you doing here? Are you working with her?"

Shannon groaned as blood spurted out of her nose. "No, you crazy bitch, I'm trying to help you."

I wasn't sure if I should believe her and I certainly was in no position to second-guess my own instincts. A knot was forming on her head as I unsheathed my sword. I backed her up against the hood of the car with the tip of the blade. It was centimeters from her throat and she had to arch her spine to successfully avoid it.

"Why should I believe you?" I demanded.

She tilted her head to the right. "There's a note in my pocket."

"Get it."

She carefully reached into her pocket and pulled out a piece of paper. I snatched it from her trembling hand and read.

Give me the skull or the author dies.

The same kind of note with the cutout letters that Blade had received the other day. There were instructions to leave the skull near the old church where we had found it.

But who was it from? Was it from the Leanan? Or someone else? And why on earth was the paper so familiar?

"Where did you find this?"

"On the door of your cottage. I didn't get a chance to tell you before you left," Shannon said. She glanced around, confused. "But what are you doing here?"

"If I lower my sword, do you promise to behave?"

Shannon said, "I just want to help. Honest."

"If you really want to help, get to Blade. Make sure he's protected."

I stared at the note again. Then I folded it and stuffed it into my pocket.

"But if you're not here to trade the skull for Blade's life, then who are you here for?" Shannon asked.

"For someone I love."

I told Shannon my suspicions that whoever had written the note must have knocked me out and likely had the skull now. "It has to be someone who knows Amethyst. Who knows Blade's staying at Birdie's and knows where I live. Get to the reunion and tell Birdie and the aunts. Then round up the coven."

"But what about you?"

I looked at the house. "I'll be fine. Just go." I tossed her the keys. Then I hesitated. "How did you know where I was?"

"Fiona's tracking spell."

I gave her a curious look.

"I figured since it didn't attach to Monique, it had to land somewhere. You seemed like the most likely source for it to adhere to. So I used a crystal ball to search for it."

"That's pretty resourceful."

Shannon smiled.

"Now go."

Shannon hopped in Cinnamon's car and left.

I took a deep breath, held my sword tight, and readied for battle.

Chapter 43

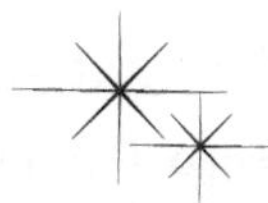

The door yawned open with a gust of wind. Candles flickered all around the dark room eerily. A giant cauldron anchored the center. I winced at the sight of it. I was standing in an open-floor-plan living room that spilled into a large kitchen. To my right was a hallway. To the left, a doorway. Directly ahead was a kitchen missing a refrigerator. The countertop was layered with nails and dust and there was pink paper covering the floor. Tiles were lined up in colorful stacks, waiting to be chosen, and a hammer lay on the windowsill next to a power drill and a circular saw.

The front door slammed shut behind me and I jumped, gripping my sword tighter, ready to slay whoever got in my way.

That's when I spotted Chance sitting in a corner chair, calmly sipping a glass of red wine. I rushed over to him. "Chance, are you okay?"

He wasn't tied up, didn't look to be in any distress whatsoever. In fact, he was spookily calm.

He gave me a chilling look with dead eyes that beamed right through me. "Of course I am. I'm here with my lady. We're going to have a fun night."

His voice sounded far away, as if he were speaking through a tin can. As if we were separated not just by the coffee table, but by years of neglect and heartache.

"Chance, sweetheart, I'm your lady. Come on. We have to go."

I grabbed his hand but he wrestled it away, spilling some of the wine onto my sleeve. It leaked through to my skin. It was wet and warm. Like blood.

"No. I don't think so. She said you'd come. Said you'd try to seduce me." His face darkened and his voice deepened.

There was a truth charm in my belt and I pulled it out and put it in his hand. "No, Chance. *She's* trying to seduce you. I'm the one who wants to help you." I clasped his hand shut, opened my third eye, and said, "Believe me."

He ripped the charm apart and tossed it over his shoulder. "I don't need your help. I have everything I need right here."

He took another sip of his wine and greedily licked his lips. His eyes were black and lifeless, like a shark's. I considered Tasing him, but I wasn't sure I could carry him all by myself.

Instead, I moved to shake him out of the trance, but he blocked my arm and seized my wrist. He stood up, still holding on to me. My left hand gripped my sword.

His face blazed with hatred. "I think you should go," he growled.

"I'm not leaving without you."

Behind me, I smelled sawdust and caulk, and a sultry voice said, "Oh, I think you will. Not through the door, of course, because that would mean I spared your life, which I have no intention of doing."

I turned to see Frieda standing in the kitchen, wearing a red negligee. She was standing in the kitchen of the vacation home she had mentioned, I assumed.

Or more accurately, the Leanan Sidhe incorporating Frieda's body. She stepped forward out of the shadows of the hall and as she did so, the mole faded from her face and her hair grew longer, shinier, her bosom swelled, and her legs lengthened.

She was growing stronger. Had she already siphoned some of Chance's blood?

A sinister smile spread across her face and she picked up the power drill. "Boy, I love these new tools. Don't you? They smell of must and men." She looked at me, then pointedly at Chance and back to the drill. She flipped a switch and the long, grooved metal bit shrieked to life. The fairy mistress shouted over the noise. "So much easier than the old days. Just apply directly to the temple and voila! A hole in the head. Best way to gather the nectar."

I turned back to Chance and grabbed his hand. "Come on. We have to get you out of here. Now!"

"*No!*" he shouted and shoved me so hard I knocked into a painting and cracked the frame.

I peeled myself off the wall as the Leanan called to Chance, "Come here, my pet." She turned the drill off, set it down, and tested the saw. It zipped on, whirring in her hand. She extended it toward Chance. "Bring me a present from our guest." She raised the saw. "Her matrimonial finger, perhaps. She won't be using it."

Chance stepped forward and I pulled a five-pointed blade from my pocket and fired it at the fairy mistress.

She raised her other hand and the star burst into flames midair. The remnants of my weapon showered the carpet with molten sparks.

The Leanan tossed her head back and laughed. "Is that all you've got, Geraghty?" she shouted over the buzz of the saw blade.

There was a binding charm on my belt. I unclipped it and held it in the air, spinning the ribbons of the pouch in a tight circle with my left hand, gripping the sword with my right. I chanted the Latin phrase for banishment over and over. "*Pello Pepulli Pulsum.*" I didn't know much Latin, but it is more powerful to use than my mother tongue because it harkens back to the ancients.

Chance took the saw from the Leanan and eyed it curiously as if he had never used one before. The Leanan buffed her nails on her negligée and laughed again. She waved her arm and the enchantment pouch froze in my hand. So icy cold it burned. I yelped and dropped the binding charm. It misted over the rug like dry ice.

"Really, Geraghty, give it your best effort, at least. I need a challenge."

She cackled.

There were more charms, potions, and weapons on my belt that would have worked on any human easily. But this was a creature of the Fae and a powerful one at that, so I decided to use the one thing in my possession that contained the most magic. My sword.

I leapt over the cauldron, spun in the air to gain speed, and swung the sword at the Leanan's head with every bit of energy I could muster.

I saw her eyes right before the sword connected with her neck. There was a doubt in them that said she didn't think I had it in me, replaced by a fright that said this might do some damage. Foolish of her to doubt me. She didn't know me or what I was capable of, especially when it came to the people I loved.

To my astonishment, the strike didn't decapitate her. The sword sailed right through the fairy mistress as if she weren't even made of flesh and blood and bone.

Which, on this plane, at this moment, she may not have been. I was too late.

Judging from the electricity that flared from the sword when it sliced through the Leanan's neck—and her screams—the attack did cause her pain, if not dismemberment.

Chance screamed too as I smacked the floor and crashed into a brick wall.

I flicked my eyes to him and shifted my body so that I could see them both. He wasn't screaming for me. He was screaming for her.

He railed at me, eyes wild, saw lifted over his head, and charged.

Chapter 44

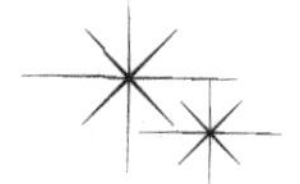

Luckily, the cord wasn't long enough and it lurched from the wall, cutting the current.

I managed to roll away just as Chance smashed the tool into the brick with a roar that shook the foundation of the house.

Behind us, the Leanan whooped. Chance shifted at the sound of her voice as I hauled myself up to standing.

She seemed to have recovered from the pain, but her eyes were flaming red. She wasn't laughing in amusement anymore. It was with determination. With purpose.

"We're going to have such fun," she snarled.

Chance repeated, "Such fun." He laughed and sent me a look so malevolent, I could have sworn he was another person entirely.

My gut wrenched. It was awful not to trust him. To be afraid of the man I loved. I felt alone again, like that young girl who had lost her parents. Except back then, I had Chance to turn to in my grief.

Now, there was no one.

It was the worst moment of my life.

The Leanan walked over to my love, put her arms around him, and kissed him deeply. He responded enthusiastically, hands running all up and down her back, through her thick hair and to her buttocks.

I cringed and jerked my head away.

The fairy mistress broke away from Chance and said, "What shall we do with her?" Her arms trailed up and down his chest, admiring the build of him so openly, she bit her lip and a trickle of blood dripped to her cleavage.

Chance studied me a moment. "I suppose she could serve as a fun toy." He looked at the succubus with so much desire in his eyes, my heart cracked wide open and I thought I might vomit.

"Get the rope, my darling," purred the fairy mistress.

Chance shuffled off into another room as I desperately tried to come up with a plan to bind the Leanan.

Or kill her. Whichever came first.

"I have the skull," I lied.

"What skull?" The Leanan walked over to a shelf and extracted a long, pointy dagger from a vase. She examined it as if it were a long-lost friend. "Old-school tools really are the most faithful," she said absentmindedly.

"Your only creation. The obsidian skull. Let him go and I'll return it to you."

She looked for a moment as if she had no idea what I was talking about. Then she said, "That old thing? Why ever would I want that back?" She scoffed and ran a finger along the side of the blade. She pricked herself then sucked the blood with rabid passion. "You humans and your silly treasures. The only real treasure, dear Geraghty, is magic, because with magic comes power."

She lashed at the air with the blade.

Now I was really nervous. If she didn't want the skull, then that meant she wanted—

"You poor, daft thing. You think that's why I'm here?" She stepped forward, the tip of the knife aimed inches from my throat.

I backed away slowly. "Then why are you here?"

There was another spell in my belt that Birdie had insisted I carry. I unsnapped the pocket where it was tucked.

"For you, of course. To get my revenge for what the Geraghtys did to me. And for everything I've been denied so long." Her eyes looked past me as she put the dagger to her tongue. "Carnal pleasures are really what this world is all about."

Chance came back into the room, a golden rope in his hand.

"But before I kill you, I'm going to make you watch and suffer as I had suffered at the hands of your ancestor." She flared her eyes at Chance, who was waiting for instructions. "Bring her into the bedroom," snapped the Leanan.

He advanced on me and yanked my arm.

"Chance, baby, come back to me. Don't do this. Don't help her," I pleaded, holding onto his wrist.

He didn't look at me. He just shoved me through the doorway.

I sheathed the sword and clutched the amulets hanging from my neck. My locket, Shannon's dharma, and Adia's Tibetan skull. Then I pulled out Birdie's beacon potion, bit the cork off the top, and gulped the contents of the vial down.

When the Leanan followed through the threshold, I whirled on her and aimed the three talismans at her face. Then an image flashed in my mind and my father's voice whispered, *warrior.*

I shouted to the Blood Moon through the open window in the bedroom. To the Samhain night and the spirit world and all the Fae that respected the earthly plane and the species who inhabit it, I called. Then, still gripping the amulets, I bellowed an incantation.

"I bind thee, Leanan Sidhe, I bind thee in the name of the sacred treaty of Queen Maeve and Mother Danu. I bind thee to uphold peace between our worlds and to serve out your punishment against the human race in the Otherworld under the laws of the ancient Druids and the Tuatha Dé Danann."

When I was finished, my chest heaved and I was light-headed. It took all the oxygen in my lungs to attempt to invoke the spirits. Nothing else had worked. Not the spells, not the skull, not even my sword. This was our last hope. A Hail Mary pass designed to penetrate the veil that separated the worlds and call for help.

Because I didn't think I could do it alone.

The fairy mistress crossed her arms and cocked her head. "You think human trinkets will work on me? Did no one teach you anything, Geraghty?" She trained her dagger at me, gliding forward until I was forced into a chair. "I was once a goddess, worshipped by men the world over, the inspiration of countless art born from both brush and quill. Do you know what that means?"

"It means the only power you have is between your legs," I said.

She sneered and slashed at my face, but I kicked the knife from her hand. It flew past Chance and stuck in a potted plant.

The Leanan put her face right next to mine. Her breath was hot as she hissed, "It means you are beneath me." She looked back at Chance, still standing there like a zombie. "Tie her up," she spat.

Chance wrapped the rope around my chest and the chair, knotting it off to the side. He bound my feet together and my hands to the arms of the chair, while the entire time I pleaded with him to stop.

My words fell on deaf ears.

I closed my eyes and chanted the last spell I had worked on for this moment.

"Geraghtys of the past, come back. Aid my quest and thwart this attack. Goddess Danu and queen of the Fae, join my people to carry her away. Queen Maeve of the Emerald Isle, banish this Sidhe to exile."

I repeated the words over and over again, but nothing seemed to be happening.

The fairy mistress knelt over me, her breasts spilling into my lap. "Would you like me to cut out your tongue first?"

I stopped talking, opened my eyes, but kept the words echoing in my head. The chanting in my brain grew louder and louder as I tried to drown out what was happening to me. And who it was happening with.

"That's better." She stood and walked over to the bed.

"Now what?" Chance asked.

"Now you kill her." She said it as calmly as you might order a latte.

My unuttered chants grew louder, as if it was more than my own voice inside my head. As if I had a whole team of witches in there assisting me.

Chance flashed his eyes to me, and there was just a flicker of doubt. Albeit brief, still it was there. She hadn't completely bespelled him. A part of his soul lingered; I could feel it, taste it, smell it.

Which meant I could still reach him.

He looked at her and said, "I thought you were going to do that."

The fairy mistress lay down on the bed and put her hands behind her head. "I've changed my mind. But I promise we can have fun after."

At the word *fun*, Chance let out a moan.

He looked at me and I could see a tiny hint of recognition. Then it was gone. The room electrified as he walked over and plucked the dagger from the dirt. He approached me slowly.

"Any last requests?" the Leanan asked.

Warrior.

"Just one." I held Chance's eyes in mine. They swirled with black clouds, but I knew in that moment, I wasn't alone anymore.

"Well, what is it?" she barked.

"One last kiss."

Chance turned to look at her. Seeking permission.

She considered it. "A girl after my own heart. Very well."

He faced me again, his back to the bed, and I whispered under my breath.

"Tibetan skull around my neck, use your power to break this hex. With one kiss last and one kiss first, let our bond shatter this curse."

Chance leaned in and locked eyes with mine.

I whispered, "I love you."

Then he kissed me for one long, passionate moment.

When he pulled away, the blackness had faded and there were gold specks in his eyes again.

He stared at me for a time, shifted his gaze to the dagger in his hand.

To my sheer horror he didn't put it down.

Instead, he held it to my neck.

Chapter 45

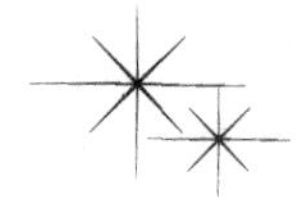

Chance looked at the dagger, then at me. He pulled back and turned to face the Leanan on the bed. In that same soulless, monotone voice, he said, "I want to use the sword."

She said, "How very King Arthur of you. Fine. Whatever. Just get on with it already. I'm bored."

He set the dagger down near my feet and reached for my sword. He held it tightly, his breathing steady, calm, his face void of any emotion.

I could not believe I was going to die by my own sword, my true love at the helm. It was like a freaking Greek tragedy.

Chance raised my weapon and held it to my cheek as one fat tear rolled down it.

I looked at him, begging him with my eyes to find himself. To remember me. Feel my love for him in this moment, despite what he was about to do.

Then he winked.

I tried to hold my reaction, tried not to move a single muscle, not to let even the tiniest twitch ripple my face.

A voice—Birdie's voice—whispered in my head, reminding

me that the curse had been cast when the first drop of Geraghty blood hit the ground all those centuries ago.

So maybe, just maybe, it could be broken the same way.

I steadied my gaze on Chance.

"Do it!" I yelled, another tear streaming down my cheek.

The authority in my voice visibly startled him. He gave me a questioning look and I said, "Get on with it already. I don't want to live if I can't have you."

From the bed, I heard the Leanan Sidhe say, "How touching." Then she shouted, "Kill her!"

Chance raised the sword and slashed my arm.

The second my blood spilled, the room exploded with energy. The lights flickered off and on, first blinding me, and then dissipating into blackness, then flashing to life again. I saw shapes and shadows outside through the window. It could have been the coven, it could have been my spirit guides—heck, it could have even been the Tuatha Dé Danann.

After all, it was Samhain.

The radio on the bedside table roared to life and the television screamed.

Actually, that was the Leanan.

From the other room, I heard buzzes and bells. The drill screeched on at full power.

Chance turned toward the bed, his arm around my shoulders, and we watched as the body that lay there transformed back into Frieda's. There was a struggle and we could see both the vampire and the human fight for control until, eventually, Frieda regained use of her vessel and the fairy mistress was wrenched from Frieda's body. Her ethereal form scratched at invisible hands, clawing at faces we couldn't see, but I knew they were there all the same. My people.

My team.

In a frenzy of screams and swirling light, the Leanan Sidhe was sucked back into the Otherworld. Back to her prison.

Chance stared at the bed where Frieda now lay, unconscious. I was certain she'd be all right, but I didn't know how much time we had before she awoke, and I didn't have a whole lot of answers to give her.

"We have to go. Hurry. Untie me."

Chance rushed to sever the ropes. I grabbed my sword and we got the hell out of there.

Chapter 46

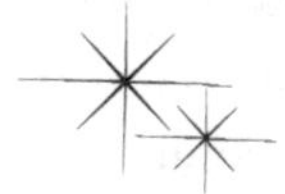

Outside, the coven was waiting. One by one, they broke the circle they had formed around the property. I wasn't sure how long they had been there. I was just grateful that they were.

Birdie approached me first. "See how much more efficient you can be when you use all the resources at your disposal?"

"Yes, Obi Wan." I bowed.

My grandmother bopped me on the head with her broom and rolled her eyes. I thanked her for the beacon spell. Clearly, I would not have been able to both bind the Leanan Sidhe and call forth the spirits without it. The locket itself may have worked on any other night, but tonight the spirits were jittery with so much to do in such a short time span.

Plus, if a witch wasn't careful, she could summon a dark one. And I didn't need two of them to deal with on Samhain.

Birdie called to Shannon and Adia to assist the "cleanup," whatever that meant. Maybe they were going to erase Frieda's memory of the last few days or maybe they were actually going to cleanse the house of the negative energy from the Leanan. Either way, I was happy they were here so that I could properly thank them for the use of their personal talismans.

Adia said, "We're sisters. Remember that." She hugged me and I dropped her Tibetan skull in her hand.

"Until next time." She disappeared into the house.

Shannon's nose was taped and she had a pretty large bruise on her head where the car door had nailed her. I removed the dharma from my neck and placed it around hers. "Thank you, Shannon. I'm sorry I misjudged you. And um"—I scratched my neck and pointed to her face—"about that."

Chance gave me a questioning look.

To her credit, Shannon smiled. "I understand."

I leaned in to hug her, but she jumped away. She stuck out her hand. "No hard feelings."

I shook it and the young witch trotted into the house.

"Where's Pickle?"

"Home," Birdie said.

"The inn?" I asked.

"No. His home. It's done." My grandmother looked at Chance and said, "How are you feeling?"

"Confused." He looked at me. "And happy." He pulled me into his arms for a kiss and buried his head in my chest. Then he sneezed. He pulled back, wrinkling his nose.

"Is that a new perfume? You know I'm allergic to roses."

"I'm not wearing perfume," I said.

Lolly approached us then. "That reminds me, Birdie, the manager at Briar Rose called. He tracked Yvonne down through the grapevine and said she left her phone charger there Monday evening."

"Briar Rose? I thought she didn't get into town until Tuesday, the night of the book signing," I said.

Birdie shrugged. "Perhaps she wanted to explore another hotel on her own. It's a very feminine place. They put—"

"Roses in every room," I said.

I pulled out the note that Shannon had given me earlier.

Give me the skull or the author dies.

It did smell of roses. That's why the paper had seemed so familiar.

And the chipmunk noise I heard before I was knocked unconscious. That wasn't an actual rodent at all. It was a sneeze.

Lolly gave me a funny look. "What is it, dear?"

"Where's Blade?" I asked, frantically.

"Packing, I suppose. They checked out."

"Yvonne has the skull. Meet me back at the inn as soon as you can," I told Lolly. To Chance, I said, "Come on."

All the while, I had been wondering: Who would shoot my window out? Who would know where I lived? And who would actually threaten Blade, but not follow through with it?

Someone who wanted him alive. Someone who *profited* from him being alive. Someone who knew where I lived. Someone who was staying right next door.

As we raced back to the inn in Chance's truck, I explained everything. Everything about what had happened to him, who I was, and why I couldn't tell him. About how it was dangerous and I didn't want him to get hurt, but seeing as how that ship had sailed, I figured it was more dangerous to keep him in the dark.

The Council could punish me as they saw fit.

And then, when Chance parked the truck, I told him the most important thing of all, the words he had longed to hear, but I could never say. I told him I loved him.

He smiled. "Thank you," he said.

"For what?"

"For trusting me."

"Always."

The house was dark when we pulled up and Blade's car was there. The Taser was still on me, but I had a lot more faith in the tranquilizer gun. I told Chance to head inside through the back door and call Leo. I jogged over to the cottage to see if the tranq gun was still in the bushes where I had knocked it out of Shannon's hand. I spotted the nunchucks, dangling from a branch, but no gun.

I sifted through the brittle leaves and the evergreens to no avail. Where was it?

"You looking for this?"

Uh-oh. I slowly turned around to see Monique standing in my front yard, aiming my dart gun at me.

This was getting embarrassing. I really needed to figure out a security spell for my weapons.

"Hey, Monique."

"Don't 'hey' me, Stacy Justice. I know you've been drugging me, you crazy bitch."

Twice in one night I'd been called that.

I reached for the locket and she put both hands on the barrel. "Don't you fucking move!"

I held my hands up.

It was clear to me that Monique hadn't thought through her next step in this plan. She looked disoriented but pissed. Kind of like she usually did.

"Monique, calm down. I can explain everything."

"Shut up!" A trail of spittle dribbled from her mouth. She was wearing the same clothes Lolly had dressed her in, although they were dirty and torn. Her hair had wrestled free of the chignon and was lashing out around her face in wild tendrils. She looked a lot like Tippi Hedren after the birds had gotten to her in that Hitchcock movie.

"Monique, please. Let's go to the inn. Chance is there and Leo is on his way. You are in danger, but it's not because of me."

"Bullshit. The last thing I remember is being in that nuthouse. It has everything to do with you!"

I crooked my finger behind her. "Take a look. His truck is right there. You trust Chance, don't you?"

She bit her lip, but she didn't move her head. "Empty your pockets!"

"I'm wearing a costume. I don't have any pockets."

"You know what I mean! Take everything off. That necklace, the belt, the cape. All of it."

Wow, she was really agitated. I couldn't blame her, but if I did as she said, I'd be defenseless. I decided to go with honesty since lying hadn't worked out so well for me this week.

I said, "Look, I'm not kidding. There's someone at the inn who wants to harm me and if I do as you ask, I'm an open target." There was still a blade in my boot heel, but it would be no match if Yvonne had a gun.

I had to get that skull. There was no telling what damage it could do in the wrong hands. But I was pretty sure Yvonne would only give it up over her dead body. Somehow she knew the skull lent creative juices to whomever possessed it and since she wasn't a writer herself, but an agent, her livelihood depended on Blade's output. There was no doubt he was her star author. From what I had learned over the last few days, his books consistently hit the #1 bestseller lists. I had no idea the kind of money high-list authors raked in but judging from his car and Yvonne's wardrobe and shopping sprees, my guess was six or seven figures a year.

Agents. Talk about bottom-feeders.

Monique smirked. "Oh, don't worry. I'll protect you. Now do it before I pop a cap in your ass."

"How long have you been wanting to say that?"

Monique trained the gun at my chest.

"Okay, okay." I blew out a sigh and slowly removed my cape, the belt, and the locket.

"Toss it all over in the shrubs. Not a girly throw, either. Launch it."

I did as she asked.

"Now take two steps forward."

I did. She further instructed me to walk slowly toward the inn, hands clasped above my head, and I wondered what the hell was taking Leo and the coven so long.

"I think we should go through the back door."

"I don't care what you think, She-Devil Barbie. We go through the front door like normal people."

When I got to the porch, the house was still dark.

"Open the door," Monique barked.

"Monique, I'm not bullshitting you. Something's wrong. Chance would have turned on a light." Unless he was still in the kitchen, but there was a front-porch switch back there. I was sure he would have flipped it on for Leo.

"Well, then I guess you're going in first."

I took a deep breath, put my hand on the knob, and twisted.

Instantly, the sack I had packed the skull in came swinging at my head. I belly-flopped on the porch and heard a scream, then a thud.

And another thud.

I stood up to find Monique flat on her back, out cold, gun still in her hand, and Yvonne—also out cold—with two darts in her throat.

Chapter 47

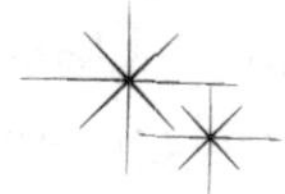

Two weeks later . . .

Chance and I were making tacos on a drizzly Saturday and he was still quizzing me about the nature of my role and my witchiness.

"So you can't fly." He was smashing an avocado into a bowl.

"No."

I grabbed a lime and sliced it into tiny bits to plop in the Corona.

"But you can talk to dead people."

"Yes."

Chance grabbed one of the limes and squeezed it into the guacamole. "Are there any here right now?"

"No. They usually don't bother me at home."

Thor came wandering over to take a good long whiff of the spicy meat. I tossed him a tortilla chip. He snapped it up and crunched it down.

"Show me a trick. Show me something you can do."

I rolled my eyes. He kept wanting me to perform parlor tricks, which really wasn't my specialty, although I had been honing my spell crafting lately.

"I can make you fall in love with me," I said and tapped his behind.

He grinned at me. "Yes you can. But I want to *see* something. Like . . ." He held up a tomato. "Slice this with your mind."

"I can't do telekinesis."

"Okay." He thought a moment. "Tell me what I'm thinking."

"I'm not a telepath. I'm a necromancer."

I plucked the tomato from his hand and began chopping it.

The doorbell rang then and I was so startled by it that I automatically summoned my sword. It tore off the wall and flew into my hand.

Chance dropped his jaw and his beer. "That. Was. Awesome."

I looked from the door to him. "I'm not expecting anyone; are you?"

He shook his head.

No one rang my doorbell. Ever. If Birdie or Cinnamon were coming over, they would just walk in. And any packages I ordered were delivered to the inn. Derek would text me first, Gramps would call.

"Maybe we should go into the den," I said.

"Don't you think you're being a little paranoid?"

"Hello? Vampire succubus. Wanted to drill you for blood."

Chance rolled his eyes and walked to the door. He looked through the peephole and said, "Looks like a messenger."

The bell rang again and I joined Chance behind it.

I kept the sword in my grip as I opened the door.

A stout man was standing there holding a white envelope and an electronic gadget. He glanced at the sword with a perplexed look and said, "I have a delivery for Stacy Justice."

"That's me."

"I need you to sign here." He handed me the device and I signed my name.

"Have a good day," he said and passed me the envelope.

Thor lumbered over to inspect the package, gave it his approval, and jumped on the couch. Inside was a letter and a key.

The letter read:

To my favorite witch,
Thank you for everything you've done for me. It was truly a pleasure getting to know you and your family. From the bottom of my heart, please accept this small token of my gratitude and know that you are magic.

Yours truly,
The Scribe

The key said *Jeep* on it.

Chance raised his eyebrows. "He bought you a car?"

I swung the door open wide just as a flatbed truck pulled up with a shiny Jeep Wrangler perched on top of it.

I was shocked.

"I guess with the money he'll save on an agent, he can afford it," Chance said. Yvonne's father, we had since learned, was Blade's father's college roommate. The two of them were in fact a part of a secret society that hunted down legends. It was a history professor at the university who organized the society that Blade's father and Yvonne's father belonged to. That professor was the Council member who had contacted Blade's parents to tell them that there was a lineage link that traced from Blade's mother back to the original author of the unfinished work in the *Book of Dun Cow.*

The reunion Blade's dad had mentioned in my vision took place a few weeks before the murders and involved just the three of them. Yvonne's father, already a literary agent at the time, didn't believe that Blade's parents had no idea where the skull was located. He threatened that if they didn't produce the skull and "share the wealth," harm would come to their son. We surmised that Blade's father thought there were clues hidden in the Robert Silverberg book, which was why he had studied it so intently.

When Yvonne and her father showed up to collect the skull, the man knew instantly it was a fake. But it was his teenage daughter who delivered the blows that killed Blade's parents. According to Yvonne, her father had no intention of hurting anyone. When the two stole the computer and read the stories Blade had written, seeing how prolific and talented an author he was as a mere boy, they knew that if they got their hands on both him and the skull, they would make a fortune. He was in college himself, searching for an agent, when Yvonne offered to represent him.

Before he left, I warned Blade Knight not to publish anything that wasn't filtered and scrubbed through the Council first. Who knew how many more secrets his work would lead to? He assured me that Birdie had already made him promise that much, upon threat of being turned into a sniveling troll. And he believed her.

As for the obsidian skull, the Council was sending someone to collect it today and I was more than happy to get rid of it. I wanted no part of keeping that much power in my guard.

I realized later that evening that I hadn't talked to my mother in a week. I decided to give her a call and went into the Seeker's Den to connect through the scrying mirror.

"Hi, Mom."

"Hello, honey." Her eyes darted toward another part of the room. "Everything all right?"

I said, "Yes. Just wanted to talk."

"Oh. Well, listen, sweetie, can I call you later? I'm just heading out."

I heard a door open then and a voice boom, "Sloane, come on. Shake your ass and let's go."

I knew that voice. I knew it like I knew my own, but I hadn't heard it in years.

"Uncle Deck?"

My mother cut the connection.

Author's Note

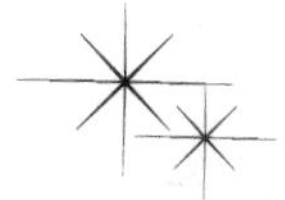

This is the book where our reluctant witch is no longer entirely reluctant, which is why I thought it appropriate to set around the Samhain holiday. Samhain is the pagan New Year, when resolutions are made, rituals are performed, and divination is on the agenda. It's the most magical night of the year, when the veils between the worlds are thin and witches can communicate with—and sometimes see—those ancestors who have passed over to the other side. In a sense, it's a time of rebirth, and that's exactly what is happening to Stacy in *Obsidian Curse*. She's becoming a new woman, a stronger witch, and a loyal Geraghty.

I wrote most of this story upon returning home from an energizing writers conference, so you'll see many literary references between the pages. If you want to learn more about *The Book of Skulls* by Robert Silverberg, hop over to Amazon. As for the *Book of Dun Cow*, the Royal Irish Academy has several fascinating online articles. Or, if you're lucky enough, you can visit the text there in person.

Until next time, stay magical.

Barbra Annino

Recipes for Samhain

Hot Buttered Cider

There are as many varieties of apples as there are ways to prepare them. Originally, apple cider was a fermented alcoholic beverage, called hard cider, and was manufactured across the world in countries like Spain, France, and England. Early American settlers began making the drink almost as soon as they arrived and it was quite popular in most households.

In pagan cultures, the apple was a symbol of immortality and used in many love spells. For a simple love charm, cut an apple in half, remove the seeds, and share it with the one you adore. Then bury the seeds beneath a full moon for a long and prosperous relationship.

Ingredients:

1 gallon of real apple cider
6 whole allspice
½ of a nutmeg seed
3 cinnamon sticks
8 cloves
4 pats of butter
Chamomile flowers
Suggested liquor: spiced rum

Directions:

To a large pot, add cider and spices. Add rum if desired. Simmer for twenty minutes. Strain into a pretty punch bowl and dot with butter. Garnish with chamomile flowers and serve warm. Serves twelve.

Warm Mead

Mead dates back to ancient times and is thought to hail from Ireland, where brides and grooms toasted with the drink for a month after the wedding, hence the birth of the term "honeymoon." Traditional mead is an ancient fermented beverage made from honey, water, yeast, and occasionally spices. The process is very involved, but this is a simpler, heated version.

Ingredients:

1 bottle of Chardonnay wine
6 sprigs of sweet woodruff, washed and dried
1 vanilla bean
¼ cup honey

Directions:

Add wine, woodruff, vanilla, and honey to medium saucepan. Gently heat until honey is dissolved. Remove woodruff and vanilla and serve in goblets. Serves four.

Acknowledgments

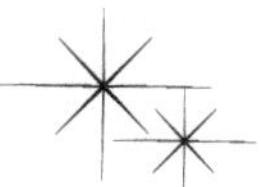

Thanks to Terry Goodman for pulling Stacy out of the slush pile and introducing her to more readers than I ever could have on my own. Huge thanks to Alison Dasho, my editor, for sifting through a very unpolished draft, finding the holes in the plot, and helping me to fill them. Your encouragement and enthusiasm for this book and the series as a whole have been instrumental in my work and confidence as a writer. For Tiffany Pokorny, Jacque Ben-Zekry, and the whole T&M Author Relations team, your efforts of hand-holding, marketing, and streamlining the production process have not gone unnoticed. When I turn a book over to Amazon Publishing, I know it's in steady, professional, competent hands. Thanks for all your ingenuity.

Much appreciation goes to my sharp beta readers, who never shy away from the daunting task of digesting a first draft. George Annino, Selena Jones, and the great Leslie Gay—your feedback is invaluable.

Finally, thank you to my husband for sacrificing Sunday football to help throw a launch party, Saturday mornings to read my work, evenings when you'd rather be relaxing but I insist on storyboarding, and most of all, for your continued, unwavering support. Just you and me, baby.

About the Author

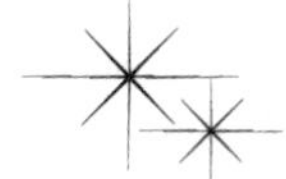

Photo by George Annino, 2011

Barbra Annino is a native of Chicago, a book junkie, and a Springsteen addict. She's worked as a bartender and humor columnist, and currently lives in picturesque Galena, Illinois, where she ran a bed-and-breakfast for five years. She now writes fiction full-time—when she's not walking her three Great Danes.

Connect online:

authorbarbraannino@gmail.com

barbraannino.com for contests, upcoming titles, and more

facebook.com/AuthorBarbraAnnino